W9-CNY-631

DEAD GIRLS DON'T LIE

ALSO BY JENNIFER SHAW WOLF

Breaking Beautiful

DEAD GIRLS DON'T LIE

Jennifer Shaw Wolf

WALKER BOOKS
AN IMPRINT OF BLOOMSBURY
NEW YORK   LONDON   NEW DELHI   SYDNEY

First published in the United States of America in September 2013
by Walker Books for Young Readers, an imprint of Bloomsbury Publishing, Inc.
www.bloomsbury.com

For information about permission to reproduce selections from this book, write to
Permissions, Walker BFYR, 1385 Broadway, New York, New York 10018
Bloomsbury books may be purchased for business or promotional use. For information on bulk
purchases please contact Macmillan Corporate and Premium Sales Department
at specialmarkets@macmillan.com

Library of Congress Cataloging-in-Publication Data
Wolf, Jennifer Shaw.
Dead girls don't lie / by Jennifer Shaw Wolf.
pages   cm
ISBN 978-0-8027-3449-5 (hardcover) • ISBN 978-0-8027-3450-1 (e-book)
[1. Murder—Fiction. 2. Secrets—Fiction. 3. Best friends—Fiction. 4. Friendship—Fiction. 5. Dating
(Social customs)—Fiction. 6. Single-parent families—Fiction. 7. Washington (State)—Fiction.
8. Mystery and detective stories.] I. Title. II. Title: Dead girls do not lie.
PZ7.W81855213De 2013   [Fic]—dc23   2013012063

Book design by Nicole Gastonguay
Typeset by Westchester Book Composition
Printed and bound in the U.S.A. by Thomson-Shore Inc., Dexter, Michigan
2 4 6 8 10 9 7 5 3 1

*For my dad, Dale Shaw, for always believing in me,
and for my mom, Linda Shaw, the one person I know who
always does the right thing*

DEAD
GIRLS
DON'T
LIE

CHAPTER
1

Rachel didn't wear shoes. She had that kind of sexy, "small town girl" style that works with bare feet. Long dark hair, thin but with all the right curves, and delicate, pretty little feet. I can't pull off bare feet. I have huge feet and clunky, square toes, and anyway, Dad would never let me go without shoes. But for as long as I can remember, summertime meant Rachel went barefoot.

She wasn't wearing shoes when we went to the old house at the edge of the woods last summer. That's why she cut her foot on a piece of broken glass. It bled like crazy and left a long pink scar on the bottom of her foot and another narrow white one, like a little ring around her middle toe.

Standing in the sweltering chapel, three people from Rachel's mom, all I can think about are those scars, and whether Rachel is wearing shoes now.

But I can't see her feet.

I'm not sure what I'm supposed to be feeling, but I'm pretty sure right now isn't the time to be obsessing about whether Rachel is wearing shoes or not. Dad says I'm in shock. Rachel was my best friend from grade school through about six months ago, but I haven't cried at all. Not even when Dad picked me up at Claire's house and told me what had happened. He didn't come until almost nine o'clock Saturday morning, but I know Rachel died before three. One hour after Skyler kissed me for the first time. Thirty-five minutes after she sent me her last text.

I step back behind the man in front of me and wrap my fingers hard around my phone. It's attached to my wrist by a little beaded cord. I forgot until just this minute that Rachel made it for me. It reminds me of what's on my phone: the text from Rachel, maybe her last words. She was asking for help, but I didn't answer her. And now she's gone.

The man hanging on a cross at the front of the church accuses me. I was taught better. A good friend, a good Christian, would have answered the text immediately. A good girl would have gone to the police.

Even though she told me not to.

Dad nudges me from behind. I look up and realize that the only thing between me and the casket is an empty space, kind of like the emptiness in my chest. I hesitate, but he half directs, half pushes me forward.

As soon as she sees me, Rachel's mom, Araceli, gasps and pulls me against her so hard that I can barely breathe. She smooths my hair and whispers, *"Mija, mija, mija,"* and other words in Spanish that I don't understand. Her voice and her chest heave against me, thick with pain. Over her shoulder I try not to look at Rachel's face, but I can't help it. She looks like a wax doll. Her eyelashes lie on powdered pink cheeks, paler than her usual golden tan, and even her satiny black hair looks fake. I've never seen a dead person before. Dad told me that she would look like she was sleeping, but to me she looks dead.

Her dress is all wrong. It's too formal, white satin with buttons that go all the way up to her chin, choking her. I've never seen Rachel in a dress before. Skirts sometimes, long and flowery, like the one her mom is wearing, but never a dress. Usually she wore cutoff shorts, tanks, and T-shirts.

Maybe the collar on the dress is so high to hide the hole in her chest where the bullet went through.

The silver ring through her pencil-thin eyebrows and the streaks bleached red in her hair, both added after we stopped being friends, look wrong too. They don't belong to the Rachel I knew. They belong to the stranger she became.

Whispers follow me to my seat.

"Friends for years."

"So horrible."

"Something like this, here?"

"Do you think she knows anything about . . ."

And then, "Shh, of course not."

I glance up, but I can't tell who was talking. People's eyes lower as I raise mine. The air is heavy with something more than the scent of wilted flowers and the above-average June temperatures. The looks that I feel as I walk down the aisle aren't from people who are grieving. Most of the people here knew Rachel her whole life, but lately just by reputation. A mix of curiosity and fear is written in their faces—curiosity, because it always accompanies anything tragic in a small town, and fear, because Rachel's death represents a crack in the shell of their security. Something that only happens in L.A. or New York, or even Seattle, has happened here.

Twice.

This time it feels closer, more personal. The first time it was an outsider, a gangbanger hiding out in our small town, but Rachel was born in Lake Ridge; no matter what they all thought of her by the end of her life, she was one of us.

I catch furtive, suspicious glances aimed at the knot of Mexicans in the back. In spite of myself, in spite of everything I've been taught about charity and about God loving everyone the same, in spite of all the time I spent with Rachel and Araceli, I feel it too. It's like everyone is looking for a reason, something that makes Rachel different, something that will keep what happened to her from happening to the rest of us.

I glance back at them. Some of the kids I recognize from school, but as small as Lake Ridge High is, I only know a few of their names. They stick to their own group, and I guess, so do we.

Taylor slides over to make room on the bench for me. I sit between her and Claire, like we were good friends again, the way we were in grade school before they decided Rachel was too different or maybe just too pretty to hang out with them anymore.

Claire nudges me with her elbow and nods toward the door of the church. Skyler is there, standing by himself. I wonder if he's here for Rachel or if he's here for me. A heavy weight of guilt presses down on me, and I turn away before he sees me.

"You should see if he wants to sit by us," Taylor hisses. Her voice carries over the solemn organ music and muted whispers.

I shake my head and glance toward my dad, but I don't think he heard. He's still standing with Rachel's mom, his hand on her arm, almost like they were a couple. When Rachel and I were little, she used to talk about what it would be like if my dad and her mom got married. How then we'd really be sisters. I didn't tell her I didn't want that to happen, not because I didn't love Araceli, but because it would mean my parents would never get back together.

I don't know if Taylor motioned him over or if he decided on his own, but when I look up, Skyler is standing at the end of the bench. "Can I sit here?" he asks.

It's the same question he asked two weeks ago, just before school got out. I was sitting on my usual lunchtime perch outside the library, hunched over a book, pretending I didn't care that I was alone. I said yes then, but I can't make my voice work now. Taylor intervenes, scooting to one side to make room for Skyler between me and her.

He sits down, and I get a whiff of sweat and too much cologne, just like at the party that night. It feels like someone poured all possible emotions into my stomach and put it on the spin cycle. Sitting by Skyler brings back all the guilt, fear, anger, and elation that I felt at the party, and all the pain, regret, and pitch-black horribleness from the morning after, when Dad told me that Rachel was gone.

I knew it was my fault.

I wasn't supposed to be with Skyler. I wasn't supposed to be at the party at all. It was the kind of party Dad has warned me to stay away from. But I was stuck at Claire's house for the night, and she and Taylor were going. Staying behind would have destroyed my nearly nonexistent social footing. After being there for about ten minutes, I was done. I was looking for a way to leave, even contemplating calling Dad, disrupting his business trip, and begging him to come pick me up, even if it meant confessing that we had lied to Mrs. Rallstrom and snuck out.

Then I realized my phone was gone. My "only because I think you're responsible enough now" and "so you can get ahold of me if something happens" phone.

I was frantically searching for it. Peyton Harris, too drunk to even stand up straight, tried to convince me that he had taken my phone and I had to reach down the front of his jeans to get it back. Skyler rescued me. He told Peyton to leave me alone and helped me find my phone in the laundry room, behind a pile of dirty clothes where someone had hidden it.

Then he offered to take me home.

People file toward their seats, the organ plays, and I can feel Skyler breathing beside me. His hand is inches from mine, but I can't look at him. I wonder what he thinks about all of this. If he realizes the phone calls I silenced were from Rachel. If he knows I let her die. I wonder what he thinks about me now.

I'd never thought of Skyler Cross as a "potential boyfriend candidate" as Claire would put it. He's quiet, and nice, but kind of all alone. I was too busy being my own kind of quiet and all alone to pay attention to him, until he started sitting by me during lunch. Until then, he was just Evan Cross's younger brother.

Thinking about Evan pours jealousy into the churning concoction of pain inside my stomach. In a stupid, horrible way, Evan is responsible for the six-month silence between Rachel and me. Correction: I was stupid and I was horrible, and it was my fault.

I remember the sheer joy in Claire's voice when she made a point to find me at church so she could tell me, "Rachel and Evan Cross on New Year's Eve! All night long, can you believe it?"

And I remember the venom in Rachel's voice after I confronted her with the disloyalty: "You don't know anything about anything, Jaycee. You live life in your own little bubble, so when Claire tells you something, you believe her without even asking for my side of the story. Maybe there's a good reason I was with Evan. Maybe you should trust me for once."

I had answered her back with at least as much venom, because she had admitted to being with him and she wasn't even sorry. "Don't talk to me about trust. You're barely around anymore. You're always with your other friends. You don't have time for me, but you still want me to keep your secrets. You told me to keep my mouth shut about what happened at that old house—you won't even let me talk to you about it— and then you go behind my back with Evan?" I choked on stupid tears as I said his name. "You know how I feel about him."

Her face was pale with anger, and something else, fear, because I had dared to go there. "Grow up, Jaycee. There are more important things going on here than your stupid crush on Evan Cross. If you can't get that, then maybe you should just stay out of my life."

I look up at the white casket and Rachel, racking my brain for a follow-up conversation, wondering if those were really the last words we ever said to each other. I think they were.

I wonder what we would have said to each other if I had answered the phone the night she died. The groove on the side of my phone digs into my hand as I think about the text, the only words from Rachel I have left:

We're in trouble. Meet me at my house NOW. Don't tell your dad. Don't call the police. Don't tell anyone what you saw.

I wonder what I'm supposed to do now.

CHAPTER 2

The floorboards creak under my feet as I follow Rachel's footprints across the dusty floor. I know I have to find her because something bad is going to happen, but I don't know what it is. I stop, afraid to follow the trail up the stairs. I call her name, but no one answers. I lift my foot to go upstairs and step in something wet. The stairs are covered with blood.

— —

My phone buzzes. I panic at the sound and reach to turn it off with my heart pounding in my ears. It takes a minute to pull myself back from that horrible place where memories are twisted into nightmares, as if reality wasn't bad enough. I don't remember falling asleep, but I must have, because I dreamed, and now it's morning.

I check my phone. It's another text. This one is from Claire, a generic:

Lake today.

I put it back on my nightstand and stare at the clock. Rachel's funeral ended less than twenty-four hours ago. I guess Claire thinks that's sufficient mourning time for an ex–best friend.

I'm not sure why she's suddenly so interested in me. I've been pretty much a loner since Rachel and I stopped talking. Maybe Dad told her mom he was "worried" about me and I'm some sort of church charity project. Maybe she's afraid if she isn't nice to me, I'll tell her mom that she snuck out and went to Evan's party. But I'd be in at least as much trouble as she would be, and I've learned that shared guilt doesn't cement a friendship like you think it would.

The phone buzzes again.

U know who might be there.

I sit up in bed, contemplating that. She could only mean Skyler. Do I want to see him again? It makes me feel guilty to think about it. Especially after the look Dad gave me when he got to the bench and realized Skyler had taken his place beside me.

Lake Ridge High is pretty small, but I didn't think Skyler knew who I was until we started eating together. I didn't really know him either. It wasn't until then that I realized how sweet and funny and utterly good looking he was. I hadn't noticed the dimples that only appeared when he laughed, or how much his blue eyes looked like his brother's, or how the muscles in his arms bulged under the flannel shirts he always wore, even when it was hot. But it wasn't just the way he looked, and definitely not his resemblance to Evan. It was the way he made me feel.

I always get stupid and tongue-tied and awkward if a guy so much as looks at me, but with Skyler it was different. At first it was just questions and small talk about classes we had together. Then one day he asked me about my running. Until then, I didn't think anyone else knew about it. He said he had seen me on the road behind his house. I wasn't brave enough to tell him I was trying to get my speed up, and that if I got fast enough, I might try soccer again.

He remembered a comment I had made in government about how the migrant workers should have some kind of health care, even if they're only here for a few months. "And you stood up to Justin Capp when he was a jerk about it," he said. "That was impressive."

He talked to me like he was interested in whatever I was interested in, like he already knew me, like I was important.

I was so grateful when he found me at the party, that he offered to take me home, that he didn't tell me I was a goody-goody for wanting to leave. "I don't want to be here either," he said. "This isn't really my thing."

He drove me back to Claire's house, taking the long way around so we could talk. We kept talking even after he stopped in the alley behind Claire's house to let me out. When he finally opened the door for me to say good-bye, he kissed me.

My first kiss.

After I made it back inside, I lay awake on Claire's bedroom floor, thinking about that kiss. How his lips had touched mine—more than just a brush, less than a movie kiss—how he had blushed and turned away. He left with, "We should hang out this summer. A lot."

And then I got Rachel's text.

When I saw it, part of me wanted to call her back and tell her about Skyler and everything that had happened. I was dying to tell someone, and I was hungry for the old Rachel and the friendship we'd lost. But when I read her text, I remembered the months of secrets, what it felt like to be all alone, and something else.

When we were walking home at the end of ninth grade, she turned around and saw Skyler walking behind us. She leaned close to me and whispered, "Do you see that guy behind us? Skyler Cross? I think he's been following me. Don't you think he's weird?"

Rachel, who could have any guy she wanted, judged Skyler without even knowing him. And now that I knew him, now that he had kissed me, that was unforgivable.

I ignored her and turned off my phone.

She's been dead for four days and I still haven't shown anyone the text.

"Jaycee, you up?" Dad pokes his head into my bedroom.

I shove the phone under my pillow. "Yeah. I'm up."

"I'll wait for you, then." He shuts the door and leaves.

I get out of bed like I'm on autopilot, afraid to think or feel too much. I pull on my swimsuit and shorts and work my hair into what Taylor would call a hideously unflattering ponytail— apparently I'm too pale to pull my hair back like that, and it makes my cheekbones stick out so I look like a fox. She should know; her mom has been a beautician for, like, ever. I instinctively reach to put my phone into my pocket and then pull back from it, as if it were a snake. I haven't answered Claire, and I don't know what time she wants me to be at the lake, but I don't want the phone with me today. I don't want to remember what's on it. I don't plug it in either. Maybe if it dies completely, maybe if I never charge it again, the text will go away. I won't have to look at Rachel's last words. I won't have to show anyone else, and I won't have to remember. I leave it under my pillow with my dark thoughts and everything else I don't want to deal with right now and go downstairs.

Dad has the newspaper in front of him. He folds it in half as I read GANG VIOLENCE SUSPECTED IN TEEN SHOOTING. I want to read the rest of the story, but he slides it to the other end of the table so I can't see it. Typical. Dad has decided to shelter me from any details about Rachel's death, the same way he shelters me from other bad things, like television and the Internet and, until this year, cell phones. Maybe because he spent too much time as a defense lawyer in the other Washington—DC, before I came along.

Before our ultimate breakup he hinted that I shouldn't spend so much time with Rachel, that maybe I should find friends at church, girls like Claire and Taylor. But I stuck with Rachel, even when she pierced her nose and dyed her hair, even when she plucked her eyebrows, penciled them in thin, and wore heavy makeup, mimicking the girls she started hanging out with at school. I stuck with her even as she pushed me away.

It wasn't that Dad didn't like Rachel. When we were younger Araceli would watch me during the day when Dad was at work, and then he would watch Rachel while her mom took evening classes at the community college. He was like her second dad, or her only dad, since hers disappeared before she was born. I know it was hard for him the day he sat me down and gave me the "Rachel seems to be heading down the wrong path, and while I don't want you to stop being her friend, it would be better if you didn't hang out with her any-more" lecture. It was after she got caught with drugs in her locker. At that point it didn't matter. I didn't even argue with him. I was already through with her.

"How are you, hon?" Dad says as I sit down. I shrug and he reaches for my hands across the table to say grace. I close my eyes as Dad begins to pray. "Dear Lord, we are thankful for this meal and for this glorious day and for all that we have been given . . ."

I settle myself in for a long one. My grandpa was a minis-ter, and Dad learned how to pray from him.

Dad's voice rises as he goes on. "We are mindful of the many souls who are lost and seeking for thy light in the dark-ness. We are aware of many who struggle with addictions, and sin, and transgression. Please keep a watchful eye on those who walk in darkness."

I open my eyes to see if I can read at least some of the article about Rachel before Dad is finished praying, but I can't quite see it.

Dad's tone changes. "Lord, you know we have lost a dear friend, a companion who has spent many hours with us at this very table."

He squeezes my hand, and I swallow an ache in my throat, but it doesn't go away. "Please bring her to your bosom, keep her in your heart. We pray for her soul, that the darkness that filled her at her life's end may be taken from her, that she may be forgiven . . ."

I think about the text. About how I should tell Dad about it. About what it would take for me to be forgiven for not answering Rachel.

"How are you doing?" Dad asks again.

I look up and realize the prayer is over, but Dad is still holding my hands. I pull away. "I'm okay."

Dad reaches for his coffee. "Your mom called last night, but you were already in bed and she said not to wake you up."

I take a breath. "Did you tell her about Rachel?"

He nods. "She said to tell you she was sorry, that she'd try to call later." There's more, I can see it in his eyes, or rather in the way he avoids my eyes.

"What else did she say?"

He wipes his hands on the napkin in front of him, still not looking at me. "She said that your trip at the end of the summer will have to be postponed. She has some big case she's working on. She doesn't think she can get away."

"Oh." I'm not sure what to say. Dad and Mom met in law school. They got married after they both passed the bar. Dad will never say it, but I think I was an accident. I know Mom loves me and everything, I'm just not sure she ever wanted to have a kid. When Dad left their law office in DC and moved here to live the "quiet country life," Mom didn't come with him.

He starts eating, still without looking at me. "She feels really bad. She said that maybe the two of you could do Europe at Christmastime."

"Europe" has been Mom's all-purpose apology bribe. The only problem? We've never actually gone.

He sits back down. "What would you like to do this morning? I was planning to take the day off anyway, in case you need to talk or something." Dad hovering all day, worrying about how I'm doing and overcompensating for Mom's neglect, is almost worse than a trip to Europe that will never happen.

"Claire invited me to go to the lake."

Now it's Dad's turn to say "Oh," but I'm not sure if it's a relieved "oh" or a worried "oh." "Are you sure that's what you want to do?"

I'm not sure of anything anymore. Rachel is dead. Maybe I could have saved her. But I can't talk about that. I'm stuck pretending everything is normal. I'll pretend I want to go to the lake with Claire just like I keep pretending that Mom and I will go to Europe someday. And maybe no one will ever ask me what I know about Rachel's death.

"Who's going to be there?"

For a second panic hits me. He must know about Skyler. One of the women from church must have told them I was with a boy late at night, that I snuck out, that I went to a party. I try to stay casual. "I'm not sure. Claire and Taylor probably."

He looks like he wants to say more, but instead he says, "I have some things I need to get done around the house."

"I could come back early and help you," I offer, like his hesitation is because he needs my help.

"No. Have fun with your friends." He looks up again, like maybe that's the wrong thing to say. I'm not sure what the right thing to say is either. "Maybe tonight we can go visit Rachel's mom and see how she's doing?"

I swallow hard. I don't want to go see Araceli tonight, or maybe ever. "We might go hang out at Claire's house after the lake." It's a stretch. Claire and Taylor haven't voluntarily had me over for years, but the lake thing is a start.

Dad looks relieved. "I'm glad you have friends like Claire and Taylor." The way he says it feels like a knife to the gut, like somehow Claire and Taylor are better friends than Rachel was. I'm even more convinced that he said something to their parents—or worse, to them—about being nice to me. "Just make sure you call and let me know where you are if your plans change."

"I will," I answer, even though there's no way I'm going back for my phone.

It's not even ten yet when I leave the house. I don't think Claire or Taylor or anyone will be at the lake this early. They probably aren't even out of bed, but the lake is a couple of miles away; if I walk slowly maybe someone will be there by the time I get to it.

My house is on the very edge of town, or the closest thing we have to a town in Lake Ridge. "Town" consists of a gas station, a café, the schools, a post office, the town hall, a couple of little shops and offices like my dad's, and a grocery store. Beyond that the town fades to acres and acres of rolling hills and farmland.

The fields are already full of migrant workers. They're all ages, from kids younger than me to men and women with leathered brown faces, silver hair, and arched backs. It's already hot, but they're covered from head to toe in long-sleeved shirts, hats, and long pants. They're harvesting asparagus, bent over and cutting the stalks by hand. Rachel and I tried it for a couple of weeks last summer to earn money for school clothes. It was excruciating.

A few fields down, a swather slices a path of sweet-smelling, fresh-cut alfalfa, so strong it makes my nose hurt. As the machine gets closer, the person driving it leans out of the cab and waves. I wave back, even though I'm not sure who it is. It stops at the end of the row. I hesitate, not sure if the machine stopped for me; then Skyler climbs out. My heart leaps in my chest and a lump forms in my throat. I do want to see him again.

He's wearing a baseball cap, jeans, and a long-sleeved blue shirt, unbuttoned enough for me to see inside to the muscles of his chest. His hair is damp with sweat so it looks darker than I remember it. He's dusty and gross, but when he smiles I remember what it felt like to have his lips against mine, and what he said about us hanging out this summer. He stops when he gets about four feet from me, takes off one of his gloves, slaps it against his leg, and says, "Hey."

"Hey," I reply. Something close to a smile forms on my lips.

"Um, I wanted to talk to you after the funeral but, um, I had to get back to work." In a heartbeat his easy expression fades to a nervous one. Truthfully, I was grateful for Skyler's quick exit after Rachel's funeral. I wasn't sure what I would say to him either, or how I would explain his presence to Dad. He pounds his gloves again. His blue eyes won't quite meet mine, and they're full of awkward sympathy. For some reason that makes me angry. I want to tell him that I'm a fraud. That I haven't been Rachel's friend for months, and that I could have saved her but I chose not to, because of him.

"It was a nice service, though."

"It was." My answer comes out strained and polite. Three days ago Skyler kissed me, my first-ever kiss, maybe even the start of something, but thanks to Rachel, we're strangers again. Something horrible inside me resents her for that.

I gesture to the swather, looking for safe territory. "I didn't know you knew how to drive one of these things."

He slaps his gloves against his leg again. "I've known how to drive it since I was, like, ten." His voice swells with a bit of pride, like driving it is a big accomplishment. "My dad put me in charge of this whole field." He looks over at the big machine; maybe he's looking for safe territory too. "I'd better get back to it." He moves away. I don't blame him for not knowing what to say to me, but I wish he would at least try.

I take a step backward too. "Oh, okay."

He keeps moving away. "Um, were you heading to the lake?"

Swimsuit, flip-flops, towel in a bag, not exactly a hard thing to figure out. "Yeah."

"Maybe I'll see you there, maybe when I'm done working?" He's so close to the combine now that he has to shout above the engine. "But it might be late. You don't need to wait for me or anything."

"Sure," I shout back, even though I don't think he can hear me.

I watch him for a minute while he turns the monstrous piece of equipment around and starts up a thousand blades that tear into the field, leaving it shorn and bare.

I turn back to the road, wondering how long I should stay at the lake in case Skyler shows up. Wondering if he'll ever kiss me again. Wondering if I want him to. Are girls whose best friends were just murdered supposed to care about things like being kissed?

I step out of the field and look up. There's a pair of dark eyes staring back at me. One of the workers from the field across the road is drinking from the hose and watching me. He stands out from the other migrant workers because he's wearing a gray tank top, jeans, and a baseball cap. He looks like he's close to my age. When he straightens up, water from the hose drips down his deeply tanned chest.

For a second our eyes meet and recognition flashes between us. I don't know his name, but I've seen him around school, and most recently, I've seen him with Rachel, a lot. He was at the funeral, sitting in the back of the church with the other migrants, but like he didn't really belong there. I read pain in his eyes. For a second I want to cross the road and ask him about Rachel, about the last six months of her life, if he knows why she sounded so afraid in her last text.

But before I can move, his face goes blank and he turns away.

I've been going to the lake since I was a little kid, by myself since I was twelve. I know the way. But for some reason, I leave the main road and head for the dirt road that cuts across the field in the opposite direction. I keep walking, alongside the irrigation canal, past piles of rusting farm equipment and a fallen-down barn, to where the sparse trees thicken into a little grove that someone planted years ago. It's the closest thing we have to a forest around here.

Rachel's house is on the other side, hidden from my view, but that's not where I'm going. Instead, I head toward what looks like a towering clump of weeds. The only hint that there's a house buried inside is the sun glinting off a broken upstairs window. This was where Rachel and I went last summer, two weeks before school started. This is where I went in my dream last night.

This is where everything changed.

I was sleeping over at Rachel's house. We were sitting

around talking, like we had at a hundred sleepovers before. She said something like, "What do you most want to happen at school this year?"

I hesitated. She already knew, and saying it out loud sounded painfully desperate, but because I knew Rachel wouldn't laugh at me, I answered, "I want Evan Cross to fall desperately in love with me."

Rachel shook her head and rolled her eyes. "Don't waste your time. He's a player. And anyway, your dad would never let you date a guy like him."

"You don't even know him," I protested.

"I know the type," Rachel said.

"Once he's with me he'll reform his evil ways." I said it like I was joking, but that was my deepest fantasy, that once Evan noticed me he would forget all the other girls he had ever known.

"And you'll have a glorious church wedding and the whole town will be there. And five years and four kids later, when he cheats on you and runs away with some stripper from Vegas, I'll try not to say 'I told you so.' "

I threw a pillow at her, but I threw it too high, so it hit the wall and knocked the picture above her bed crooked. She stood up and adjusted it. I watched her mess with it until it was just right before she sat down again.

"Okay," I challenged her, "what do you want from high school?"

She gripped her pillow and fell back dramatically on her bed. "I want to be in love; madly, desperately, and completely."

Now it was time for me to roll my eyes. Boys had been drooling over Rachel since sixth grade when she got all the curves I have yet to acquire. "Haven't you had enough boy-friends already?"

She sat up and looked at me seriously. "I want someone who will love me, not another guy who wants to go up my shirt." She lowered her voice. "And maybe I've already found him."

"Who?" I was shocked. We never kept secrets from each other. I used to tease her that I knew she was in love before she did.

She smiled mischievously and shook her head. "I'll let you know when I'm sure."

"C'mon, Ray," I begged. "Tell me."

She shook her head again, but this time she looked sad.

"Don't you trust me?" I pushed. "You know I won't tell."

She squirmed for a minute, and I was sure she was going to tell me, but she shook her head harder.

"Why not?"

"I just can't, okay?"

I pushed her until she finally said, "Look, if I can really trust you not to say anything . . ." She reached under her bed and pulled out an old jewelry box, her treasure box. I expected her to show me a picture or a note from the guy she was talk-ing about. Instead, she pulled out a phone.

"You have a phone?" I practically screamed the word. Rachel and I were the only kids at the middle school who didn't have phones. Her mom couldn't afford it, and back then, my dad was convinced personal electronic devices would allow bad guys to get ahold of me.

"Shh," she said, thrusting the phone under her pillow and looking around. "My mom doesn't know. And you can't tell her. I mean it." She sounded afraid, like she really believed I would rat her out.

"Why do you think I would tell?"

She got annoyed. "I don't know, maybe because sometimes you're just too perfect, with all your church stuff."

Her words stung. I'd heard them since grade school: goody-goody, tattletale. There were worse ones from middle school, but until now, Rachel had never used any of them against me.

"I won't, okay? I promise." She still didn't look convinced, so I made an attempt to sound excited about the phone. "It's really cool. Where did you get it?"

"It was a present from my dad, for my birthday." She kept her eyes down, like she felt guilty for that. I felt a sick wash of jealousy: my mom could easily afford a nice phone like that, but she'd never even tried to give me one. "But you can't tell anyone. Please, Jaycee. If Mom finds out, she'll never let me keep it."

My mind raced. If Rachel got the phone for her birthday, that meant she'd had it for almost two months. Two months of her not telling me. Two months of her not trusting me. And she didn't trust me with the new guy thing either. I tried to push all of that away, along with the jealousy, even though it stung, and be happy for her that she'd finally heard from her dad. "So what did your dad—"

But I didn't get to ask her about her dad. The phone vibrated to life, and I leaned forward, afraid and eager as a text message came through.

She held it away from me and smiled.

"What does it say?"

Before she could answer, we heard Araceli coming down the hall. Rachel shoved the phone back under her bed, and we both tried to look casual. I was sure we were busted, that Araceli would ask about the phone and somehow I would slip and give away Rachel's secret and then she would never speak to me again. But Araceli just said that she'd been called into work, she needed to leave right away, and she wanted us to call my dad to come get us so we wouldn't be alone.

Once her mom drove away, Rachel got the phone out again. She looked at the message and whispered, "Are you up for some excitement?"

As I move closer to the house now, remembering how it looked as we approached it in the dark, I was terrified, already worried about what my dad would say if he ever found out what we were doing. I was scared about what the text said and who it was from, but she wouldn't tell me. "Trust me" was all she would say.

I wanted her to think I was as brave as she was, that I wasn't always a goody-goody, and that she could trust me with her secrets. So I went with her, out in the dark, across the field, to the old house. I was so afraid, but I was loyal to her . . . then.

I hesitate, looking around to make sure I'm alone before I put one foot on the sagging front stairs.

My heart pounds; I shouldn't be here.

It was the same thought that echoed with every thump of my terrified heart against my chest that night, with every creak of the stairs that led up the front porch, toward the hollow-eye front windows and the door of the old house.

I take another step; the porch creaks so much that I wonder if it will hold my weight. I reach out and touch the sign nailed to the railing.

I remember how I licked my lips and dared to say it out loud. "The sign says NO TRESPASSING."

It wasn't more than a hoarse whisper, but Rachel whipped her head around defiantly and grinned at me, her "you're going to be part of this whether you like it or not" grin. "C'mon, Jaycee, don't be such a baby. It's not like the cops are going to jump out of the bushes and arrest us for going inside. Kids hang out here all the time, at least big kids do."

I got the jab, Rachel implying that I was immature, and so I kept moving, the fear of losing Rachel's respect greater than the fear of the old house. I had one last hope. "It's probably locked any—"

"Shh." She touched her finger to my lips. "Did you hear that?" I froze so fast and so solidly that it felt like my heart stopped too. She shook her head, still grinning. "I don't think we're alone." She giggled like this was a big joke, a big adventure. For her it was.

Her laugh sounded evil and horrible, but I huddled close to her, so close that I got a face full of long hair. Tears collected at the back of my throat. "Let's just leave, okay, Ray?"

"Not a chance." She kept moving toward the door, turned the knob, and it swung open without a sound. Somehow the door's silence terrified me more than if it had made a horror-show door creak. "See. Unlocked."

I followed her inside that night because the only thing more terrifying than going inside the old house was staying outside in the dark by myself.

I peer through the windows, dust and grime making the shapes inside almost as dark as they were that night. My eyes adjust to the dark room, and the shapes morph into semi-recognizable forms: an overturned chair, bits of garbage, boxes, things that were left behind or brought in by vagrants after the last people to own the house left permanently. It doesn't look like anything has changed since that night, like anyone has been inside since then, but I know someone has.

I touch the doorknob; this time it's secured with a big silver padlock. I remember the odd mix of smells inside, musty and old, with a hint of cigarette smoke and mice, but there was something else, a strong, lingering odor that smelled too new, like someone had just painted.

"He-llo," Rachel said when we walked inside, and she waited, like she was expecting an answer. Then she stepped toward a narrow staircase. I stayed by the door, frozen with my own fear, half admiring, half despising her courage as she headed up the stairs. She turned once. "Are you coming?" I shook my head and she shook hers back at me, with disgust or whatever, but I was too scared to follow.

I stayed back by the door, still close enough to run if I had to, but also close enough to the wall so my back wasn't exposed to the darkness behind me. The odd paint smell got stronger. I listened to Rachel's footsteps going up and then moving across the floor above me.

I rub one of the windows, and pitch-black dust comes off on my hand. On the far end of the room, pillars of dust stream through big windows, framed by long black drapes on one side of the room. It's the drapes I remember more than anything. I saw them move after Rachel went upstairs. I tried to convince myself that it was the wind or a mouse, something harmless, but my imagination kept coming up with things that were much worse.

I stayed completely still, holding my breath, searching the dark for whatever or whoever might be there. Wondering if it would be better to follow Rachel or run through the door behind me and all the way back to her house. I stepped backward toward the door, feeling for the wall behind me. My hand touched something solid; I jerked it back. It was wet.

I turned around to face a huge, dark circle. It had a symbol in the middle that looked like an eye glaring back at me. The paint was so fresh that it ran down the wall and clung to my hand where I had touched it, staining it red.

Before I could process what the symbol might mean, Rachel's scream pierced the darkness. I jerked my head back toward the stairs in front of me. Beyond them, the curtains moved again. For a heartbeat I saw something white, the number eighteen and a face. Then the curtains parted and someone disappeared into their folds.

Rachel screamed again.

I was so terrified that I couldn't move. I was too scared to even run away. She ran to the bottom of the stairs before I could get to her. I could tell her foot was bleeding, but she didn't stop. "We have to get out of here now!" She took my hand when I didn't move, dragging me out the door, down the stairs, and through the woods. I knew she was hurt, but she ran like she wasn't. By the time we got to her house, her foot was covered in little rocks, dirt, and leaves, all clinging to the sticky blood. Her hands were covered in blood. There was even blood in her hair and on her T-shirt—too much blood to have been from the cut on her foot. She was whispering something in Spanish over and over that I didn't understand, "*Lo atraparon.*"

She washed her foot and wrapped it in a bandage. She threw her clothes into the washer. She cleaned every speck of blood off the floor with a washcloth, threw that into the washer, and added a ton of bleach. She washed her hands over and over again, and when she saw the paint she made me wash mine too.

I rub my hand against my cutoff shorts, trying to erase the paint stain from my memory. I have to swallow back a gag because I can almost smell paint now. I look sideways through the window. I can't get the right angle to see if the circle or any of the other markings are still there, so I go to the other side of the porch and look through the window framed by the tattered drapes.

My face reflects back to me from a dusty mirror on the other side of the room. It's a distorted, ghostly image. The mirror is cracked and missing pieces. The shattered glass on the floor is reflecting chunks of light on to the ceiling. I turn my head, wondering if the symbol on the wall is still there, wondering if Rachel's blood is still soaked into the wood on the stairs, like in my dream. I wonder if there's blood on the floor upstairs.

Mom picked me up the next morning for our end-of-summer visit, one of the few that didn't have to be rescheduled. I found out after school started that a Mexican kid had been murdered in the upstairs bedroom of the old house. The notice that grief counselors were available for anyone who had known him was tucked in with the emergency information cards, club info, and picture order forms we got at the beginning of the school year. I asked a dumb question about it when someone brought it up in advisory, and Claire looked at me like I was a moron. "You really have been living under a rock, haven't you?" She was ruder back then, before we became friends again.

I didn't know very much about the boy who was murdered. Just that he was from L.A. and living with relatives here. It didn't seem like anyone knew him. He had moved to Lake Ridge sometime during the summer. I looked up the news story on the school's computer. It said he was killed because he was part of a gang. It also said his body was found two days after Rachel and I went into the old house.

When I finally got brave enough to ask Rachel about it, if she had seen anything when we were in the house, her eyes went wide with fear, but she said, "I didn't go all the way upstairs. I got scared because I saw a mouse, and I cut my foot on the stairs when I was running away." I knew she was lying. Rachel wasn't scared of mice or anything else. When I pushed her, mentioning the kid who was murdered, her voice got cold and expressionless. She said, "He was a gangbanger. He got what he deserved."

Around the left side of the house there's a broken window, maybe big enough for me to climb through. The urge to get inside the old house is so strong that I'm already thinking about how I'll put my towel across the glass so I can climb in without getting cut. I don't know what I'll find inside the house, or if there's anything there I want to find. I only know I have to. I should have gone to the police and told them what I saw that night. I should have made Rachel go too.

At the window I pause. There's something tucked behind an overturned couch, a backpack or a duffel bag maybe. It looks too new to have been there long. I lean forward, trying to see it better—

"Hey!" A guy's voice startles me so badly that I scream and spin around.

"I, I—" My heart pounds and my voice cracks. I turn to face the voice, momentarily blinded by the sun coming through the trees behind him.

"You shouldn't be here."

"I was just—" My eyes adjust to the light, and I recognize the guy standing in front of me.

Evan Cross.

CHAPTER
4

I stumble back and try to say something, but I can't.

His voice softens. "I mean, this isn't the safest place for you to be. There's broken glass all over, and druggies sometimes hang out here. What are you doing, anyway?"

"I was on my way to the lake," I manage to reply. I think this is the first time Evan has ever talked to me.

He looks at me with suspicion. "The lake? You seem to be a little lost."

The truth sounds completely insane. I go with, "I took a detour. I was on my way to my friend's house to see if—" I remember Rachel's dead and bite off "to see if she could come with me," and finish, "I just wanted to check on her mom, to see if she's doing okay."

"Oh." Evan looks down. "You mean the girl who lives on the other side of the woods. The one who . . ." He trails off and his face twists. I hate how he says "the girl" like Rachel meant nothing to him. Maybe she didn't. Maybe I lost Rachel's friendship over a stupid rumor. He takes a breath. "I just went by there. Her mom isn't home."

"You went to Rachel's house? Why?" Curiosity completely overcomes my fear, and I look up enough to make eye contact with him.

"Oh." He crosses his arms and avoids my eyes, like now he's the one who was doing something wrong. "I went to tell her mom that my uncle is willing to fix her window. For free."

"Oh." Evan's uncle owns Cross Landscape and Construction, the biggest, actually the only, landscape/construction company in town. "That's really nice of him."

He smiles a sad smile. "Considering everything her mom's been through, it's the least we could do." Something about the way he says it, something about his smile, makes me think there's more to it than that. "Anyway, nobody's home, and it's still kind of a mess. I don't think you want to go there."

When he stops talking I realize I'm still looking into his eyes, the clear blue eyes I memorized from his yearbook photo. Eyes that look like Skyler's. I drop my gaze and neither of us says anything for a long moment. Finally he says, "Hey, I know you. Jaime, right?"

"Jaycee," I correct him. I know I'm blushing all the way up to my red hair. Blushing, another bad look for someone as pale as I am.

"Right. I didn't recognize you at first. You look different, older or something." He smiles, but the fact that he doesn't even know my name makes me realize how invisible I've been to him. He fidgets for a second, playing with the strap to his helmet. "Well, *Jaycee*. It's getting hot and you're a long way from the lake. How about I give you a ride?"

I look up at him, startled. "Me?" I touch my hair, wishing it was curly blond like Taylor's or stick straight and shiny black like Rachel's used to be. Instead, I'm not wearing makeup, I didn't shower this morning, and my hair is in an "unflattering" ponytail. There's nothing about me that would make Evan remember my name.

"Unless you're afraid of motorcycles."

"Um." I hesitate, not daring to look above the level of his lips now. I can almost hear Claire's voice screaming at me that I'm an idiot if I don't go with him. But I can also see my dad, shaking his head with disapproval. I'm not allowed to accept rides from guys, especially not on motorcycles. "I'm not sure."

"Not sure it's safe?" He pats the helmet under his arm. "I'll let you wear this. Trust me. I've ridden these trails since I was younger than you." I get it, a jab about my age, even though I'm only two years younger than he is, but he's still being really, really nice and his lips have formed into a grin that threatens to melt me.

Besides, Evan might be the only person who could tell me what really happened between him and Rachel on New Year's Eve. Not that I'm brave enough to ask. I glance at the dark windows on the old house. They feel dead and hollow. Like eyes, watching me. The empty, creepy feeling of death settles into my chest. I need to get away from this place as soon as I can.

"Okay." A nervous laugh bubbles out of my throat. "Okay, I'll go with you."

"Cool." He puts his hand on my shoulder, propelling me away from the house to the edge of the path where his yellow dirt bike is parked. He settles the helmet on my head and then buckles the strap under my chin. It smells like sweat and guy, a smell that reminds me of Skyler. I wonder what he would think about me riding his brother's bike.

Evan looks beyond the woods toward Rachel's house. "I'm sorry about your friend." The sympathy in his voice makes me remember that everything isn't okay. "Eric says this is a lot like the other one, the kid who was killed last summer, but he's not sure how the two cases are connected."

Evan and Skyler's older brother, Eric, is the sheriff. He was elected last fall, even though he's only about thirty. If I'm not brave enough to ask about the date with Rachel, at least I can ask about that. "How are they the same?"

Evan sets his hand on the seat of the motorcycle. "Eric says they're still investigating, but it looks like a gang thing, like before. Rachel's house was tagged."

"Tagged?"

"Gang symbols. Graffiti. Like that." He points to a faded red symbol on the side of the house, a leftover from the last time gangs visited Lake Ridge. I shiver despite the heat. It matches the dripping red symbol I saw last summer—a circle with an eye inside and a dot above the eye.

"He said they questioned all the Mexicans who have ties to gangs, but they clam up whenever he tries to talk to them about anything." He shakes his head like he's disgusted. "You'd think they'd want to help. She was one of them."

"No, she wasn't." The words come out before I can stop them. "She lived here her whole life, and her dad was white. She wasn't like them." As soon as I say it, I know it sounds awful, racist, and stupid. I shrink farther into his helmet.

Evan just shrugs. "Scary that this kind of stuff is coming here. Eric says Yakima has major gang stuff, and Moses Lake, even some other smaller towns, but Lake Ridge always felt safe."

"Yeah," I answer.

"Anyway, somebody from the gang task force in Spokane is coming to take over the case. That's what they did the last time."

He straddles the motorcycle and waits while I climb on awkwardly behind him. "Hold on tight; this road is pretty rough." I wrap my arms around his waist, thinking about how many times I've dreamed of riding on Evan Cross's motorcycle. I didn't imagine looking this bad or being this scared. He kickstarts it. The bike lurches forward in a cloud of smoke and rocks. I lean into Evan's back, but I can't help but look behind us at the broken window and the faded graffiti on the side of the house.

E v-an Cross." Claire repeats his name again, slowly, in disbelief.

"And you look like that." Taylor indicates my ponytail, my face, my outfit. Maybe she doesn't mean it as rude as it sounds. She's just more concerned about appearances than the rest of the world. She shakes her bleach-blond curls that will never touch lake water and takes a sip from her Diet Pepsi.

There was no way Claire or Taylor or any of the other kids lounging around the edge of the lake could have missed me showing up with Evan. His motorcycle blasted the announcement from a mile away. Then he helped me take off the helmet and said good-bye in front of the gawking crowd. "I have some stuff to do for my uncle," he said like he had to explain why he wasn't staying. "But I might be back later. I kind of miss hanging out at this place."

"He saw me walking here and offered me a ride." All the attention is making me feel dumb, and showing up at the lake on Evan's bike feels like cheating on Skyler, or Rachel's memory, or maybe both. And what if my dad finds out? One way or another, everything I do seems to get back to him.

"Next time I'm walking," Taylor says, "if he's willing to pick *you* up—"

"At least you're keeping it all in the family." A nasty edge creeps into Claire's voice, an edge I heard all the time before she started being nice again.

I cringe, thinking about how bad that sounds. "I don't, I didn't—"

"Oh, come on," Taylor says. "Skyler is a good starter boyfriend. An okay first kiss, but Evan is eighteen and totally drool-worthy."

Claire and Taylor keep talking, analyzing my ride with Evan, strategizing the next step in our relationship. Arguing about whether I should let Skyler down easily, so there's no bad blood between brothers, or if I should hold on to him until I'm sure about Evan. The conversation is getting to me, like my ride with Evan is the most important thing in the world. Like Rachel isn't dead. Lying between them on my beach towel is making me claustrophobic.

"Are you, like, having the best summer or what?" Taylor says, spinning her sunglasses around in her fingers. "I mean, first Skyler and now Evan. Wow. Just wow."

"Yeah," I throw back at her. "If it weren't for Rachel getting herself killed, this would be, like, the perfect summer."

Taylor freezes, her mouth wide open. "Jaycee, I'm sorry. I just—"

"Forget it, okay, just forget it. I need to cool off." I stalk across the beach to the end of the dock and dive in, deep. I stay submerged, opening my eyes to the green-gray world that surrounds me, pushing myself forward until my lungs feel like they're going to burst. When I finally have to surface I keep swimming, ignoring Claire and Taylor yelling at me from the shore. I'm nearly to the middle of the lake and beyond any of the other kids before I realize it. I catch my breath and dive under again. I've never swum across the entire lake before. I'm not allowed to, even though it's probably less than a half mile across. Now I feel like I have to. Like making it across will erase Taylor's stupid comment, or the text, or even the last six months.

Like it will bring Rachel back.

I'm almost to the far side when my fingertips meet something dark and stringy. It feels like hair. It looks like hair too, long, dark, silky hair. Rachel's hair. I'm surrounded by a sea of dark hair, waving back and forth, accusing me, pulling me under. It tangles around my wrists and ankles, dragging me down. I strike out against it and get more tangled. I picture Rachel's face in the water in front of me, her eyes closed like they were at the funeral. Her hair swirling, swirling around me, holding my arms down so I can't move. I gasp for breath and take in water. I'm freaking out. Drowning.

Something grabs my shoulders, pulling me up instead of down. I'm fighting against the pull, too panicked to realize what's happening. Strong arms wrap around my waist and jerk me upward. My face breaks the surface. I choke out lake water, my chest heaves with relief, but I'm still freaking out.

His skin against mine feels cold, like a dead body. I fight to get away, but he's holding me tight with one arm and untangling the lake weeds from my wrists with the other.

"You're okay, you're okay, you're okay." He's lying to me. Nothing is okay.

When I look up, my eyes meet his. They're brown and deep and calming. As soon as I stop fighting him, I realize who he is. Rachel's friend, the guy who watched me across the field earlier today.

I push him away, hard. "Let me go!" But he holds me in a grip that feels like steel bands.

"Calm down," he says. "I saved you."

"I didn't need your help!" I yell back. He looks at me with a mix of amusement and something like pity. Then I realize that if he's standing up in the water, so can I, even if he is a good head taller than I am. I put my feet down and stand up; only then does he release his grip.

He stares at me long enough that it's uncomfortable. Finally he says, "You're her friend, *Jaycee*." He emphasizes my name like it's important.

"*Was* her friend," I correct him. I feel horrible for the way that sounds.

His eyes turn cold and hard, like they're made of stone; all the comfort I saw before drains out of them. He nods stiffly, and his chin clenches with pain. I get the feeling if I could push past the stones in his eyes, I'd see pain in them as deep as mine.

The lake weeds brush against my legs, and panic bubbles inside me again. "I have to get out of here."

Without looking at me, he takes me by the arm and drags me out of the water. As soon as I'm on dry ground, I sit down on a log and tear off strands of lake weeds that are still sticking to my legs. I'm so scared and confused, I want to slump forward and cry. If I were alone, I think I would.

He sits beside me, leans in, too close, and whispers in my ear. "I have a message for you." He looks around. "From her."

I jerk back, startled, my heart pounding as hard as it was in the lake. I shake my head. "What?"

"From her."

I shake my head again, afraid, but I don't move as he picks up a drawstring bag sitting by the log. He pulls out a piece of paper and presses it into my still-damp hands. I take it from him. I'm trembling with fear or cold or what, I'm not sure. He watches me as I unfold it, gingerly around my wet hands. I gasp as I realize what's inside. It's the loyalty pledge that Rachel and I wrote in grade school, signed in Rachel's blood and mine.

The paper is yellowed and creased, written in Rachel's elegant handwriting and signed with my fourth-grade scrawl and two thumbprints of dried brown blood. I close my eyes so I don't have to read the words, "We promise to always stay friends and always protect each other."

I hate blood, even the little dried fingerprints of blood on the note. The sight of it always makes me sick. Rachel knew that. Even when we were little kids and we cut our fingers, she knew that, but she still made me do it.

He takes the note from me and turns it over. He looks around him again and points at something written on the back.

It's Rachel's handwriting, but not from fourth grade. There are two lines that look like they were written at different times:

Don't trust anyone but E. And then, *The cross has the answer.*

My blood runs cold. I know the message is for me, but it doesn't make any sense. "The cross has the answer" sounds like something religious, but Rachel hadn't gone to church for months before she died.

He leans close to me, reading over my shoulder.

I whip my ponytail around to face him. "Where did you get this?"

"She wanted me to give it to you. She said you would know—"

"I'd know what?" My voice raises with fear.

"Shh," he says. Then I realize why he was leaning so close. We aren't alone. I turn around and look farther up the bank. It looks like I swam into some kind of party.

Tan faces and dark hair, like Rachel's, surround me. My eyes flit from face to face, but none of them are familiar, and they're all watching me. I stand up quickly and shove the paper back into his hand, like it is evidence I shouldn't be caught with.

He leans into me again. "We can trust them. At least"—he looks around again—"most of them." He stands up and turns his back on me. "Later." Then he melts into the crowd of people. I'm alone. It feels like I've crossed the border into another world. I'm not sure if I should go back into the lake or how to get away. Maybe the reason my dad didn't want me to swim across the lake didn't have anything to do with the distance.

Someone touches my shoulder and I jump. "Are you okay?" The girl talking looks like she can't be much older than me, but I've never seen her at school.

"Fine." My voice sounds hoarse and shaky.

"Hungry?" As young as she is, she's hovering over me, the way Araceli used to. "There is plenty."

A few feet away, tamales wrapped in corn husks sizzle over an open fire. Next to them a woman is flipping fresh tortillas over a propane burner.

"No, I'm okay." But despite everything, the smell of fresh tortillas is making my mouth water.

"Please." She pushes a fresh tortilla into my hands.

I accept it, still shaking.

Another woman with a curved back and gray hair drapes a scratchy wool blanket across my shoulders. "To make you warm." She chooses her English words carefully, like she doesn't have very many to use.

I roll up the tortilla and take a bite of a thousand afternoons in Araceli's kitchen, telling her about our day while she made homemade tortillas and gave us advice on everything from makeup to boys—things I couldn't ask my dad about. But when the tortilla hits my throat it changes to a dry lump that gags me. I finish eating it because everyone is watching me, but I want to throw it into the lake.

The girl who gave me the tortilla bends back over her cooking. I glance around at this other world, still wondering how to escape, but at the same time fascinated. Men, women, and children are milling around, coming in from the fields and going back to them. The women cooking over the fire fill the tortillas with a mixture of rice and beans from the pans in front of them. Then they pile the tamales and tortillas on paper towels. They speak in quick Spanish, too fast for me to pick out anything but a couple of words. Everything has a hurried but close atmosphere. The word "community" flashes across my brain, but this is a different community than the rest of Lake Ridge.

While I watch them, somewhere between frightened and fascinated, a cloud of dust rolls in, a big silver pickup in the center. As soon as I see it, I know it's out of place, but I don't recognize it until Skyler steps out. The men stop eating and look up at him with suspicion. A little boy steps forward and points at the truck, a little girl hides in the skirts of the old woman. Skyler glances around him, looking almost as nervous as the little girl. There are two other people in the truck, Claire and Taylor.

Claire stays in the truck, but Taylor gets out behind him, hurries over and throws her arms around me. "Cee Cee, I'm so sorry."

"It's okay." I stiffen and can't return her hug.

She leans into my ear. "Why did you come *here?*" She emphasizes the word, like crossing the lake is equal to crossing into enemy territory. "I thought you were going to drown. And when that guy . . ." She looks around, maybe realizing that her voice is too loud.

I pull away. "I'm okay. The weeds at the edge of the lake kind of freaked me out." I glance over and see Rachel's friend watching me. He's still wearing his gray tank top, soaking wet from going into the lake after me. Taylor shrinks against Skyler. He looks from me to my rescuer, his face a weird mix of fear and suspicion. Skyler says something under his breath to him in Spanish. It doesn't sound like "thank you for pulling her out of the lake." When Rachel's friend answers back, it doesn't sound like "you're welcome."

I pull the blanket off my shoulders and set it on a log beside the woman who gave it to me. "Thank you," I say. She smiles and nods as she fills another tortilla to give to the man waiting for it. I turn to thank Rachel's friend, but he's gone. I didn't even find out his name.

Skyler, Taylor, and I walk back to Skyler's pickup. Claire is still sitting there, looking terrified. "Are you okay?" she says dramatically.

"Fine." I squeeze between Skyler and the gearshift in the cab of a truck that wasn't made for four. Not wearing my seatbelt makes about the millionth of Dad's rules I've broken today, along with no motorcycles, no talking to strangers, and no crossing the lake.

"That's so gross." Claire points through the window. Next to the lake, two little boys, about two or three, are playing in the water, completely naked. Beside them, a woman is nursing a baby, her breasts only covered by the baby's head. "They have, like, no shame at all." Claire adjusts the straps on the tiny cups of fabric that pass for her bikini top. It's the kind of swimsuit Dad would never let me wear. I stare at her, but she doesn't catch the irony.

I shake my head and look out the window, trying to catch another glimpse of Rachel's friend.

"I didn't know you could speak Spanish," Taylor croons to

Skyler over the top of me. Maybe she's in the market for a starter boyfriend.

Skyler keeps his eyes on the road. "My dad has a lot of Mexicans that work on the farm. I picked up a few words." He shrugs. "Most of them bad."

"What did you say to him?" Now Taylor is leaning so close to me that I can see the silver cross she always wears, crushed between her boobs. If he turned his head, Skyler could see it too.

He doesn't look, but after he shifts gears he sets his hand on my bare leg. "I just said hi." The look on Taylor's face tells me that she doesn't believe that either.

Skyler stops on the other side of the lake. Claire gets out, but Taylor lingers until Claire drags on her arm. When they finally shut the door, I'm left sitting next to Skyler, closer now than I need to be. I slide over, but not far enough that he has to move his hand. I'm not sure what I should say. The radio doesn't quite cover our silence. Finally he says, "I need to get back to work. I drove over on my lunch break, to cool off."

"Oh," I answer, moving toward the door.

He grips my leg to keep me from leaving. "And to see you. Like I said I would."

"Oh," I say again.

"I got to the dock when you were about halfway across. I saw . . ." He grips the steering wheel with one hand and my leg with the other. "Where were you going?"

I twirl my fingers around my wet ponytail, trying to figure out how to explain why I had to leave, why I felt so smothered by Claire and Taylor. "Nowhere, I just—"

"Do you know that guy who pulled you out of the water?" His voice has a flash of jealousy, a flash of suspicion, or maybe just concern.

"No," I answer without looking at him, but the thought that he actually cares makes my heart thump. "But I think he's one of Rachel's friends, I mean he was—" I swallow.

Skyler nods. "His name is Eduardo." I look up quickly. Eduardo? Like the "E" Rachel told me to trust? "He worked for my dad last season. He's kind of rough. Dad fired him after he caught a bunch of them smoking pot behind the silos."

"Oh." I think about the headline I saw this morning. More than once I've heard people use the word "drugs" when I knew they were talking about Rachel. If he was a drug addict, why would Rachel tell me to trust him?

"Anyway, not exactly the kind of guy you should be hanging around with."

If I were quick or brave, like Claire or Rachel, I would say something like, "Maybe you could give me an idea about the type of guy I should be hanging out with?" But I'm not them and anyway my mind is too full of other things.

"I need to get back to work. My dad will kill me if I don't finish that field today. Do you want to stay here and swim, or should I take you home?"

The thought of going back into the water freaks me out, and I don't think I can stand listening to Claire and Taylor barrage me with questions again. "Do you have time to take me home?"

"Sure. No problem." He turns around to back out, but Claire comes to the window.

She taps on it, and Skyler rolls it down. She passes Skyler my bag and towel. "I got your clothes. In case you need them or something."

"Thanks," I reply. When Skyler turns to hand them to me, Claire makes kissing faces at us through the window. I think Skyler sees her when he turns around. I want to dissolve into the seat.

Between shifting gears, Skyler keeps his hand on my leg for the short ride home, but when he pulls up in front of my house, I get out quickly and don't wait for him to walk me in. I'm not sure if we've reached the point where good-bye requires a kiss. I'm pretty sure I want him to kiss me again, only not right now, and not in front of my house where Dad might see. I wave and yell thanks from the front porch.

"See ya later," he yells back. He peels out as he throws the truck into reverse. I cringe, wondering if Dad saw him, and count to ten before I open the door.

Dad is waiting for me, my phone in his hand. I freeze, terrified that he's seen Rachel's text. "I heard your phone buzzing from your bedroom. You got a text." He holds out the phone. "Would you like to explain it to me?"

My hands are shaking, but I try to hide it as I take the phone from him. I look down, bracing myself to read Rachel's last words again. Instead I read:

We need to talk.—E

CHAPTER
6

"Who is E? And where have you really been? And why did Skyler Cross bring you home?" Dad's questions come at me fast. I blink, trying to process what he's saying and how to answer. "Well?" His voice is calm, but I hear shakiness behind it, like he's really mad, or scared—maybe both.

I choose the easiest question to answer right now. "I was at the lake. Like I told you." I indicate my stringy, wet ponytail, evidence that I really was where I said I would be. "I didn't feel very good, so Skyler brought me home." That's mostly true.

"And the text?" I can feel Dad's eyes searching mine for traces of guilt. I've never been a good liar.

"It must have been a mistake." I pretend to study the message so I can avoid his eyes. "I don't recognize the number, and I have no idea who E is." That part is mostly true. Evan? Eduardo? Neither one has my phone number. It probably is a wrong number. But it makes me remember what

Rachel wrote on the back of the paper Eduardo tried to give me.

Don't trust anyone but E.

Could this be the same E? The idea that this is a wrong number slips away.

Dad lets out his breath, like he's trying to stay calm. "I guess it could be." He doesn't sound sure. "But with everything that's happened with Rachel and with . . ."

Now I'm trying to get him to look me in the eye, mentally begging him to keep talking, to tell me something about what happened. To give me the chance to talk about it. Maybe even tell him about the paper and the lake and Eduardo. Maybe even about the night at the old house.

But he shakes his head. "It probably is a wrong number." I reach for my phone, but he holds on to it. "However, since you came home with Skyler without telling me you had changed your plans—"

"I told you I got sick, and Skyler offered to—"

He holds up his hand. "If you would have called, I would have come and got you."

"I didn't have my phone, obviously."

"You know the rules, Jaycee. I gave you that phone so I could get ahold of you when I needed to and so you could tell me where you are and what you're doing. If you aren't going to use it for the purpose for which it was intended, I might as well keep it."

I stand there, tried, convicted, and sentenced. I don't usually argue with Dad, but I can't let him take my phone. "That doesn't make any sense. I couldn't call you to tell you my plans changed because I forgot my phone, so now you take my phone away so I can't call you at all."

"Ironic, but fair I think." Dad's voice has a "the discussion is over" edge to it.

"For how long?" I'm trying not to panic. Dad has a standing rule: he can check my texts at any time, for any reason. Until now there hasn't been any reason for me to worry about that, but I can't let him read the text I got from Rachel.

"Three days sounds about right."

That's it, no first-offense warning, no leniency because my best friend is dead. It isn't fair and he knows it. He's just keeping the phone in case "E" texts me again.

I'm afraid he will.

"Have you eaten lunch yet?" Dad steps out of the way so I can come inside, but I don't move. I'm already feeling sick because of what Dad might see, but it gets worse as a breeze picks up a horribly familiar smell.

Everything inside of me goes in reverse. I run to the bathroom and throw up.

Dad follows me but stays outside the bathroom door, like he's not sure what to do.

The smell is even stronger here.

I keep vomiting until there's nothing left in my stomach, but my body still wants to throw up. I lean over the toilet, my shoulders shaking with dry heaves, but nothing more comes. It's like my body is trying to empty out everything inside: tortillas and lake water, Rachel's text and her murder, and a long-buried memory of a place we never should have been.

"What is that smell?" I choke out as I lean over and try to throw up again.

Dad steps into the bathroom, reaches across the tub, and shuts the window. Then he turns on the fan. The paint smell dissipates, but I can still smell it, and taste it, and feel it clinging to my hands.

"I'm sorry. I was painting the patio furniture. I didn't think . . . you really are sick."

"I told you I was." I say it because I want him to believe me and feel sorry for me, but I wasn't sick, not until I smelled the paint. The smell of spray paint has made me nauseated since the night I saw the symbol on the wall at the old house, but it's never been this bad.

"I'm sorry, honey." His voice is quiet and gentle, but I can still hear fear in it. "Are you okay?"

I can only shake my head. I reach for the toilet handle and close my eyes as everything I ate swirls down the pipes.

I stand up shakily and rinse my mouth out in the sink, then I wash my hands over and over again, even though the stains are only in my memory. When I look in the mirror I'm surprised to see tears running down my cheeks.

Dad turns off the sink and pulls me into his arms. "It's okay, it's okay, it's okay." He's lying, just like Eduardo at the lake. "Let it all out."

But there's too much inside me that I can't let out. And it will never be okay again.

I pull away from him. "Maybe I should go back to bed." I don't wait for him to reply. I go into my bedroom, close the window, and climb into bed, burying my face in my blanket so I don't have to smell the paint.

Outside Dad is dragging the patio furniture to the far side of the lawn, away from my bedroom window. I feel guilty. For being mad at him about my phone. For getting sick over something stupid like paint fumes. For getting a weird message and making him worry.

For ignoring Rachel's calls and not answering her text.

Maybe it's better if Dad sees it. Maybe when he sees it he'll realize what a horrible person I am. He'll know that everything he taught me about doing the right thing meant nothing. He'll know that I'm the kind of girl who's more interested in a boy than in helping my best friend. He'll know that it's my fault that Rachel is dead.

I lie in bed, waiting for him to find the text, but he doesn't come. Eventually I fall into a semiconsciousness that might be considered a dream. I'm half-aware of what's going on around me. Dad starts the lawnmower, and the smell of cut grass cancels out the leftover paint smell. My mind fills with shadows and memories.

Rachel and I are in fourth grade again. We're building our own world out of sticks and leaves in the old brick fireplace at the end of the playground. She finds a broken glass bottle buried in the leaves. She holds up the biggest piece, and her voice gets serious. "We have to swear a blood oath. We have to mix our blood together and swear that we'll be friends forever, that we'll always stay together and protect each other."

I was afraid then too. I didn't want to cut my finger. I didn't want to bleed. But I loved Rachel, and I would do anything for her.

It was a little cut, a few drops of blood, but I thought I was going to pass out. We pressed our fingers together and let our blood run into each other. When our blood was sufficiently mingled we left our fingerprints on the contract, signed in blood.

Then we got caught by the playground duty. I remember that Rachel got in more trouble than I did.

The memory slips away as the door to my room opens; it's Dad. "I hate to leave you, but I'm out of gas for the lawnmower. Will you be okay alone?"

"Yeah. Sure." I sit up. "I'm feeling better."

"I won't be too long."

I lie in bed, listening. As soon as I hear Dad's truck pull out of the driveway, I get up. I have to find my phone and erase Rachel's text before Dad sees it.

I scan the kitchen, but it isn't on the table or on top of the fridge. I go into Dad's office. The room is tiny but organized. On the wall behind his desk there's a tall black filing cabinet and a bookcase that's a mix of law books and how-to parenting and religious books. The only thing on Dad's desk is a picture of me, a plant, and my phone. I take a deep breath, pick up my phone, and scroll back through the incoming calls, *Ray, Ray, Ray, Ray, Ray, Ray*, it says over and over again. How many times did she try to call me after I turned off my phone? I count them as I hit erase. She tried to call twenty-five times while I was riding around town with Skyler, twenty-five times, and then one text.

I go to my messages. Besides the one from E, I have one from Taylor:

SKYLER or EVAN??? I want dets!

And one from Skyler:

What r u doing 2night?

I consider deleting those texts too. I'm not ready to answer questions from Dad about Skyler yet, especially not anything to do with how we got together. But maybe it would look suspicious if too many were gone. I decide to stick with the one I came to erase. My heart aches as I scroll back to Rachel's text, maybe her last words:

We're in trouble. Meet me at my house NOW. Don't tell your dad. Don't call the police. Don't tell anyone what you saw.

What was she doing when she sent that text? Was she alone? Was she scared? Did she know she was going to die?

Why didn't I answer her?

I sink into Dad's big chair and trace the words again.

Don't tell anyone what you saw.

She could only have meant the night we went to the old house. I close my eyes and think about the last time I brought it up. We were walking to her house after school. It was raining, and I tried to take the shortcut through the field that would take us in front of the old house. She stopped me, gripping my arm. "Let's stay on the road."

I was wet and frustrated with her so I resisted. "This is faster, and I'm soaked. What are you so afraid of, anyway?"

She looked at the house. "Nothing, it's just . . . I can't, okay? He died in that house."

There was something about the way she said it, different from before, like someone she knew had died there. "Who died in that house? That guy, the one they found after we—"

"Shh." She looked around, like she was worried someone was listening, but we were alone.

I moved closer to her and spoke quieter, but I wasn't going to let her avoid the question this time. "You saw him, didn't you? That's why you screamed, that's why you ran down the stairs—"

She stood there, shocked, like I had slapped her. I waited for her to deny it again, but she didn't. Instead she turned pale and gripped my shoulders. "You can't tell anyone."

And then I knew that everything I was afraid of was true: Rachel had seen the body. I remember the guilt and terror that hit me with that revelation. I had been in the same house where someone had been murdered, and I hadn't done anything about it, I hadn't gone to the police. I loved Rachel, and I trusted her, maybe too much. "You saw him, I know you did. Why didn't you tell the police?"

Then she got angry. "They have pictures, they collected evidence, they have everything they need. Us being there or not doesn't change what happened. If we go to them now, we'll be in major trouble."

I knew she was right. We would be in trouble, more trouble than I'd ever been in before. I was suddenly furious with her.

"Then why *didn't* we go to the police that night? Why didn't you tell them? Why didn't you at least tell me?"

She glared back at me, but she was fighting tears. "Because I knew you'd want to tell, and then the people who killed him would come after us."

I saw the fear in her eyes, and I felt it too. I thought about the person in the curtains. What if he had seen me? "How do you know that? Wouldn't the police have protected us? We could have at least made an anonymous tip or something." Even as I said it, I heard doubt in my own voice.

Her fingers dug into my shoulders. "You didn't see what I saw. You don't know what they can do. No one is safe from them. The police didn't protect him, and they can't protect us."

"Who are *they*?"

"Don't ask that question. It's better if you don't know." She started walking away, holding back tears.

"Rachel."

"I mean it!"

"No. It's not that, it's just . . . did you know him?"

She shook her head but didn't turn around. "He was just a gangbanger." Her voice choked. "He got what he deserved. It's not worth risking our lives to tell the police what they already know."

I stand up, thinking about what I should have said to her that day. My foot knocks against Dad's recycling bin. On top is another newspaper with Rachel's picture splashed across the front. I pick it up and read:

Local Teen Found Shot in her Bedroom

LAKE RIDGE—The town of Lake Ridge is still reeling after the discovery of a local girl who was found shot in her bedroom on June 16. Police are continuing to investigate the death, said Grant County Sheriff Eric Cross. "We suspect that gang violence was involved. There were gang tags found at the scene," said Cross. "We're still looking into it."

Rachel Araceli Sanchez, 16, was found by her mother, Araceli Sanchez, after returning home from work. Sanchez could not be reached for comment.

"It's horrible," said Claire Rallstrom, 16. "She was, like, really amazing."

This is the first case of gang violence in Lake Ridge since another teenager, Manuel Romero, 17, was murdered last summer, the victim of an alleged gang retaliation.

"At this point the two crimes do not appear to be related," Cross said.

After the initial investigation, according to the statement released Tuesday by the sheriff's department, the case will be turned over to the Spokane Violent Crime Gang Enforcement Team.

I reread the story, choking on the irony of what Claire said, since she and Rachel have hated each other forever. The words blur together: "gang violence," "gang retaliation," and the phrase "the two crimes do not appear to be related." But I know they are.

My phone vibrates, making me jump. I pick it up, a little afraid of what I might find. The message comes through slowly. It's a video file, a forwarded message from a number I don't recognize. I scroll back to see who sent it originally.

It's from Rachel.

CHAPTER 7

I stare at it in disbelief. What if they're all lying? What if Rachel isn't really dead? What if she needs my help? What if it's not too late? My heart aches to believe that's true. But I saw her lying in a coffin.

The image is small and grainy, but it's Rachel, sitting in her bedroom, alive. I stare at it a minute before I hit okay. As she starts to talk, pinpricks of pain find something solid in the hole in my chest.

All hope that Rachel is still alive drains with her first words.

"Jaycee, if you're watching this, it either means this whole thing ended as badly as I think it will, or this is our twenty-year class reunion and we're drinking champagne, eating expensive chocolate, and toasting the fact that we survived all of this and high school too.

"If the second part is true, and I really hope it is, I'm going to bet that by now Claire Rallstrom has six kids, three ex-husbands, and weighs at least two hundred pounds. Taylor

Brice married the richest guy she could find, divorced him, and now she has so much plastic surgery that her face will crack if she smiles." She laughs at her own joke, but her voice sounds sad.

"But if the first part is true, and I'm gone, I need you to know how sorry I am. I shouldn't have taken you to the house that night. His secret was mine to keep because I loved him, not yours. I should have never let you get close enough to be involved. I was stupid, and now it's too late for either of us to go back."

She pauses a second, swallows, and I hear fear in her voice when it starts up again. "I guess I should have told you everything from the beginning, but I thought it was more important for you to be safe than it was for us to be friends. I'm sorry for that. I probably would do the same thing again, but I've missed you so much." Her voice cracks.

My throat closes over with pain.

"I'm sorry to ask you to do this, but if I'm gone, you're the only one who can find out the truth." She waits, like she wants to give me time to take that in.

"I've learned a lot in the last ten months. Like who I can trust, and it boils down to two people, you and Eduardo. You, because you always do the right thing, and Eduardo, because he has as much to lose in this as I do. You can trust him, Jaycee: him and no one else. Not the police. Let me repeat that. Do. Not. Go. To. The. Police."

She looks behind her like she's worried someone is listening. "Eduardo has a huge attitude problem. He hates this town and gringos and probably even fuzzy yellow kittens. He's a hothead. If I left this up to him, someone else would probably end up dead." She laughs, but I'm not sure she's joking. "But he has a good heart. Trust him. You'll need each other.

"I'm sorry to dump this on you, especially now, when you're confused and grieving the best person you've ever known." She smiles her mischievous smile. "Okay, maybe not the best person you've ever known, but certainly in the top ten." I can't believe she's making jokes about her being dead, but it's so much the Rachel I used to know that I want to replay that part again and again. Then she gets serious.

"I thought I had to do this alone. I've done a lot of things you wouldn't approve of to find the answers I needed. Even broke my best friend's heart." She looks away, but I can tell how sorry she is. She shakes her head like she's struggling to get control.

"I've worked so hard, but there's still something missing, something I think will end this whole thing. I'm going tonight to try and find it. If I do, you'll probably never see this, except maybe at our twenty-year class reunion." She smiles again, but it's a sad, scared smile. "If I don't make it, it's up to you to find the truth. I told Eduardo to give you something, something that only you will understand. I know you can help me. You're the best person I know. You always do the right thing."

She presses her index finger against the screen, so I can see the tiny line across the tip of her finger, the leftover scar from when we bled together. "I love you, *chica*. I'm sorry for everything. I miss you."

The video stops on that image. I press my index finger against hers through the glass on my phone, sharing the signal we've had since that day on the playground, the signal that we would always be friends.

I sit back, my mind reeling with questions. She knew she was going to die. I'm sure of that now, but why? Whose secret was she trying to keep? Eduardo's? But she wants me to trust him? Was it worth getting killed for? Eduardo gave me the loyalty pledge, "something that only you'll understand," but I don't understand any of it.

I close my eyes and slump in Dad's chair, heartsick, wanting to help but knowing I can't do what she needs me to do. I'm not strong, not like she was. I'm the quiet one, the one who hangs out with little kids and blushes when a guy tries to talk to her.

What can I do?

I'm startled by my phone vibrating. Another text comes through.

tomorrow 10 am answer then delete all

It's attached to a picture of the grade-school playground.

I don't know what to do. Answer? Delete? Pretend I never saw the messages? Take it to the police and finally tell them everything? Somehow the video from Rachel is harder to ignore than the text. Maybe because it's more like she was asking in person.

I scroll back to the text from "E" and compare the number from the forwarded text and from the text I just got. They're the same. Eduardo. What does he know? What does he think I know?

A truck drives by. It sounds like Dad. I panic, pick up my phone, and delete the last two texts and the original one from Rachel.

I set the phone on the desk, shove the newspaper back into the recycling, and head for the door. As soon as my hand touches the knob, my phone vibrates again. I turn around and pick it up.

4 her

I close my eyes, breathe in, and then quick, before I can change my mind, I text Eduardo:

I'll be there.

CHAPTER 8

Evan said Rachel's house was still a mess, but I wasn't expecting this. I stare in disbelief at the front yard that until a few months ago was so familiar. The house is small, only one level, and old, but Araceli had painted it a bright yellow with white trim and a red door. There were always flowers in the yard, red geraniums in the boxes in front of the window, and the wide front porch was always clean.

Now the house looks like the wounded remnant of a war zone. The flowers in front have been trampled. Yellow police tape, now ripped and blowing in the breeze, hangs around the perimeter of the porch, and shattered pots of dying geraniums litter the ground. The front door, the porch railing, the sidewalk in front, and the shed have all been tagged with red graffiti—circles full of the same eye shapes painted in red. I don't know what they mean, but they're familiar enough to make me shiver.

Rachel had the front bedroom because Araceli works

nights and it was easier for her to sleep in the back of the house. I expected a bullet hole, or maybe two, but the front of the house is peppered with them. Rachel's bedroom window is shattered. The leftover bits of glass line the frame like jagged, gaping fangs. The window is covered by a quilt, tacked on the inside. I wonder what I would find if I went inside Rachel's bedroom.

Dad reaches for the door handle and rests his hand there without opening the door. "I'm sorry. I would have never brought you here if I'd known it looked like this."

I should have told Dad I was still sick. I don't want to face Rachel's mom, or go to a house Rachel will never come back to, but my conscience got to me, so I said I would come. After everything, visiting Rachel's mom felt like the least I could do.

I'm half a breath away from asking him to take me home when the front door opens and a man in a dark suit comes out, followed by Rachel's mom. For the first time I notice the blue car parked in front, too clean to have spent much time in Lake Ridge. Araceli looks small, alone, and lost. She's wrapping what looks like a dish towel around and around her hand. Dad opens the door and climbs out. He stands between my door and Araceli's porch, like he's trying to be a human shield between me and the awfulness. At the same time I know he's waiting for me to get out. I force myself to open the door. When I reach him, Dad wraps his arm around my shoulders and we walk toward the house.

We're almost up the stairs before the man on the porch

turns. "It looks like you have visitors, Ms. Sanchez." His eyes fall on us only for a second, but in that second I can feel him measuring our guilt and innocence, like someone who does that kind of thing on a daily basis.

"Jaycee, Travis." Araceli says our names with a mixture of shock and relief. "I'm so glad you came."

Dad steps forward, and since his arm is still around me, so do I. He kind of herds me up the steps to the front porch and toward the door. I keep my eyes on Rachel's mom, the only thing about this place that feels familiar anymore.

"This is Rachel's best friend, Jaycee Draper," Araceli says. The title makes my stomach twist around itself. As soon as I'm within reach she pulls me toward her, the way she did at the funeral. For a second I don't think she's going to let me go, but as soon as she does, I want to bury my face into her chest again, anything to avoid the hard black eyes of the man standing next to her.

"Rachel's best friend." The man repeats it slowly, like being Rachel's friend makes me a criminal.

"Since kindergarten," Dad says, pulling me away from both of them. He reaches his hand to Rachel's mom. "Araceli, I want to extend my deepest sympathies." I've never heard Dad talk to Rachel's mom so formally, but when he extends his hand Araceli takes it as if he were keeping her from falling into a bottomless pit.

"If you're Rachel's friend, maybe you could answer some questions for me." If the man speaking has a complete face, I can't tell. All I can see are his eyes drilling into me.

"We haven't been friends for a while," I blurt out. To the left of the dark eyes, the pain lines on Araceli's face deepen. I feel the weight of my disloyalty, but it feels like an association with Rachel spells guilt to the eyes in front of me. "I mean for a few months. We stopped hanging out about six months ago."

"Oh? Why?" His stance stays stiff, and his eyes don't leave mine.

I lick my lips, but I can't find an answer that would satisfy his accusation.

"Rachel and Jaycee just took different paths," Dad intervenes. "You know how teenagers are."

"That's all it was? No fight or anything?" The man directs his question back at me.

"No." I say it slowly, positive he's not interested in a fight between two teenage girls over a guy.

"Well, Jaycee. That being said, I still have a few questions I'd like you to answer." The dark eyes find me again, shrinking behind Dad.

"And you are?" Dad's voice holds a challenge that I've only heard a couple of times, when I watched him in court.

"Special Agent Herrera." The man reaches inside his coat and pulls out a badge. "I'm part of the Spokane Violent Crime and Gang Task Force. Through the FBI." *FBI?* My heart stops. "I specialize in drug- and gang-related crimes." He slides the badge back in his pocket. "When was your last communication with Rachel?" I swallow hard. I can feel him weighing my expression, my breaths; my every move. "Her last phone call, or text?"

I'm suddenly confused. Does the video message I saw this afternoon count? It was from Rachel, but not directly. She told me not to talk to the cops, begged me. In spite of everything I've been taught about telling the truth, I'm not sure what's right anymore. I start small. "She tried to call me a few nights ago."

He flips open a little notebook. "When exactly?"

I want to look away, but I don't dare. "Friday."

His eyes flash with surprise, and I hear Dad and Araceli both draw a breath. "The night she was murdered?"

I flinch. "Yes."

He writes something down. "Approximately what time was the first call?"

"Late. I'm not sure when." I glance up at Dad, wondering if Detective Herrera is going to ask me where I was when Rachel tried to call me, knowing I can't lie to him.

"I see. And did you have a conversation with her that night?"

"No. My phone was off. I didn't see that she had called until later," I say. His eyes are still boring into me so I include, "But she sent me a text."

Dad and Araceli exchange shocked looks.

Agent Herrera stays steady. "And what did the text say?"

"I'm not sure. I didn't read it. I deleted it." The lie and the truth come out with one breath. If I don't admit what it said, I'm not responsible. Phone records can be traced. I'm sure Detective Herrera can find out what the text said without me.

"Oh?" Special Agent Herrera says.

Araceli looks shocked, hurt, and confused. She turns to me. "Jaycee, I don't understand. A text? Rachel didn't have a cell phone."

Now it's my turn to look shocked. Somehow I didn't think that Rachel would have kept the phone a secret from her mom this whole time.

But Agent Herrera is nodding. "You aren't the first of Rachel's friends to tell me about her having a phone. But the other person couldn't tell me where she'd gotten it. Can you?"

I swallow, look from Araceli's hurt face to my father's disappointed one. "She said her dad sent it to her. That he was paying for it."

Araceli's eyes widen. "No. No. She has no contact with her father. He wouldn't have given her a phone."

"But it seems she did have a phone." Agent Herarra writes something down. "Perhaps of unknown origin." He turns to me. "How long would you say she had this phone?"

"Almost a year." I look up at Dad for help. "She showed it to me last summer. I didn't know she hadn't told her mom about it."

"Do you have any idea where that phone is now?" Agent Herrera's eyes are measuring me even more closely than they were before.

"No. I thought . . . I mean, she had to have had it with her. The text came the night she died." I'm floundering again, not sure what the truth is.

"So I assume you have the number?" Agent Herrera holds his little notebook, poised and ready to write.

"It's in my phone," I answer, "but I don't have it. My dad . . ."

"I've got it right here." Dad pulls my phone out of his pocket. I don't know why he brought it with him; maybe he was planning to give it back to me.

"I'm going to need to take that as evidence." Detective Herrera reaches for my phone and Dad passes it to him. I feel like he's handing over my life to a complete stranger. I'm suddenly very grateful I deleted everything, including the text I sent to Eduardo. But I'm not sure how cell phones work. Can Detective Herrera see what I've deleted? Can he tell I got a video message I didn't tell him about? And what if I get another text from Eduardo? He turns the phone on and goes to my contact list. "I assume the number is listed here."

I nod. "Under Ray." When my dad gave me the phone as a surprise the day I started high school, Rachel's number was the first one I put in. I've gone to delete it a hundred times, but I couldn't bring myself to do it.

He writes down the number and then seals my phone in a plastic bag from his pocket. "Now, back to the text message you got the night she died. Why did you delete it?" The question comes from Agent Herrera, but I can feel it coming from all sides.

I stare at the graffiti under my feet, a hollow eye. "Rachel was into some bad things. I didn't want anyone to see it." I can't face Dad or Araceli, and if I look at Agent Herrera he'll know I'm not telling all of the truth.

"Bad things?" He leans toward me. "Like what?"

I step back. "I don't know. I just heard rumors." He's still breathing down my neck. "And they found drugs in her locker." Araceli takes in a wavering breath. I hate that I brought that up in front of her. I whisper, "I'm sorry," as Dad grips my arm.

"Anything you have firsthand knowledge of?" Agent Herrera seems to fill the entire porch. I can't escape his eyes.

I think about telling him everything, about the text, about the old house; maybe if I tell him, this could all be over. I wonder what the penalty is for withholding evidence. I wonder if the police could really protect me. But I promised Rachel I wouldn't.

He's already moved to the next thing. "Could you tell me anything about who Rachel has been associating with lately, or what she might have been doing?"

Eduardo's face comes into my brain, but I can only form one word. "No."

"I see." He steps back and I breathe again. "I'll check the phone records and see if we can retrieve the contents of the text, but usually the phone company only keeps that data for twenty-four to forty-eight hours." I wonder if that includes the other text I received today, if he'll search through all my texts, including the video message and the one I sent Eduardo. Agent Herrera writes something down. "Ms. Sanchez was telling me that Rachel sometimes kept a journal, but the journal hasn't been seen since Rachel died. Do you know anything about it?"

I lick my lips, but can't think of anything incriminating about telling the truth. As long as I've known Rachel she's had some kind of journal. "Yes."

"So you're saying you know where it is," Agent Herrera says eagerly.

"No, I'm saying I know about it." The graffiti moves in red swirls around my feet, making me dizzy. I lean against Dad for support.

"You don't have any idea where it might be now?" Agent Herrera's eyes glitter, like some kind of bug, or a spider, moving in for the kill.

"No," I answer firmly. My face is getting hot like I'm about to throw up again, or pass out. I close my eyes.

When I open my eyes Detective Herrera is holding a business card. He reaches it toward me, but Dad intercepts it. "If you remember anything you think might be important to the case, please give me a call." He turns to Araceli with a stone-cold look. "I'm sorry for your loss. We'll do whatever we can to find out who did this." His speech sounds canned, like he's said those words without hope a thousand times. The way he looks at Araceli, without any real sympathy, makes me dislike him even more.

"Who's responsible for all this?" Dad indicates the porch with a sweep of his hand. "Who do we need to talk to in order to get this cleaned up?"

Agent Herrera shakes his head. "We're done gathering evidence. As far as what's left, that's the homeowner's responsibility."

I can see the sides of Dad's jaw working, like he wants to say something, but he just nods.

"I'll be in touch." Detective Herrera's monotone voice makes me think he's pretty much done with this case.

"What about my phone?" My voice sounds small and selfish. It was just a hand-me-down, Dad's old phone, but it's been my social link to everyone for the last year, and even though I deleted the text, it was my last link to Rachel.

"We'll send it to you when we're finished with it," Agent Herrera says briskly.

He nods to Dad and then leaves us standing on the porch. We all watch him climb into his car and drive away. When he's gone, Dad reaches for Araceli's arm. He looks down at her. "I'm sorry for this. Why don't you come stay at our house for a couple of days, and I can get some people together to help you clean this up."

Araceli shakes him off, drawing herself into a stance I know too well. Rachel and Araceli have always been independent. "I'm leaving for work in an hour. The boy from the construction company said they would be here to replace the window tomorrow morning. I'll take care of the rest when I can."

We stand in silence for a few minutes. Araceli doesn't invite us in. Finally Dad says, "We'll let you go, but please call us anytime, day or night, if you need anything."

Araceli looks at me with an expression that feels cold for the first time ever. She can't forgive me for deleting Rachel's last words. "Thank you very much, but I have friends I can go to if I need help."

The way she says "friends" cuts through me, like she's implying that Dad and I aren't her friends anymore, when once we were more like family.

Dad reaches for her hand. "Again, I'm so sorry. Rachel will be missed by all of us."

Araceli pulls away and nods. She doesn't look at me again before she closes the door.

CHAPTER 9

W e really appreciate Jaycee coming today." Dawn, the head of the church children's program, is talking to Dad at the door. "She's so good with the kids."

I can't hear Dad's response over the noise the kids are making while they paint animals from Noah's ark. I've been helping with Vacation Bible School since I was thirteen. I love being around little kids, but because of everything, this is the first time I've made it this summer. I feel guilty that the only reason I came today was so I could be close enough to the school to meet Eduardo at ten. I couldn't exactly tell Dad about that. I just have to figure out an excuse to leave the class for a few minutes. I hope it's only a few minutes. I'm not sure what Eduardo has to say to me.

"And she's turning into such a pretty girl—the big brown eyes, the auburn hair," Dawn says.

I turn on the faucet to rinse out the paintbrushes and look in the mirror. I wonder if Dawn is right about my being pretty. The skinny girl who looks back at me doesn't look any different to me. My hair isn't auburn, just plain reddish-brown, my face is pale and plain, and while I'm not quite a size zilch in bras anymore, my body doesn't compare to Taylor's or Claire's, and not even close to Rachel's. I'm sure Dawn is only being nice.

Dawn continues. "I'm glad she felt good enough to come today. I'm sure she's heartbroken over what happened to Rachel. Those girls were quite a pair. It's so sad the path Rachel chose, so unexpected."

"Yes, it was," Dad says. I can hear the sadness in his voice.

"Cee Cee." One of the little girls, Nicki, tugs on my elbow. "I made a picture for you."

I bend down and accept the picture, either a short-necked giraffe or a horse with blue spots. "It's beautiful." Nicki's face glows, and my heart swells as I give her a hug, wishing some of her innocence could rub off on me.

"Was that my dad?" I ask Dawn after I'm done hanging up Nicki's picture.

"Yes, it was. He didn't want to disturb your art class, but he said he wanted to check in and see if you're feeling okay."

"Oh." More like he was checking up on me. Dad's always been overprotective, but it's gotten worse since Rachel died.

Being with the little kids keeps me busy and keeps my mind off everything else, at least mostly. I still glance at the clock every few minutes, wondering what Eduardo wants to talk to me about and whether I dare meet him.

It's not even 9:45 when I see Dawn standing by the window, looking out toward the field behind the grade school where I set up a soccer game. Some guy is kicking the soccer balls we left in a pile next to the portable net. He slams it into the goal so hard that the cheap net is about to collapse in on itself. "Who is that boy? He's going to destroy that net," she says. The boy turns and I recognize Eduardo.

I hesitate and consider hiding out in the church, but I said I'd meet him. "I'll go talk to him."

"Are you sure?" Dawn says. "I mean, he looks like he could be dangerous."

"I'll be fine," I say, and try to laugh to cover my shaking voice. "As long as you're okay being alone with the minions." Instead of waiting for her answer I head for the door, afraid that if I don't go now I'll lose my nerve.

I walk outside and cross the street to the school. "Hey," I call. The soccer ball slams into the net and the post leans closer to the ground. "Hey!" I yell louder, running toward the goal as a second soccer ball makes the other post tip over. "You're going to ruin that." The third soccer ball shoots toward me. It surprises me, but I manage to block it with my foot and send it back toward Eduardo. When it hits his foot, he looks shocked that I was able to return it. Maybe even a little impressed. When I was a little kid Rachel and I played soccer together. I haven't played for years, but I've been practicing behind the house, where no one can see me.

"What are you doing?" I demand in a voice that's braver than I feel.

He catches the ball with his foot and launches it straight up, then catches it smoothly. "You said you would meet me."

I glance over my shoulder at the big window where Dawn is still watching us. I walk closer so I don't have to yell. "Yeah, in fifteen minutes. I'm kind of busy right now."

"You didn't get my text about coming early?" he says.

I freeze. "You sent me another text?"

"Is that a problem?"

"Only if you sent me something you don't want the police to know. They have my cell phone now."

The whole time we've been talking he's been kicking the ball back and forth between his right foot and his left, but as soon as I say "police" he stops and his dark skin goes a shade lighter. "You gave your phone to the police?"

"No. The FBI," I say slowly, watching for his reaction.

He gets even paler. "FBI?"

"There was some special agent from a gang task force at Rachel's house yesterday." I tug at one of the goal posts to straighten it, avoiding his eyes. "He asked me some questions and he took my phone."

"You talked to the feds?" He says it like I'm a traitor. "You gave them your phone? With Rachel's message?"

"Yes . . . I mean no." His reaction is making me more nervous. "Yes, I talked to them. Yes, I gave them the phone, but I deleted the message, like you told me to."

"Did he have a warrant to take your phone?" He sounds scared, as if Agent Herrera's having a warrant for my phone would be a bad thing.

"No, I was just trying to cooper—"

"Don't."

"Don't what?"

"Don't cooperate with them. You can't trust them. You can't trust the police, the feds, anyone."

"Except you?" I'm trying to sound ironic, but I'm not sure he catches it.

"Except me." His voice is so serious that it scares me.

I finish straightening the posts and stand to face him. I'm not sure where this is going. "So, you want to talk? Okay, let's talk."

He looks back at the church. "Not here."

I roll my eyes, but his need for privacy makes my stomach clench. "No one in the church can hear us." He shakes his head. I'm not sure how to handle this situation, or if I should be alone with him. I point to the far end of the field. "I'm supposed to set up an obstacle course for the kids out there. Help me with that and we can talk." He looks around the empty field and then nods. I head for the shed next to the church. "Bring the soccer balls."

In the safety of the shed I take in a breath, contemplating what Eduardo could possibly want to talk to me about. I grab an armload of spikes with flags on the end and a stack of orange cones. Eduardo is heading down the field, a ball in each arm, dribbling the third one between his feet. I stop and watch him, wondering if I'm being stupid or paranoid. He kind of saved my life in the lake. I would have probably figured out I was in shallow water before I drowned, but still, he came in after me, or maybe he was already there. Maybe he was watching me. That thought sends chills down my spine.

Whatever he's here for, at this point being friendly is probably my best option. "Do you play soccer?" I say when I catch up to him.

"No," he says flatly. He drops the balls from his arms but continues dribbling the other one between his feet, like it was a nervous habit. "Why do the feds have your phone?"

"Because I had Rachel's number, which apparently not even her mom had."

"Why did you tell them you had her number?" He eyes me suspiciously.

"Because they asked. Because they're trying to figure out what happened to her, and I thought I should help." Not exactly the whole story, but it sounds more noble than my getting a text from Rachel and then deleting it. Except to him, I don't think it sounds noble at all.

"The cops are idiots. They don't want to find out what really happened. They just want to find some Chicano to pin it on." He keeps dribbling the ball between his feet. I don't want to keep arguing with him, so I look for neutral territory. I drop my armload of flags and cones on the ground. "You're really good at that. You should try out for the high school team—"

"The high school soccer team is a joke." He shoots the ball toward me so hard that it stings my foot, but I block it and send it back to him.

"They went to state last year, and the year before," I point out.

He catches the ball under his foot and rolls it back and forth. "Really? How many soccer games did you watch last year?"

I pick up the first flag, not sure why he sounds so hostile. "I didn't—"

"And how many football games?" His gaze goes through me.

"I don't—"

"All of them?"

I hesitate, not sure of the animosity in his voice. "I don't know what that has to do with any—"

"And they lost every one." He crosses his arms. "But you watched them anyway. And probably painted your face and wore the school colors and screamed for them."

He's right. I didn't paint my face, but I wore the school colors and I went to every game, alone. Even though Rachel and I were still friends at that point, I couldn't get her to come with me. The rest of the town went though. We all screamed ourselves hoarse as the football team was trounced again and again. Why does Eduardo care?

"Nobody goes to soccer games because they're a conciliation sport for the Mexican kids."

I plant another stake while I think about that. "So you texted me and made me come all the way out here so you could give me attitude about high school sports?"

"No."

"Then what do you want?"

He looks like he's sizing me up. "Rachel said you were different, but you're just like the rest of them."

"You don't know anything about me."

"I know you stopped talking to Rachel when she changed the way she looked. I know you were ashamed to hang out with her."

"That's not true. She—" But I can't explain about Evan to Eduardo. "Look, we just . . ." What did Dad say? "We just took different paths."

He doesn't look convinced. "Are you sure?"

That stops me. I remember Rachel's voice when I admitted to her that she wasn't invited to Claire's New Year's Eve party but I was, probably because Claire's mom made her invite me. Rachel wasn't mad, just quiet. "It's okay. I have plans." But I half believed she was lying to protect my feelings, so I could go to the party without feeling guilty.

On New Year's Day, I called so we could laugh together over how stupid Claire's party was, but she didn't answer and she never called back. Claire told me about Evan and Rachel's date at church, the day before we went back to school after winter break. My last conversation with Rachel happened the next day.

He's still watching me, his eyes narrowed. I know what Rachel meant. The chip on his shoulder is so big I can almost see it.

"If you want to talk, talk," I snap at him.

"She said you knew things. That you were with her that night."

His reference to the night I've buried in the black corners of my memory, the night in the old house, makes my blood freeze. I wonder how much Eduardo knows about it.

"No." I shake my head hard as fear pulses through me. "She was wrong. I wasn't there. I don't know anything." I turn away so he can't see my face. We promised we'd never talk about it; Rachel made me promise. I don't know this guy. For all I know he was part of the gang that murdered her. Just the mention of the word "police" makes him freak. "I can't help you."

"You mean you won't help me. But you'll help the pigs in blue." He shakes his head in mock disappointment. "Rachel said you were different, *boba*, but I don't think so. You're just like the rest of them."

"Whatever, okay?" I throw down the cone I was holding and start back to church.

"Boba!" he yells. When I turn, he boots the ball to me one more time. I stop it with a header that sends it flying to the other side of the field. When I turn back around he yells, "Why don't *you* play high school soccer?"

It was the wrong thing for him to say, like he knew exactly how to get to me. Like Rachel told him.

It was the regional championship. The score was tied, and for once I was in the game. The ball came to me. For one beautiful moment, everything ahead of me was clear. I started dribbling down the field, getting in position to shoot the winning goal. I was getting closer, so close I could almost see myself being carried off the field on the shoulders of my adoring teammates. She came from behind me, so fast that all I could see was her long blond ponytail and the flores-cent green of our matching shorts. Claire was going to steal the ball from me, her own teammate, because she didn't trust me to make the shot. Rachel blocked her so I could shoot the ball. I missed, and we lost the game on a penalty kick. I don't think Claire has ever forgiven me or Rachel for that.

We were eleven. Rachel said it was no big deal, that it was just a game, but I quit after that season because soccer wasn't fun anymore. Not because of what Eduardo was implying, that soccer is beneath me because it's a sport for the Mexican kids.

Dawn is coming out of the church with the children, but I don't care. I'm done with his attitude and everything about him. I march back to Eduardo. "You don't know anything about me. I gave my phone to the police to try to help, because it was the right thing to do. Because I wanted to help. Rachel was just fine when she was my friend."

"She was fine." He scoffs. "That shows how much you didn't know about her."

"And she was better off with you?" I'm so angry, I'm shaking. Eduardo stands his ground, his eyes hard, but I step toward him, so close I'm in his face, my anger pushing aside all fear. "How can you stand there and accuse me of being disloyal to Rachel"—the words come out before I can stop them; I have to blame someone—"when she's dead because of people like you?"

His attitude melts into horror and pain. He lowers his head. "You're right. It is my fault."

He looks so hurt that I reach for him, sorry for what I said. He jerks away, and my hand catches the edge of his tank top.

It slips off his shoulder, and for the first time I see a red mark on his back, a tattoo that looks like the symbols I saw on Rachel's porch. A gang sign.

I back away and Eduardo runs.

CHAPTER
10

D ad isn't home yet when I'm finished with Vacation Bible
School, so I go for a long run. I plug in my earbuds and
try to concentrate on the music, my breath, and moving forward. Running is my release. Sometimes it feels like my runs
are the only time I have to myself, the only time I have to be
in my own head. After my talk with Eduardo, I need to think.

I make a wide circle and then run into town. For a while I
head to the high school track, thinking I might try some
sprints. Instead I end up back at the grade school, the place
where I first met Rachel. I'm thinking about the piece of paper
she gave me, our loyalty pledge, signed on this very playground,
hidden here until she gave it to Eduardo. I think this is where
she wanted me to go.

At one end a mom and her kids are playing on the swings,
and there's a lawnmower going behind the building, but oth-
erwise I'm alone. I slow to a trot as I get closer to the fireplace
at the far corner of the school. It's a stone structure with two

ends where you can build a fire and a long chimney in between that makes it look kind of like a castle—at least it did to a couple of little girls. There's a grate across the top of either side for cooking over the fire, but it's old and rusty. I'm sure no one has used it for years.

At the end of fifth grade a little boy jumped off the top of it and got a bloody lip and a chipped tooth. We were banned from playing on or near it after that, which sucked because until then the castle fireplace was our haven, where Rachel and I went to pretend at recess, far away from the rest of the kids.

I slow down as I get closer. Somewhere in the back of the right side, up underneath a loose brick in the chimney is where we left our proclamation of loyalty, signed in blood. I'd forgotten about it until Eduardo tried to give it to me at the lake. I wish now that I had kept it instead of shoving it back at him. Agent Herrera said Rachel's phone was missing and that she had a diary. Maybe she hid one of them in the fireplace. I have to look.

I glance around again. I'm hidden from the view of the mom and her kids by the corner of the school building, the lawnmower still sounds far away, and there's no one else around. I have to sit down and slide backward across the soot-stained cement to get to where I can reach the back of the fire-place. I turn sideways, wedging myself farther into the narrow opening and reach up. I don't fit into this spot as easily as I once did.

Solid, solid, solid, I count the bricks as I touch them. The fourth one gives way like a loose tooth. Rachel and I used to hide notes for each other in the space behind the loose brick. I work it out with one hand and heft it beside me. From the angle I've shoved myself into it's impossible to see if there's anything inside. Trying not to think about spiders, I reach my hand back into the hole. It goes back farther than I remember. I strain to reach, and my fingers touch something like a plastic bag.

I stretch farther sideways, my arm scraping against the bricks, until I get the plastic between my fingers and slide the bag out into the light where I can see it. It's full of black beads and a thick cross.

My heart throbs. The cross is Rachel's, the only gift she ever got from her dad, except for the phone. She used to wear it all the time. I swallow hard as I trace the roses carved onto the front. It's gaudy and huge, but somehow it seemed to fit her. I try to remember the last time I saw her wearing it. Or even the last time I saw her.

I remember now, her eyes following me as I walked past her, but she didn't say anything. Not "hi" or "have a great summer" or anything. Just watched me walk away as she left school with Eduardo. It was like we'd never known each other.

I don't know if she was wearing the cross.

I reach to replace the brick, but suddenly the lawnmower sounds like it's on top of me. I scramble to get out of the fireplace. Just as it gets to me, I scoot out and stand up, stumbling forward. The lawnmower's engine kills, and a tall guy wearing a baseball cap gets off and comes toward the fireplace.

He laughs when he sees me, and my heart sinks. Evan

Cross. Again. He's shirtless, his T-shirt tucked into the back pocket of a pair of ripped jeans. "Jaycee, what are you doing?" His grin makes me feel like a slow little girl again, standing alone on the sidelines of the soccer field.

"I was just—" I stop when he reaches over and brushes my cheek with his hand.

"You have a little smudge there." He brushes my other cheek. "And there." He touches my forehead. "And there. Were you climbing around in the fireplace?" I step back, bump my elbow against the bricks, and drop the bag. I lean to get it, but he's faster than I am, so he picks it up first.

I reach to take the bag from him, but he holds it up to take a look. Frustrated, I step back. "I came to see if that was still here. I hid it when I was in grade school."

"How long ago?" He's studying the cross through the bag.

"Fourth grade."

"And it was in the fireplace all this time?" He pushes his baseball cap back, leaving a streak of soot on his own forehead. "Amazing that it didn't burn up years ago, but I guess no one uses this anymore."

"What are you doing here?" I ask to take the attention off the bag of beads before he recognizes it.

He rubs his hand on his jeans. "The pursuit of higher education."

"Higher education?" I glance over at the grade school, not sure if he's making a joke.

"College. I'm working for my uncle. To earn money to go to school." He walks over to the lawnmower and picks up a bottle of Coke that's sitting by the seat. He wipes the lid off with the T-shirt from his back pocket.

"I thought you had a football scholarship," I say. He looks confused, and I push forward stupidly. "Weren't there scouts from WSU and everywhere else coming to the games, checking you out?"

"Junior year, yes. Last year, when the team went 0–9? Not so much." He takes another drink like he's disgusted. "I'll be lucky if I make Walla Walla Community College. But one way or another, football or not, in a couple of months I'm outta here."

He sits on the edge of the fireplace and takes a long drink of the Coke. He watches me as he lowers it and wipes his mouth. "You want a drink?" I shake my head. "Are you sure? You look hot."

The way he says, "You look hot," makes me shake my head harder and tug my T-shirt down to cover the sliver of skin between it and my shorts. Everything Evan says sounds like he's flirting, like it's impossible for him to have a conversation with a girl without turning on the charm.

As he tips his head back to drain the last bit of Coke, I'm distracted by a tattoo on his shoulder, black-and-purple symbols surrounding a sloppy eighteen, his football jersey number and my lucky number for most of my life. The number I saw in the old house.

I think.

The swirls remind me of the symbols I saw on the porch at Rachel's house and the tattoo on Eduardo's back.

He leaves the bottle on the fireplace and stands up. "I need to get this finished." He nods toward the lawnmower. "I'd offer you a ride again, but this isn't nearly as fun as my motorcycle."

"That's okay." I back away, trying not to stare at Evan's tattoo. "I need to get home."

"If you wait, my little brother will be here to pick me up." His lips twitch into a smile. "I think he'd like it if you were here." I duck my head, wondering what Skyler might have told Evan about me or about us kissing. "You might want to clean up a little, though." He pushes a piece of hair that escaped from my ponytail back around my ear. His ease at touching me makes my heart beat faster but bothers me at the same time. He doesn't move his hand. "Skyler was right, you are—"

Before he can finish whatever it was that Skyler said about me, a door slams and both of us turn toward the parking lot. Evan freezes with his hand on my cheek. Skyler stops and stares at us. He's close enough that I see his expression change from shocked to hurt to angry in about a heartbeat.

Evan pulls his hand away and swears under his breath. He turns toward his brother, and says, "Skyler, don't . . . ," but Skyler turns back around and climbs into the truck. He slams his door again and tries to restart the engine, but it won't turn over. "You better go talk to him before he tears out of here. Skyler has a tendency to flip out over stupid stuff."

I head for the parking lot, trying to figure out what I'm supposed to say to Skyler. I only know I want to erase the hurt from his face. Before I can reach him, he peels out and screeches away.

Evan swears again, louder this time. "Now it looks like I need a ride home. You have a car?"

"No, I ran here."

"Looks like that's what I'll be doing too. Insecure little punk." He throws his hat down.

"Sorry," I say, but I'm not sure what I have to be sorry about.

"Not your fault. Skyler's just a hothead." He leans over and picks up his hat. "Can you make it home before dark, or do you want to wait and I'll walk you home?"

"No, I'm okay." I glance at the sky; the clouds are just starting to turn pink. I must have been running longer than I thought. "I need to go." For a second I remember that there was a time when I'd have given anything to be alone with Evan Cross. But after two conversations he's already starting to annoy me. Maybe it's because of the rift he caused between Rachel and me, and now with Skyler.

"Okay." Evan puts his hand on my shoulder. "Be careful, there's a lot of crazy stuff going on around here."

I pull away and shiver. I'm not sure if it's because of his touch or because of the warning in his voice.

CHAPTER
11

I hurry, but the sun is setting faster than I expect it to. I've been gone a long time, and Dad is going to be worried. As the shadows get longer, my imagination keeps inventing things in the bushes. A cat running across the road makes me jump sideways. I pull out one earbud, because not being able to hear is freaking me out. The fastest way home would be to cut across the dirt road that eventually leads past the old house. No way am I going by it now. I skirt around it on the paved road, but I can't help but look at the top of the house, at the one broken window. It reminds me of Rachel's bedroom window, hollow and empty.

I stop dead in my tracks, remembering the bag of beads. Evan didn't give them back to me. I was so worried about Skyler being mad that I forgot to get them from him. I look up at the darkening sky. I'll have to be quick if I'm going to get the beads and make it home by dark. I hesitate just a second before I turn around and head back toward the school.

It's almost completely dark when I make it to the playground. Everything smells like cut grass, but the lawnmower and Evan are both gone. I slow to a walk as I approach the fireplace, hoping he left the bag here. The fireplace is covered by shadows from the trees around it. I'm almost to it when I see something move. I freeze and watch for a second. At first I think it's just the shadow of the trees moving in the wind. Then there's a light dancing around inside the opening, like a flashlight. I back up against the side of the school building, hiding in a little alcove between windows, watching.

Someone stands up from the fireplace. He's tall, but he's wearing a black hoodie and his face is shadowed by a baseball cap, so I can't tell who he is. He starts walking toward me. I press my back hard against the brick wall, trying to keep my breath still, but my heart is pounding so much that if he gets any closer, I'm sure he'll hear it. He keeps walking until he's just to the side of me, where I can't see him around the corner of the school.

I jump as another voice to my right whispers, "Did you find anything?"

For a second I think the first guy saw me move; he stops like he's scanning the side of the school. I cram myself farther into the corner. After an eternity, he walks by me.

"No," the first guy says. I don't dare look around the corner to see if I can see their faces.

"Are you sure she was looking for something?" the second voice asks. It's a boy, someone closer to my age than the first voice. They're just a few yards to the side of me, but I'm too afraid to look.

"Why else would she be digging around inside a fireplace?" They're talking about *me*. Were they watching me, following me? I strain my ears, trying to decide if the voice is familiar.

"She wasn't carrying anything when she left, at least nothing I could see."

"Maybe there wasn't anything for her to find."

"He said she had a journal—"

Who is he?

"Maybe he was wrong. Anyway, why would she have written it all down? It's not like she knew she was going to—"

"None of us did." His voice is thick with regret. He pauses for a second. I smell cigarette smoke.

My blood chills; they're talking about Rachel.

"Just in case, we'd better make sure there isn't anything here to find."

For a few minutes I hear shuffling and the cracking of branches; something sloshes and the air fills up with first the smell of gasoline and then the spicy, musty smell of burning leaves. The fire pours out of the hearth and for a second lights up the hat the second guy is wearing. It says LAKE RIDGE HIGH STATE CHAMPS.

I stay still for a long time after the fire dies down, after their footsteps fade in the dark, so long that I wonder if I can make my body move again. When I finally gather enough courage to leave the safety of my alcove, my first instinct is to run, and run hard.

I think about going to the police, but what would I tell them? I don't have the message from Rachel, or her note, or her necklace. And Rachel said not to go to them, not to trust them.

Don't trust anyone but Eduardo. But Eduardo hates me.

I need to sort this out. I have to get the beads back. My heart pounds in my ears in time to the pounding of the pavement under my feet; between the two I can't tell if someone is following me now. I don't dare turn around to look.

Outside of town, I pause for a second to catch my breath. Debating the route again—longer paved roads or the shorter road that will take me by the old house. I freeze. Footsteps are coming toward me. I turn. No one is there, but a shadow moves between the streetlights, maybe a cat, but I'm not sure. Headlights come up the street. The shadow disappears behind a tree.

An old truck rumbles by with a bunch of migrant workers in the back, lit cigarettes glowing red as they pass. One of them yells something to me in Spanish. I shrink farther off the side of the road. The truck stops and the driver leans out. "Want a ride, chica?" He looks older than my dad.

One of the passengers in the back leans forward, arguing with the man in Spanish. I take a couple of steps backward, plotting my escape route. I turn, prepped to run, and catch a glimpse of Eduardo in the corner of the truck. I look into his eyes, begging for help, but he looks through me like he doesn't know who I am. The door opens. I stumble backward and then run.

I cut across the field toward Rachel's house, running hard, sliding over loose rocks and uneven ground. I try to hurdle an irrigation ditch and land with my ankle sideways in soft earth on the other side. It pops as I fall. A cry of pain escapes my lips, and I land in a crumpled heap.

"Okay, chica?" the man calls.

I grit my teeth and stand, trying not to limp as I start running again, my ankle burning with every step. The truck doesn't turn down the road. I limp/run until I can see the top of the old house clearly, the upstairs window looming above the trees. I glance back, but the truck is still sitting on the side of the road, the headlights illuminating the field. I'm so scared that I can't think straight. Running away now feels wrong, like I'm confirming what Eduardo said about me, but I'm driven by fear and adrenaline; I don't know what else to do.

I slow to a walk, still trying not to limp. If they'd leave, I'd go back that way to get home. Even if it is farther. Even if my ankle is broken. I don't want to go by the old house, or Rachel's house. I'm not sure which I'm more afraid of, the men in the truck or the house in front of me. I don't dare turn around to see if they're still watching me.

A truck roars behind me, barreling through the field. Its headlights feel hot on my back. It's getting closer. They're going to run me down. I start running again, but I can't move fast enough. I won't make it anywhere safe before they catch me. Not to Rachel's. Not even to the old house. My ankle is screaming a warning with every step, but I keep running.

"Jaycee!" It's Skyler's voice. "Jaycee!" I stop and turn. When I see his face, relief hits me so hard that I almost cry. He slows to a stop, opens the door, and gets out. "What are you doing out here?" He pauses for a second, maybe taking in how horrible I look. "Are you okay?"

I look toward the edge of the field, where the truck was

parked, but I'm blinded by Skyler's headlights so I can't tell if they're gone. I take in a quivering breath and burst out with the truth. "No."

He opens his arms and I melt into his chest. "What happened?"

"I went running." I breathe into his neck. "That's why I was at the school. I ran there and your brother saw me, so I stopped to talk to him. Please don't be mad. Evan told me you were coming . . . to get him. I was going to wait . . ."

He puts his hand on my back, patting it awkwardly. "It's okay. I shouldn't have—"

But I have more to tell him, and now that it's started, I can't stop the flood. "I went back . . . I heard these guys . . . I think . . . they were following me."

He pulls away from me. "Wait? What? Who was following you?" He glances up the field. "Those guys in the truck?"

I take in a shaky breath. "I don't know. I'm not even sure—" I step back, stumble, and gasp as my ankle bites in protest.

Skyler grabs my shoulders and keeps me from falling, but he looks really freaked out. "Did they hurt you?" He's checking me over, like he's looking for a fatal wound.

"I twisted my ankle. I jumped over a ditch and fell."

"Sit down. Let me look at it."

He bends to untie my shoe, but I stop him. "I'd rather just get out of here."

"Right. Good idea. But shouldn't we tell someone? I mean, if those guys were following you."

I glance at the truck again. I'm not sure of anything right

now. "No. I'm okay." I lean on his arm and try to hobble toward his truck, but my ankle feels like it's going to explode.

"Let me help you." He slides his arm around my back trying to help me to his truck, but he ends up making me lean my weight on my ankle. I grit my teeth to keep from screaming or throwing up from the pain.

"Forget this." He opens the door to his truck, picks me up, and sets me inside. "Are you okay?"

"No," I admit, "but I'll live." When he gets back in the truck I say, "Thanks for rescuing me again."

He shrugs like it's no big deal. "I saw you running. You went into the field and it looked like those guys in the truck were coming after you. I had to help."

"But why did you come back?"

He concentrates on some dried dirt on his jeans, digging at it with his fingernail. "Actually, I was looking for Evan."

"To give him a ride home?"

Skyler shakes his head in disgust. "No. To kick his butt . . . or . . . something." He glances up to catch my reaction, but I'm not sure how to respond to that. "Sorry. I'm just so sick of him. He gets any girl he wants, treats her like dirt, and then moves on to the next one. I heard he gave you a ride to the lake on his motorcycle and I thought that you . . . and then you were together at the school." He's clenching and unclenching his fist, tendons rippling across a white scar on his wrist. "I'm tired of him thinking he can take whatever is mine." His face flushes red, like he realizes what he just said. "Not that I think you're *mine* or anything, but . . ."

Everything he said churns through my mind. He was jealous of Evan, to the point where he was ready to start a fight. He even implied that he wants me to be his. I guess that means he really likes me. I've never been in this situation before. I'm not sure what I should do or say. I like Skyler, I like him a lot. I just don't—

For a second I hear Rachel's voice in my head. "You analyze everything too much. Sometimes you just have to go on instinct."

So I do what I think Rachel would have done. I lean across the seat and press my lips against his—our second kiss, totally initiated by me.

I pull away, my face blazing, already wondering if I did the right thing. He looks shocked or . . . I don't know what. I can barely look at him, but I have to say what I'm thinking before the moment passes. "I'm not interested in Evan. At all."

As soon as I say it, I know it's true. I feel free, like the shy, awkward girl who obsessed over the high school jerk is on her way out. Skyler gathers me in his arms and kisses me back, long and deep, until I can feel it in my toes.

As he pulls away I feel a stab of pain, knowing I lost Rachel over someone like Evan and something that could never be real.

CHAPTER 12

C ome find me, Jaycee."

Rachel is calling me from somewhere on the far end of the playground. But it's foggy, one of those days where people disappear and reappear in a haze of gray. I call back, running toward her voice, but when I get there she's calling from somewhere else, over by the fireplace. I turn and run again, but then I'm underwater, trapped in long flowing weeds that turn into her hair. I'm trying to get free, but the more I struggle, the more I get tangled in Rachel's hair.

Just when I think I'm going to drown, the scene shifts to the porch of the old house. I'm huddled close to Rachel and everywhere I turn I get a face full of long dark hair. I step backward and then I'm wrapped in thick black curtains. I'm scared, claustrophobic, and I'm not alone.

I tear the blankets away from my face and sit up so hard that I jar my ankle and cry out. I'm disoriented, tangled in a quilt on the couch and my ankle feels like it's on fire. I take a breath and adjust my position. When I look up, I'm face to face with the emptiness of the front window in the living room, where I fell asleep last night after Skyler brought me home. The long drapes billow out with the breeze from the open window. I stare at them, terrified, for a second I think I see someone there; his back to me, his face hidden, a white number on his back.

Eighteen.

— —

"Jaycee, how did you get in here?" Dad looks scared and shocked, almost as shocked as he was when Skyler carried me through the front door last night.

I sit up and look around my room, disoriented. I blink in the sunlight that filters in through my closed curtains. "I walked."

Walked, limped, crawled; anything to get away from the black window in the front room last night, its hollow and gaping eyes leaving me exposed, a fragile piece of glass the only thing protecting me from whatever might be outside. Or the dark folds of the open curtains, where anyone might be hiding.

Dad crosses the room. "I'm sorry, honey. I should have helped you to your own bed last night, but you were so tired by the time I got Skyler to leave."

Skyler had stayed with me, getting me ice, holding my foot on a pillow, talking to me and Dad until he had hinted, more than once, that Skyler should go home.

"I'm okay." I slide my leg sideways and then flinch, my ankle throbbing a reminder of last night. I touch my lips and remember that not all of it was bad.

"How is your ankle?" Dad reaches to pull the covers off my legs.

I'd like to lie and say "fine," but I'm too busy gritting my teeth as he untangles the blanket from around my leg. I glance down at the purplish, yellowish, blackish lump that passes for my ankle and then have to look away.

"They always look worse on the second day," Dad says. He has two pieces of toast in his hand and he's already dressed to go into work. He hands me one of the pieces of toast and sits down on the bed. He presses his fingers into my ankle carefully. "I don't think it's broken." Worry crosses his face. "If it's still bad tomorrow I'll take you to the doctor." I get his hesitation; doctors and X-rays are expensive. Dad's a lawyer, but we still don't have very much money because he does a lot of work for free. Mom has money, but Dad would never ask her for child support.

"For today I'd say ice, ibuprofen, and stay off it. I already told Dawn you won't be able to go to VBS today." He pats my head like a puppy and then stands up and takes another bite of toast. "I'll check on you at lunchtime, but I won't be home for dinner. The ladies' auxiliary from church is having a picnic, and I'm the guest speaker. I'm talking about estate planning this time." Dad is always the guest speaker at the ladies' events. He's still young and good looking, and I know there's more than one woman in the auxiliary who would like to change his "single" status. In fact, that might be the reason Claire is being so nice to me; her mom is recently divorced, again.

He kisses me on my forehead. "Stay still today. I have some books in my office that I'll get for you to read."

— —

The knocking on the front door matches the throbbing of my foot, drawing me out of another dream, this one I can't remember. The ibuprofen must have worn off. I brush my hair out of my eyes and glance around my room. I reach for my phone to see what time it is. It isn't there, but the movement causes a stack of books to fall off my nightstand. The next sound I hear is the front door opening. Panic hits me as I remember Dad never locks it. I think about the voices in the dark from the night before and start looking for something to use to defend myself.

"Jaycee, are you here?" The voice sounds vaguely familiar, like something out of a dream. "It's Evan."

Evan? Evan Cross is in my house. I'm still wearing my running clothes from last night. I didn't get the chance to shower and my unflattering ponytail has morphed into a full-fledged plume of nastiness. I'm trying to remember if I care if he sees me like this when he knocks on my bedroom door. "Jaycee? Are you in here?"

Evan's number was eighteen. The number in my dream was eighteen. That thought sends waves of panic through me. Was he the person I saw in the old house? Did he tell those guys I was looking in the fireplace? Or has the number been burned into my subconscious so much that I saw it in my dreams?

He knocks again. "Jaycee, are you decent?"

I try to answer "no" but nothing comes out. It's like one of those horror movies where the stupid girl lets the killer into her bedroom just because he's hot.

The door handle turns, and I scoot closer to the edge of my bed. What kind of a guy just walks into your house and then comes to your bedroom door?

He pushes open the door and peers around it. "Are you in here?"

"Yeah," I answer. My voice sounds hoarse. "Yes," I say a little clearer, pulling the blankets up over my chest, even though I'm sweating. I feel exposed. My heart skips around in my chest, bouncing between panic and embarrassment, and something else, a voice that says, "Evan Cross is actually in your bedroom." That voice sounds a little like Claire.

"Sorry to barge in like this, but the door was open." He looks fairly harmless, unarmed except for a grin and those blue eyes. He takes in my outfit. "Did I wake you up?"

One hand stays on my blanket and the other one goes to my hair. I feel somewhere between a little girl being teased and a girl that's old enough to be checked out; either way I'm uncomfortable. He takes a couple of steps into my room, crossing a threshold that no guy who isn't related to me has ever crossed. "Where's your dad?"

"Gone." I lick my dry lips. "But he should be back soon." It comes out quick, like I was lying to scare him away. Truthfully,

I have no idea what time it is or if Dad will be home any-time soon.

"I won't stay long, then." But he doesn't act like he's in a hurry to leave either. He drags my desk chair over beside the bed and sits down. "I was worried about what happened to you. I heard you got hurt."

"It's just my ankle."

His face changes, softening into something like concern. He sets his hand gently on my ankle. "Can I see?"

"I don't—"

But he's moving onto the edge of my bed, uncovering my leg. He grimaces. "That looks bad. Does it hurt?" His voice deepens almost to a purr, and he leaves his hand just below my knee. "I'm sorry I didn't walk you home last night."

"It's not your fault, I just—" My heart is fluttering around in my chest like a trapped bird. I keep thinking about what Skyler said about Evan, and what I said last night about not wanting Evan. I thought I was free, but here he is, in my bed-room, being really, really nice. I'm not sure why or what he wants from me.

He leaves his hand on my leg and leans over and picks up one of the books that fell off my nightstand. He reads the first title out loud. *"Boy Meets Girl: Dating and the Christian Teen."* He grins. "Nice." He picks up another one, *The Christian Girl's Guide to Boys and Dating.* "Very informative," he says as he flips through the pages.

My face flames. This is what Dad left for me to read. Skyler bringing me home must have really freaked him out. "Don't—" I reach to grab the books.

He sets them out of my reach and then retrieves the last one. He clears his throat dramatically. *"Saying Good-bye: Finding Faith in . . . Death."* He swallows. "Oh . . . sorry." The hole in my chest rises up to choke me. "I was just, just joking around. I didn't mean to . . . I know . . . I was being a jerk." He looks down, like he's actually embarrassed. I've never seen Evan Cross look embarrassed before.

"It's okay," I say, although I don't feel like it's okay at all.

He holds up the book. "Do you really believe in all of this?" His expression is almost sincere. I can't tell if he's getting ready to mock me again.

I take a deep breath, waiting for the next blow to come, but he looks like he really wants an answer. Finally I say, "The dating stuff, maybe not. But the religious stuff"—I touch the book in his hand—"life after death. That I do believe in." As soon as I say it I'm full of doubt. Where is Rachel now?

He nods. I'm not sure if he's agreeing with me or just acknowledging what I said. "How long did you know her?" His teasing expression has gone almost tender, his blue eyes turned soft.

"Forever." I run my thumb over the satiny edge of my comforter, suddenly wishing it were pink-and-white checked again, the way it was when Rachel and I did our bedrooms together in fourth grade.

He traces the tattoo on his shoulder. "I only knew her a little bit." I bite the side of my cheek against the pain that engulfs me when he says that. "My senior year we worked on a project together for digital arts and—"

"Wait." My throat closes over the word, I have to swallow

to finish. "She never told me that." I can't believe Rachel didn't tell me she had a class with Evan Cross. That she actually worked with him on something without even mentioning it. I wonder how long that was before the New Year's Eve date.

"She was cool. Really pretty, but she didn't, like, throw herself at me like other girls did. I even asked her out a couple of times, but she totally blew me off."

I try to wrap my mind around everything he's telling me. Evan asked Rachel out before New Year's and she didn't tell me. How many times did she say no to protect my feelings?

"I was totally putting my ego on the line when I asked her out for New Year's, but I guess third time's the charm. She said yes."

I swallow away a bitter lump that turns to pain when it hits my chest. Did Rachel really like Evan? Is that why she went out with him? Is that why she didn't tell me? What would I have done if she had?

He rubs at the tattoo again. "Did she tell you what happened that night? The night we went out?"

"No. What happened?" I lean forward, hoping Evan will tell me what really happened.

He looks at me like he's worried. "Oh, actually, I was hoping you could tell me. You were her best friend, right? I figured if anyone knew, it would be you."

I'm confused. Why wouldn't he know what happened on their date? I hesitate and then push forward. "Things got weird between us right after that. We kind of quit talking." I look down at my blankets; I can't tell him that he's the reason we quit talking. "I heard you went out with her, but . . ."

He shakes his head. "I'm not sure why, but she freaked out and left the party. She wouldn't even let me take her home." He sets the book on my bed and stands up, like he's going to leave, but he doesn't. Instead he starts pacing. "Then all of a sudden she was with Peyton, and then it was Mitch Thompson, and . . ." He pauses again, like he's trying to save my feelings, but he finishes. "The last thing I heard was that she . . ." he seems to be searching for the right word, "had been with all of them—with all of my friends."

I'd heard those rumors too, and I'd been mad enough to believe them, but hearing them from Evan makes me sick, thinking about what that means. "No!" I'm suddenly furious with him, with all of them, for whatever he did to her, for whatever he started. My voice rises on its own, the way it did when I was talking to Eduardo yesterday. "It's not true. Rachel wasn't like that, not before."

Evan backs away from my anger and the tears threatening in the corners of my eyes. "You're probably right. Those guys always talked big. I did too. It was a jock thing. Stupid."

He stands there, looking uncomfortable, like he doesn't know what to say. "Look, I didn't mean to make you mad or upset or whatever, I just . . ."

"Then why did you come here?" I'm so mad and confused that I forget to be intimidated by him. I bite off the words as they come out of my mouth.

He looks surprised. "I told you, I was worried about you. I

didn't expect you to flip out about it. I'm sorry. I shouldn't have said anything about Rachel. She was a really great person." They're the same words Claire used in the newspaper article, but Evan sounds more sincere. Maybe he really liked her.

He sits there for a minute, like he's debating something. Then he pulls a plastic bag out of his pocket. "I forgot to give this back to you last night."

I gasp and reach to take the bag of beads from him, but he holds onto it for a second, fingering the cross. "It looks a lot like the necklace she used to wear."

I take it away from him, maybe too fast.

"Did you find anything else in the fireplace?" He's trying to stay casual, but desperation seems to tug at the corner of his eyes.

Now I know what he came here for—to see if I found anything else in the fireplace. Evan has something to do with the guys I saw at the school, but what?

"No. This is all there was." My voice wavers a little, and I hope he doesn't catch the fear in it.

"Are you sure?" The tone is teasing, but he's studying my face, like he's waiting for me to crack.

"I'm sure."

He leans in closer. "You wouldn't lie to me, would you? I can tell when a girl is lying to me." He strokes my cheek with his finger, leaving a trail of heat that spreads over my whole face. I turn away. "She won't look me in the eye." His finger moves across my bottom lip. "And sometimes her bottom lip quivers."

I pull away from his hand, but my heart is thumping inside my chest. I move to the other side of my bed to get away from him. "You'd better go. My dad will be home . . . soon." I swallow, wondering if he knows I'm lying now.

He puts his hand on my leg, grinning, like he has me right where he wants me. "If you really want me to leave, I will." But he isn't leaving. "I don't want to get you into trouble."

I scoot as far away from him as I can. "Yes. Leave . . . now."

"Okay." He tucks the blanket back around my ankle. "Whatever you want." He stands and looks back at Rachel's necklace, clutched in my hand. He walks to the door but stops with his hand on the knob. "We pretty much have a party at our house every night over the summer. My dad's cool with it. You should stop by sometime." He turns and I get the full force of those blue eyes. "I'll be watching for you."

As soon as I hear the front door close I let out my breath. My face is still burning, like his touch left a trail of liquid fire. I kick the book he left on the foot of my bed. It glances off my bruised ankle as a departing shot before it lands on the floor. I grit my teeth in pain and anger, suddenly furious with Evan for coming into my house and pretending to be interested in me just so he can ask what I might have found in the fireplace. I'm more furious with myself for ever thinking he was anything but a self-centered jerk.

As soon as I hear the front door close I open the bag of beads. I put my hand inside, pulling them out, letting the necklace slide through my fingers again and again to calm myself down. I need to think. Why is Evan so interested in what I found in the fireplace? Rachel left the beads there for some reason, but why? Maybe there was more. Maybe she hid her journal there and I left it to burn because I didn't find it quick enough. Maybe it could have told me everything: what happened in the old house, what happened on New Year's Eve, who might have wanted to kill her. It might have even told me who Rachel was, and whether I ever knew her at all.

I grip the cross, take it out of the bag, and hold it up to the light. It's thick and ornate, almost gaudy, but on her it looked perfect. Like everything else she wore. Rachel was beautiful. Everyone could see it, including Evan Cross, a boy who never looked twice at me until I kissed his brother, until I had something he wanted.

For as big as it is, the cross isn't very heavy, in fact, it feels hollow and cheap. I run my fingernail down a crack in the side and it starts to separate in two. I pull back, afraid that I I'm going to break it. The crack in the cross feels symbolic, like what I did to our friendship. I put it back in the bag and lean back in my bed, but the cross keeps drawing me back to it, like something isn't right.

The cross has the answer.

That's what Rachel had written on the back of the loyalty pledge. I pull the cross out again and look at it closer. It looks like it was broken once and glued back together. I slip my fingernail in the side again, and again I pull back just when the two halves start to separate. It feels like a sin to desecrate a cross, especially Rachel's cross.

The cross has the answer. I thought it was a religious thing, but maybe she meant it literally. I pick up the cross again. This time, breathing a prayer that God and Rachel will forgive me, I slide my nail between the pieces and try to pry it apart. I almost break my nail and it still won't separate. I slide out of bed and get a nail file out of my dresser drawer, slip it in the crack, and pry hard. The cross breaks down the middle. The file slips; one side flies across the room and lands under my bed, the other falls at my feet. Something drops out and bounces under my dresser.

I drop to my knees and reach under the dresser. I pull out half of the cross and then my fingers brush against something tiny and square. I pick it up, still kneeling on the floor, and hold it up to the light. It looks like a computer chip, but for what, I'm not sure. It's only about the size of my fingernail, probably too small to fit into the card slot in Dad's computer.

It's tiny, but whatever it is, it's important. Important enough that those two guys were looking for it. Important enough that Evan came to my house to see if I had it.

I need to find out what's on it.

CHAPTER 13

Day two of ankle-induced incarceration and I'm making myself crazy trying to figure out how to read what's on the chip. I wish for dumb, easy things that other kids have—my cell phone back or clear access to a computer. The only one we have is in Dad's office, and I have to ask permission to use it. Only he has the password.

I've already compared it against the slot on Dad's computer. I was right. It's way too small to fit in the card reader. I have no clue how to get into Dad's computer anyway. I'm contemplating a long hobble to the library when the phone rings.

"Hey, you up?" Skyler's voice makes me blush and smile at the same time.

"Yeah," I answer back stupidly.

"What's going on? I've been trying to text you for days, but you haven't answered." His voice is a mix of irritation, insecurity, and maybe even worry.

"Sorry, I forgot to tell you. That cop took my phone," I say.

"Cop?" Skyler's voice goes up a notch.

"The FBI agent, the one from Spokane. He needed to get Rachel's number, and he took my phone as evidence."

"Oh . . ." He's quiet for a long time. Finally he says, "That sucks."

"Tell me about it."

"So . . . I was thinking . . . I could come over, or we could go to lunch or something? If you want to." He sounds so unsure of himself, so opposite from Evan. There's something adorable about it. "I thought maybe you'd want to get out of the house."

I do want to get out of the house, and I do want to see Skyler. Maybe I can get him to drop me off at the library. There might be a slot in the computers there that's small enough to fit the chip, or at least I could look up things on the Internet. "Sure. I mean, you had me at 'get out of the house.'" I bite down on my lip, wondering if that sounds desperate.

"Cool. I'll be over around eleven."

That gives me about forty minutes. I take the chip back to my room and put it in my purse. I hobble in and out of the shower quickly, put on a T-shirt that Skyler said he liked once at lunch. Then I start on my hair and makeup. Before I'm finished, his truck pulls into my driveway.

Unlike his brother, Skyler waits for me to limp over to answer the door. Then when I do, he stays outside. "Hey," he says, digging his hands into his pockets. "I was thinking Norma's."

"Sure. That sounds great." I grab my purse, close the door

behind me, and start across the porch, awkward on the too-tall crutches Dad borrowed from someone at church.

He watches me struggle for a minute. Then he kind of laughs. "I only have about a half hour for lunch. Dad flips out if I'm late."

"Sorry." I blush. "This isn't as easy as you might think."

"Hold on." He takes the crutches from me and carries them toward his truck.

"Stealing my crutches isn't going to make me go faster," I call after him.

He puts the crutches in the back of his truck. "Guess I'll have to carry you then." He comes back to the porch and scoops me up. I start to protest, but he shakes his head. "What? Do you think I'm a wimp?"

I bite my lip. "I'm not saying that . . . just that . . ."

"That you don't trust me?" He hoists me almost over his head so I have to wrap my arms around his neck to keep from falling. He grins.

"I'm not sure." I know we're just teasing each other, but the words from Rachel's note come back to me. *Don't trust anyone but E.*

I shake off that thought as Skyler pulls me close against his chest. "How about now?"

My heart pounds against his chest, our eyes lock, and he leans in to kiss me. I close my eyes. This time the kiss is soft and slow, but long enough to take my breath away. I pull away, but he doesn't put me down. I glance around, wondering if anyone might have seen us kissing.

"Is something wrong?" He looks around too. "I didn't think your dad was home."

I wiggle out of his arms. "He isn't. But he has spies everywhere."

He puts me down, like he's afraid. "Maybe we shouldn't go into town, then." I was kidding about Dad having spies, but Skyler seems to be taking it seriously.

"Actually, I was hoping you could drop me off at the library." I want to sound casual, but I'm thinking of the consequences of getting caught alone with Skyler at my house. This is new territory for me and Dad and I'm not sure what to expect. Maybe I should have read the books he left me.

"The library? Why? Do you need something to read?"

For a horrible second I wonder if Evan told him about the books Dad left for me. "No," I say quickly. "I need a computer."

He gives me a funny look. "You guys don't have a computer?"

My heart sinks. This is where I admit how weird my family is. "We only have one computer, in Dad's office. And I don't have the password."

"Seriously? Wow, your dad is strict."

"Or just weird."

"I bet I can get you into it. I got into the school's computer once."

"Seriously?" Now it's my turn to be shocked. "What did you do?"

"Nothing too bad, just excused some absences my dad didn't know about." I'm not sure if he's telling the truth or trying to impress me. "If you make me a sandwich, I'll hack into your dad's computer."

"I don't know." I hesitate, wondering if Dad is coming home for lunch. "How long will it take?"

"I bet I can do it in less than five minutes."

"I don't think—"

"Trust me." He opens the front door before I can stop him.

I follow him inside, trying to keep up without my crutches, guilt and fear churning in my stomach, but I need to figure out how to read the chip. Besides, it would be nice to use the computer any time I wanted to. I could find out more about Rachel's murder and the other murder and the gang signs. That's not exactly something I can ask Dad to use his computer for.

I stop in the kitchen and set down my purse. I'm still not sure I dare let him into Dad's office. "What kind of sandwich, PB and J, grilled cheese, or turkey?"

"How about one of those famous PB and Js?"

"Sure." I shared my lunch at school with Skyler a couple of times because he said he'd forgotten his.

He looks around the empty house. "So where is your dad?"

"At his office in town, I guess." I reach for the jam on the counter. Suddenly Skyler is behind me with his hands on my waist. With him so close, I'm painfully aware of the stack of dishes that are left in the sink and the countertop that still has crumbs from last night's dinner. I slip out of his grasp and move toward the cupboard where the peanut butter is. "We should probably hurry."

Skyler looks around, avoiding my eyes like he's embarrassed. "Right. What can I do to help?"

"The peanut butter is on the top shelf." I gesture above my head. Skyler leans toward me as he reaches up but purposely doesn't touch me. He smells like hay and sweat, barely covered by the same cologne. I wonder if he put it on as he drove here. The idea that Skyler might be worried about how he smells around me makes my stomach clench, but in a good way. He gets the peanut butter, retrieves a knife from the drawer, and starts spreading it on the bread I've laid out.

"Yuck," I stare at his hands, streaked with what looks like grease. "You need to wash your hands if you're going to make something I have to eat."

He looks at his hands sheepishly. "Sorry." He walks over to the sink and slides the sleeves of his shirt up. As he reaches for the soap, I notice the scar I saw on his wrist goes all the way up his forearm in a long, jagged path. He catches me staring and pushes his sleeves back down fast.

My mind races; the scar looks like someone cut him. "What happened?" I try to keep my voice even, like it's no big deal.

"Nothing." He pulls away and dries his hands on a towel hanging on the stove. "I shattered my wrist playing football. I had to have surgery to put the bones back together." His face clouds with a look I've never seen on him before. Anger? Pain?

It looks too jagged to me to be a surgery scar, but then again, I don't know what a surgery scar is supposed to look like. "Is that why you were gone so long last year?" I had forgotten about it until now, but Skyler missed almost the entire first term last year.

"Yeah," he says, but he won't look at me.

"You must have really screwed it up. You were gone for a long time."

"I dove for the ball and someone else dove on top of me. My wrist was twisted around nearly backward."

I cringe. "Ouch."

He reaches for the knife again. "Thus ended the illustrious reign of the Cross boys over Lake Ridge High sports." The peanut butter tears through the bread as he spreads it harder than he needs to.

I reach for a bowl. "I usually mix the peanut butter and jam together, so it's easier to spread." I get a spoon out of the drawer and scoop a glob of peanut butter into it. "So you couldn't play after that?"

He throws the shredded pieces of bread into the garbage. "I probably could have this year. But I don't really want to." He leans against the counter and watches me stir the jam and peanut butter together. "That looks kind of gross."

"But this is my secret recipe for making them taste so good." I spread the mixture on two new pieces of bread. "Why didn't you want to play football anymore?"

"Football was Dad's thing, and then Eric's thing, and then Evan's. I was never as good at it as they were. I'm not the hulking mound of muscle that they are." His face goes dark again. It's obviously a sore subject.

I top off the sandwiches and then cut them in half, trying

to think of some way to make him more comfortable. It was easier when we talked at lunch, but I guess we weren't technically alone. "So what is your thing?"

"Promise you won't laugh." He says it seriously, like I would honestly laugh at him.

"I won't laugh."

"Photography." He pauses like he just delivered the punch line and I'm supposed think it's funny.

I slide the sandwiches on a plate. "Photography?"

"Yeah, I guess I'm a real geek, huh?" He takes the plate from me.

"I don't think so. Actually, I think that sounds really cool."

"Thanks." He looks relieved. "I'll have to take your picture sometime." He takes a bite out of his sandwich.

"No. No way."

"Why not?"

"I hate having my picture taken. I always come out looking too pale and with a dumb look on my face." I take a bite of my sandwich and chew.

"No you don't."

"Yes I do. Every. Single. Time." I point to a picture of me on the wall. "Case in point."

"That's just because you're trying too hard to pose, and the photographer didn't know what he was doing."

"And you think you could do better?"

"I know I could." He reaches into his back pocket and pulls out his wallet. He opens it and takes out a picture. When he sets it on the counter I gasp. It's a picture of me.

My stomach does flip-flops. I'm not sure what to think. Not only does he have a picture of me that I didn't know he took, but he keeps it in his wallet. "When did you take this?"

He suddenly looks embarrassed, like he shouldn't have shown me the picture. "On the last day of school, when you were walking home." He rubs his hand across his scar nervously. "Do you like it?"

I look closer at the picture. It's black and white; the wind is blowing my hair over my shoulder, the light is just right. I don't look too pale or stiff. Actually it's the best picture I've ever seen of myself. "Is it vain if I say I do?"

His face breaks into a relieved grin. "No. It's honest."

"You're really good. I mean, really. This is the first picture I've seen of myself that I've liked since before middle school."

"Thanks." His whole face is lit up, both dimples creasing his cheeks. He takes the picture from me. "We'll have to do portraits for real, sometime soon."

I make a face but don't comment.

He puts the picture back in his wallet and looks at his watch. "We need to hurry if we're going to get into your dad's computer. Where is it?"

"In Dad's office, but I'm not sure . . ."

He waits. "If you don't want to . . ."

"No, let's do it."

I pick up my purse, and Skyler follows me into Dad's office. He sits down at Dad's desk, and I discreetly push away a stack of books with titles similar to the ones Evan saw, except these all begin with *A Christian Parent's Guide to* . . .

If Skyler notices, he doesn't comment. He brings up Dad's log-in screen. "Okay, what might your dad have for a password?" I shake my head, clueless. "Hmm, we'll start with the obvious, how about your name?" He types it in. "Nope. When is your birthday?"

"April 24."

"I'll have to remember that," he says, but that isn't the password either. He tries JC24, Jaycee4-24, and my dad's birthday.

I glance at the clock. If Dad is coming home for lunch he could be here any minute.

Skyler looks around the room. "Any other ideas? People usually choose passwords that mean something to them."

I'm staring at the bookcase beside Dad's desk and something else occurs to me. "Try Atticus."

"Atticus?"

"Like Atticus Finch. Dad's favorite book is *To Kill a Mockingbird*."

Skyler types it in and the computer opens to a web page. "Gangs: Are They a Problem in Your Community?" the headline screams.

"Wow. Good call."

I lean forward to read the web page Dad has up. "The gang thing has really got everyone scared, hasn't it?"

"Yeah, crazy that this stuff is coming to Lake Ridge." Skyler sounds disconnected, like he doesn't want to talk about it either.

But I need to talk to someone, so I blurt out, "Why would a

gang want to kill Rachel? Why would they come all the way here to do it?"

Skyler rubs the edge of the desk. "Maybe they were already here. The migrants come from all over. Eric says some of them have ties to gangs in other cities or in Mexico."

I'm thinking about the guys I heard talking by the school; they didn't sound Hispanic. "Are you sure it was the migrants? There are lots of gangs listed here." I lean forward to read through the list; I had no idea there were so many.

"The symbol on Rachel's house is from a Mexican gang based in L.A. called the Cempoalli." Skyler moves the mouse over the word "Cempoalli" on the computer screen and clicks on the link. A page of red symbols like the ones on Rachel's door comes up. I can't tell if they match the one I saw on Eduardo's back.

"But why her?" I say it more to myself than to Skyler. I lean forward, trying to read more about the gang.

Skyler is gripping the edge of the table, making the scar on his wrist stand out, white against his skin. "Maybe it wasn't her they were after. Maybe it was an accident. Maybe she was just with the wrong person."

Eduardo's face flashes through my head again. "But no one was with her when she died. It was a drive-by, right?" It hurts my chest to say that, because it was my fault that she was alone.

"Associating with the wrong gang is enough for a death sentence with these people."

I think of the red mark on Eduardo's back. He said that Rachel's death was his fault, but Rachel said I could trust him.

Maybe she didn't know who to trust. I set my purse on the desk, weighing everything before I pull the chip out, but I need answers.

"I found something." I put the chip on the desk. "I think it was Rachel's, but I don't know what's on it."

Skyler leans closer. He picks it up between his fingers and turns it over. "It's a memory chip, a micro-SD chip. I have one like it in my phone, for music. Where did you get it?"

I hesitate, wondering how much I should tell him. "She left it for me. I should probably take it to the police, but I want to know what's on it first. Do you know what I need to do to read it?"

He's holding the chip up to the light, like he's trying to see what's on it. "You could read it on my phone, but I left it on the swather. If you had an adapter you could put it in any computer." He touches the slot on the side of Dad's computer.

"I don't know if my dad—" but before I can finish, the front door slams.

"Jaycee, where are you?" My dad is home, looking for me. I'm in his office, with Skyler, and we just hacked into his computer.

I hear him walk down the hall, the doorknob turns. I freeze, but Skyler reaches for the computer and turns off the screen, so it goes black. He takes a couple of steps so he's beside the bookshelf when Dad opens the door.

"Skyler?" Dad looks from Skyler to me in surprise. "Jaycee, what are you and Skyler doing in here?"

My brain and my tongue can't coordinate anything, but

Skyler steps toward my dad. "Sorry. It was my fault." I can tell he's nervous, but he's taking the blame for me. "Jaycee wanted to show me a book she was reading. Something about dating?"

I stare at him in disbelief. His voice is shaking, and I don't think Dad is buying it. His smile is kind of frozen in place. Finally he shakes his head. "I have lots of books I could share with you and Jaycee on dating." He goes to his bookshelf and pulls out *Dating and Intimacy: Why Wait?* Skyler's face goes red, but he takes the book. I want to sink into the floor. It's like Dad just provided the literary equivalent of polishing his shotgun. Either that or he really expects Skyler to read the book. Sometimes it's hard to tell with Dad.

"Thank you. I'll be sure to read it." Skyler backs away. "I should go now. I need to get back to work."

"You're welcome. Jaycee, you can walk him out," Dad says. "Then we need to talk." I don't like the way he emphasizes the word "talk."

Skyler and I walk side by side in silence until we get to his truck. He reaches in the back and pulls out my crutches. "I'm sorry. I didn't mean to get you in trouble."

"It's okay." I glance back to the window, where I know Dad is watching. "Do you still have the little micro-whatever card?"

"Oh, I put it in my pocket." But he doesn't offer to give it back. "I have an adapter for it. You could come over and . . ." He looks at the window. "Or I can copy it on a CD and give it to you at church."

"Church?" No one in the Cross family has gone to church as long as I can remember.

Skyler nods toward the window. "I need some way to get on his good side, so he'll let me see you."

I like the way that sounds, but I'm not sure I should let the chip out of my sight, so I hesitate.

He reaches into his pocket, but he doesn't pull the card out, he just covers it with his hand, like he's protecting it. "I'll be careful with it. I promise."

"Okay," I answer. The only way I'm going to get to see what's on it is if I let Skyler help me.

"How was lunch?" Dad asks when I make it back in the house. He picks up Skyler's plate and puts it by the sink. "Did you at least offer him a pop?" I open and close my mouth a few times, trying to decide if Dad is really mad that Skyler was here, or if he's teasing me. He sighs and screws the lid back on the peanut butter jar, puts it in the cupboard, and then turns back to me. "I like Skyler. He's a nice kid. And so far, he seems to have avoided the mistakes his older brothers have made." He pauses again, and I wait for the *but*. "But I don't want you to be alone with him. Not at our house, not at his house, not in a car, not anywhere." He looks into my eyes, and I know he's serious. "Promise me you'll always have someone else with you, that you won't ever be alone with him. Promise me you won't ever go to his house."

I nod because I know that's what he expects, but somehow, I'm not sure it's a promise I can keep.

CHAPTER 14

"What did you do to your foot, dear?" Mrs. Francis says to me as soon as she walks into the church.

"I slipped when I was running," I answer with a patient smile. Church doesn't start for ten minutes and I'm already tired of people asking what I did to my ankle. I'm waiting at the door because I want to catch Skyler as soon as he walks in, so he doesn't have to wander around the church looking for me. Dad's already in his seat, but he's talking to the pastor so he hasn't noticed I'm missing yet.

"Oh, that's terrible. You need to be more careful." She pats my shoulder, picks up the church bulletin, and goes to sit next to Mrs. O'Dell.

Mrs. Francis puts her glasses on and peers at the bulletin. Almost immediately she starts to click her tongue. "'A grieving support group for teens affected by the tragedy,'" she leans over to Mrs. O'Dell and reads loud enough for me and anyone close to hear her. "I hope that doesn't interfere with bingo on

Tuesdays. Tracy Fisher had another baby? What is that, number six? Like we need another Fisher kid running wild in the streets." She shakes her head and keeps reading, this time to herself, her lips moving silently. She stops again, like she's shocked. "I thought the 'People in Need' section was reserved for parishioners."

"No," Mrs. O'Dell answers. "Pastor is big on reaching out to the community. Why?"

"Look at this." Mrs. Francis leans closer to Mrs. O'Dell but doesn't lower her voice. "'We're asking for volunteers to help with the cleanup of Araceli Sanchez's home and yard, following the tragedy with her daughter. We will be working in conjunction with Father Joseph in this effort.'" She clicks her tongue again. "Every time one of those poor Mexicans gets into trouble, we're called on to help."

"I feel for that woman," Mrs. O'Dell says, "losing a child like that."

"If you ask me, that child was lost a long time before she got herself killed. Did you see what she'd done to her hair, the eyebrow ring, and the way she walked around town half-dressed?"

Claire's mom sits down beside them. She looks at me and then lowers her voice, but not enough. "That Mexican girl who was killed? They say she was part of a gang. That she was into drugs, selling her body for money, about everything else you can imagine. I read in the paper this morning that they found a gun in the migrant housing, possibly the murder weapon. It belonged to Jose somebody."

"They're all named Jose," Mrs. Francis points out. Mrs. O'Dell chuckles.

Claire's mom nods. "Anyway, he had ties to a gang in Mexico. Looks like she crossed the wrong person and got killed for it."

I pick up my crutches as quietly as possible. Until now, I've always felt like I belong at church, where everyone knows me, where everyone takes care of one another. But I can't stay here. I can't listen to them talk about Rachel like that. I can't listen to a sermon about sin and damnation and lost souls.

I can't listen and think about the possibility that Rachel is one of them. I knew her better than anyone. She's not the kind of girl they're whispering about. At least she wasn't.

I catch Taylor coming in. "Tell my dad I didn't feel good and so I went home, okay?"

"Where are you really going?" she says. "You're going to see Skyler, right? Can I come? I really don't want to—"

"Just tell him, okay?" It comes out harsh and so loud that Claire's mom turns around.

Taylor blinks like I hurt her feelings. "Okay. Whatever."

I shove the crutches under my arms and hurry out the door, ignoring the other members of the congregation coming in.

More than anything I want to run, run as far away from the church as possible. Away from the things those women are saying and away from the feeling that it's my fault. If I had been a better friend to Rachel, if I hadn't been jealous, if I hadn't deserted her, maybe this never would have happened.

If I'd gone to the police.

If I hadn't been afraid.

I leave the church behind me and walk, skip, and hop with my crutches as fast as I can, wishing I could move faster. I don't turn around or look to see if Dad or anyone else is following me. I don't care anymore. As I reach the top of the cemetery hill, I stop, lean on my crutches to catch my breath, and look around. From here, I can see most of the town: houses, duplexes, trailers, and the buildings that the migrant workers live in for the summer, scattered around the fields.

On the hill behind the church is a long expanse of green, dotted with cement markers and flanked on one side by a wall of trees. The cemetery where Rachel is buried.

I make my way up the hill, babying my left ankle as my crutches alternately dig in and slide on the grass, still wet from last night's rain. Concrete numbers accost me from both sides, the years each person spent on this earth, literally carved in stone. I focus ahead, trying not to subtract the numbers, trying not to think about how many died young, like she did.

I'm drawn back to her grave at the edge of the cemetery, beside a row of trees that frame one side. The dark earth covering her is dotted with bits of green as the lawn starts to come through. There's only a metal plate to mark where she's buried, RACHEL ARACELI SANCHEZ, and more numbers. Darkness overwhelms me as I lean against the tree and draw in a breath, thinking about my best friend lying underneath all that dirt.

I close my eyes and try to picture her alive, but it's like my mind has blocked out her face, and all I can see is a body lying on a bed of white satin.

I brush my fingers across the top of the headstone next to her, and come back with my fingertips wet because of the rain. I think about what the women at the church said, what Evan said, and about what I've heard about Rachel. About how different the Rachel I knew was.

She changed after that night in the old house, little by little, until the Rachel I knew was gone. I tried to be loyal. I've kept her secrets, even now.

Maybe keeping secrets is what killed her.

Missing her hurts so much now I can barely breathe. A bird twitters from the tree, too cheerful to be looking down on so much pain. I shoo him away.

Skyler is probably at the church by now, waiting for me, but I can't make myself move. I can't go back to that church. I can't face those women and everyone else there. I want to tell them that they're wrong about my friend. Even after everything that happened. I have to believe that they are.

The bird flutters back down, perches on another headstone, cocks its head, and stares at me. I lean against my crutches, bend over, and brush some of the muddy dirt away from Rachel's simple marker. "What happened that night? What did you see?"

I'm sure now that it all comes back to that night in the old house: what she saw, why we had to run, and why she was crying.

I'd never seen Rachel cry before, and I was scared. I

wrapped my arms around her and let her cry into my chest. I smoothed her hair and told her it was okay. I asked her if her foot still hurt. She nodded so I got her some Tylenol, but I was afraid to ask what was really wrong.

I should have pushed harder then; I should have made her tell me what happened before it was too late. In the darkest corners of my imagination, I sometimes wondered if the guy she told me about was the one who had texted her, that he had something to do with the kid who was murdered. But I couldn't believe that Rachel would have anything to do with a guy like that. Now that she's dead, I'm not so sure.

I drop my crutches down and sit on a slanted stone with my knees tucked up in my skirt. I lean my head against my legs, overwhelmed but not sure if I have the strength to cry. The air is heavy with the smell of dirt and rain.

A twig cracks, and I jerk my head up. It feels like someone is with me, watching. I listen, but I don't hear anything else, not even the little bird. Suddenly sitting among so many dead people gives me the creeps. I reach for my crutches and try to stand, not wanting to touch the stones on either side of me. I lose my grip and slip forward.

A hand on my arm steadies me. I jerk away and scream as I turn and face Eduardo. "What are you doing here?" I screech at him.

He lets go of my arm and shakes his head. He has a half-wilted bunch of lilacs in his hand. Lilacs were Rachel's favorite flower. He steps forward and puts them on Rachel's grave without answering me.

We stand together not talking, looking across the cemetery, both hurting with something we can't express. As hard as it is, I feel like I have to say something. He might be the only one I can talk to now. The only one who understands how I feel. "I miss her," I say quietly. He nods. I take a breath and feel the weight of my guilt pressing into my chest. "I'm sorry for what I said to you, about it being your fault." I shake my head and swallow the lump in my throat. "Sometimes I think it was my fault. If I'd stayed her friend, if I'd only answered . . ." But I can't tell him about the text. I glance at him, looking for his reaction to my confession. He crosses his arms over his chest like he's shutting me out, but he doesn't leave.

I try again. "You were right about me. I lost the last six months of her life because I was stupid, because I was jealous." The truth of that word hurts my throat, and my eyes sting with tears I won't let fall. I suddenly need to confess everything to someone, "There was this"—I swallow—"guy and—"

"No." He cuts me off without even looking up. "It was my fault." His voice is hollow, like my chest. "Only me. They killed her because of me."

"Who?" Skyler's words come back to me. *Maybe she was with the wrong person.* I turn around and look at him, my hands shaking, but he doesn't notice. He seems to be in his own world, consumed by guilt or anger or something, muttering to himself in Spanish. Finally I grip his arm with a kind of desperation I didn't realize I felt. "Do you know who killed her? If you do we have to—"

He shakes me off, so hard that I trip backward, but I keep from falling. "It was them. The Cempoalli."

The Cempoalli was the gang Skyler was talking about, but why would they come here? I shake my head in disbelief. "There aren't any gangs in Lake Ridge."

"They're everywhere, boba. You can't escape them."

I don't want to believe him, but my best friend is dead, and her front porch was tagged with gang symbols. "But why her?" He won't look at me. I get closer and say it louder this time, demanding an answer. "Why her?"

He finally looks up. "Because of me, because of this." He touches the tattoo on his back. "Because I was a Cempoalli."

I stare at him in disbelief. "You were . . . one of them?"

He nods. "They were my homies, my gang, before my mom sent me here. To get away from them."

My heart races. Skyler said that was the name of the gang whose symbols were painted on Rachel's front porch. I think about what Rachel said, *You don't know what they can do.* Did she mean a gang? "Was Rachel part of . . . was she one of them? Was she part of your gang?"

"No!" he explodes. "You knew her. She wasn't like that."

"But you were." I say it carefully, not wanting to make him even angrier. I'm afraid if I push too hard he'll run away from me again. "Why?"

"Where I came from in California, Pico Rivera, gangs are life. You were part of a gang or you were caught in the cross-fire. You were in and you didn't get out."

I look at Eduardo. He can't be much older than me, just sixteen. "How long were you part of . . . ?"

"When I was ten I was a lookout and a runner. By eleven, I was jumped in."

"Jumped in?"

"Beaten. By the whole gang. To prove I could take it. To prove I was worthy."

My stomach hurts. "They beat you? To make you part of them?"

He nods.

"Why would you . . . why would anyone do that?"

He looks down, muttering again. "You wouldn't understand."

I don't understand, not at all. He talks about beatings and murder like they were the norm. To me it's sickening. Insane. "Why would anyone choose to live like that?"

He looks into my eyes, daring me to understand him. "There's no choice. It's where I was born, my home. There was nowhere else to go, no money to get out."

I take a breath. "But you got out. How?"

"Last year, one of my homies went to visit some *chola* from La Puente and never came home. We found him three days later, rotting in a Dumpster, with a bullet in his head." He says all of this without any emotion, but it makes me want to throw up.

"My mom was done with it. She didn't want that to be me, so we came here, to stay with my uncle. To get away from them."

"We?" My voice comes out steadier than I feel.

"Me and Manny. *Mi primo.*"

My mind races through the little bit of Spanish I know. "Your cousin? Manuel, the boy who died last summer, he was your cousin?"

He crosses his arms, his hands gripping his biceps hard, his eyes, harder. He nods.

"We came here to be safe, and now he's dead." He laughs a little. "Nowhere is safe."

"So you think your gang, the Cempoalli, killed Manuel and Rachel too, because she was with you?"

He nods, and his face is stone, but I can see the side of his mouth working, like he's struggling to keep any emotion off his face.

"Why?"

"Because you don't cross the Cempoalli. You don't walk away."

I hug my arms trying to keep myself from shaking. "Are they still here? I heard the police found a gun—"

"They're lying!" He turns on me, his face clouded over. "Arrest a Chicano, any Chicano, and then everyone is safe again. But Jose Ortiz isn't a gangbanger. He's an old man. He didn't even know her." He's working himself up again. "We should have stayed in our own *barrio*. We should have stayed where we belonged. At least there we had some street cred, at least there we had some protection." His voice thickens with pain. "If we had stayed, she wouldn't be here."

I step back, afraid, as he kneels down by Rachel's grave. "I swear they will pay for what they did." He crushes a handful of fresh dirt from the grave and lets it slide through his fingers.

My heart churns for him, for Rachel. I'm afraid of him, of his anger and pain, but at the same time, I feel it too. For the town who condemned her so quickly, and whoever killed her.

I've been raised to forgive, but I'm not sure I can forgive whoever did this. I whisper, "What are you going to do?"

He looks at me, his eyes blazing. "Whatever I have to do."

"Do you think they're still here? That it was someone who lives here?"

He nods. "The workers here, they come from everywhere. Some are hiding, like me. They leave the gang behind, but they keep their loyalties." He touches his shoulder again. "All I need is a name, or just a face."

"I want to help." I lean toward him, a rush of fear and exhilaration floods every part of me. I'm a part of this now. "Rachel was my best friend, I owe her—"

He turns around. "Did you find what she left for you? Her journal, did you find it?"

"No. Not a journal. I just found her necklace and—"

"Give it to me."

"No." Despite what Rachel said, I'm not sure I can trust him. "I . . . I haven't figured out what she wanted me to do with it yet."

"Just give it to me. I'll take care of it."

I'm shaking my head. After everything he's told me about where he's come from, I'm not handing over the only piece of Rachel I have left. "Rachel wanted me to help. I'll figure out what it means and then we can—"

He laughs. "What can you do?"

"I've lived here longer, I know people, I can . . ." I'm trying to come off confident, even though everything inside me is quaking with fear. "I can do lots of things."

"No!" He turns around and faces me with eyes on fire. "Do you think I want your blood on my hands too? First Manny and now Rachel!" He turns his back on me, mixing Spanish with English again, going off. I catch enough to get that he thinks I'm a small-town hick looking to get myself killed.

I stay still for a long time, arguing with myself as much as with him. He's right. I should stay out of it. It isn't safe, but I can't get Rachel's text out of my mind. Finally I speak, "I lied to you. I *was* there." I lick my lips. "I was with Rachel the night Manny died. I saw someone, at the old house. Not someone I could identify, but still . . ."

He turns around, shock and horror on his face.

I face him, pleading. "I'm already part of this, and Rachel wanted us to work together. We'll find out who it was. We'll get evidence, and we'll go to the police."

His laugh has a bitter edge. "The police don't care about us. They don't care about her. Just Mexicans killing Mexicans, another bloodstain they have to clean up. Send someone back across the border, and it's all over, the town is safe again."

"The FBI, then, someone has to listen. Once we have proof—"

He laughs again. "Give me Rachel's necklace and forget you ever knew her. Go back to church, boba, pray for her soul and pretend we never talked to each other. Forget what you saw. Keep thinking you're safe here. As long as you stay away from us, maybe you will be."

I clench my jaw to keep my voice even. "Fine. You do this your way, and I'll do it mine. But I'm keeping the necklace and anything else I find."

He clenches his fist. For a second I think he might hit me. Instead, he shakes his head. "You're just like her. She wouldn't listen to me either." He turns his back on me and heads down the hill.

I think about what he said. I'm not like Rachel, not at all. I'm not pretty and I'm not brave. Eduardo scares me. I can only imagine what the rest of his gang is like. But Rachel trusted me; she thought I could help. Maybe I can be like her. I have to do this. I watch Eduardo walk away.

And it looks like I have to do it on my own.

W here have you been? Are you skipping church or avoiding me?" Skyler's ticked. He's standing at the door to my dad's truck, dressed in a white shirt and tie. After Eduardo left, I couldn't be at the cemetery alone, but I couldn't go into the church either. My ankle hurt too much to walk home, so I curled up in the truck to think and wait for my dad to come out.

I lean forward to hide my face so he can't see the marks the tears left on my cheeks. "I just couldn't handle church today."

He opens the door, climbs in next to me, and puts his arm around me. I turn my head and stare at the door. His voice softens. "Are you okay?"

I'm not. I'm so not, but I don't know how to tell him that. As I limped back down the hill, all my bravado faded. I'm scared of what I have to do, but I can't tell Skyler that. All I can do is shake my head. He shuts the door behind him, reaches over, and gathers me in his arms. I lean my cheek against the warmth of his chest and listen to his heartbeat. My heart aches and my body feels heavy with the weight of guilt and responsibility.

"What's going on?" he says into my hair.

I lean into his arms and shake my head against his chest. Part of me wants to tell Skyler everything and part of me wants to melt into his arms and forget. "Mrs. Francis and Mrs. O'Dell and Claire's mom were saying nasty things about Rachel, so I left. I walked to the cemetery and went to her grave." His arm goes stiff around my shoulders, but he doesn't pull away. "I saw—" I stop myself, not sure how he would react to my conversation with Eduardo. "They said someone has been arrested, that she was . . ."

He nods. "I heard."

"Do you believe it?" I ask, looking up into his eyes.

"I don't know." He hesitates, avoiding my gaze. "I didn't really know her."

"She wasn't what they said she was," I say, tears pushing their way past the corners of my eyes. He doesn't move. I know my tears are making him uncomfortable, but I can't stop talking. "Maybe I could have helped her. Maybe I could have saved her. If I'd—"

"Don't talk like that." His voice is so sharp that I pull away. "She made her own choices." I stop crying, shocked, as he continues. "Sorry, I just don't think you should beat yourself up for someone else's mistakes. There's nothing you could have done."

I look up at him. "You're just like the rest of them!" I try to wiggle out of his arms. "You just said you didn't know her, but you're sitting there condemning her like it was her fault."

He holds me tight. "I didn't say that. I said it wasn't your fault. That you shouldn't feel responsible for something you can't change."

I take a breath. "I wish I—" He stops me by leaning into my lips and kissing me. I pull away, irritated that he wants to kiss and I want to talk. "What are you doing?"

He looks sheepish. "I'm sorry. I thought it might help. You looked like you could use a kiss."

"I guess . . . I . . ." But I don't know what's appropriate when it comes to kissing and mourning, I've never been here before. "It was nice."

He kisses me again, softer, slower. I close my eyes, wrap my arms around his neck, and lean into him. I want to erase everything in my brain, just let his lips take me away. We kiss for a few minutes, soft, feather-light kisses changing into longer, deeper kisses. Skyler adjusts his hold on my waist, pulling me closer to him. His mouth opens and his tongue slides across my lips. I pull back, suddenly realizing what I'm doing. I'm afraid that someone might see us. I can hear the not-so-hushed whispers from Mrs. Francis now: ". . . making out in her dad's truck during church." I wonder how fast it would take them to jump to the same conclusions about me that they did about Rachel. Skyler leans in to kiss me again, but I shake my head.

He looks at the church and nods like he understands. He twines his hand in mine. "You want to go somewhere else? We could go for a drive. Get away."

"I don't think—" My heart is still pounding. A hundred thousand reasons why I shouldn't leave with Skyler right now run through my head, not the least of which is my promise to Dad, which I guess I've already broken.

He leans over and touches my cheek, tracing the path the tears made. "Rachel doesn't want you to stop living. She doesn't want you to be sad." He twists a piece of my hair around his finger. "I don't want you to be sad."

I shake my head to clear it. "I can't just forget." He doesn't understand. What Rachel wanted, what she asked me to do, I don't know how to do. That's the problem. I'm not even sure where to start. Then I remember what Skyler has. "Did you copy that chip for me?"

He lets me go and leans back. "I pulled it up, but there was only one file on it."

"Was it her journal? Do you have it with you?" My voice comes out breathless, almost panicked.

"Hold on." Skyler looks uncomfortable, like he doesn't want to tell me something.

I'm losing patience. "Don't tell me to hold on. I need to see that file."

He pulls at his tie. "It's not her journal. I'm sorry, I wasn't going to look at the file, but I thought it was important. I mean, Rachel was murdered, and the guy who did it might still be out there. He might even be one of those guys who was following you, but—"

"But what? What was on the chip?"

"It was just a school assignment. A bunch of pictures stuck together. Something she made for digital arts."

"A school assignment?" I'm so stunned that it comes out as a whisper.

"I'm sorry." He looks defeated, like he failed me.

I lean back in the seat, trying to process what he's saying. "What were the pictures of? Why would she put a school paper in . . ." But I haven't told Skyler about Eduardo or the necklace or Rachel's message.

Skyler puts his arm around me again. "There were a lot of pictures of you and her. Maybe she wanted you to remember the good things."

I'm shaking my head. It has to be more than that. "I need to see it. Can we go to your house? There's still a little church left, and Dad always stays late."

"Okay . . . sure." He hesitates, but I'm already opening the door and pulling him out after me.

I cringe at the noise his truck makes when he starts it and look back at the church, thinking again about the promise I made Dad about not going to Skyler's house, but this is more important.

I watch the trees beside the cemetery as we drive the opposite direction. For a second I think I see Eduardo standing there, watching me drive away with Skyler, but when I look again, he's gone.

— —

Except for the party at the beginning of the summer, I think I've only been to the Cross house once before, for Skyler's sixth or seventh birthday party, when his mom was still around. She left the family when he was like eight. The only thing I remember about her was that she was very thin, very pretty, and she always acted nervous.

The house looks different than I remember it, but it was dark the night of the party, and I was pretty freaked out about being here. It has a wide circle driveway with a big barn in the back and a truck on one side. The swather Skyler was driving is parked out front.

He leaves my crutches in his truck and loops his arm around my waist. "My computer is out back. C'mon, I'll show you." Dad's warning goes through my head again, but I shake it off and let him take me behind the house, across the backyard, and to a building that looks like some kind of garden shed. It's painted white with little shutters, and there's a window box, overgrown with weeds.

He gets a key out of the window box, unlocks the door, and steps inside. The room is really dark. I look around and realize all the windows are blacked out. He turns on the light. It comes up a pale yellow/red color, then he hits a different switch and the regular light comes on.

There's a sink in one corner and a long table, like a potting bench. It holds flat basins and some kind of projector. Strung across the room is a clothesline with clothespins. There's a piece of canvas, like a photographer's backdrop, on one wall and another wall is covered in framed black-and-white pictures. "What is this place? Why does it have that weird light?"

"It's a safelight, and this is a darkroom. My mom was a photographer. This is where she developed her pictures."

"Developed? You mean like with film?"

"Yeah." He walks over to a computer set up on a desk in the corner and turns it on. "Mom taught us all how to do pictures when we were pretty young. Eric still does the crime scene photos in town when they need him to. Evan got into taking sports pictures after he broke his ankle in middle school and got stuck on the bench. He wasn't very good at it though."

"They still have the stuff for that?" While we wait for the computer, I wander around the room and look into one of the basins; the sides have something grainy stuck to it and it smells like sulfur.

"It's a little harder to find, but yeah, I can get all the chemicals I need online."

It seems like a lot of work for one picture. "Why? If you have a digital camera you can take as many as you want and print them off from your computer."

"I don't like digital pictures." He almost sounds offended.

"Why not?"

"It's too easy to fake stuff if you go digital, like all those models you see in magazines with impossibly perfect bodies and flawless skin. When you take a picture with film it has to be real."

"I never thought of that before." I walk over to the pictures on the wall and examine them. "These pictures are great. Did you take them?"

"No. My mom did." He keeps his eyes on the computer.

"This is you!" I point to one, obviously him as a little boy, blowing on dandelion fluff, a halo of light around his head.

"Yeah."

"You look so sweet." At the bottom of the photo are the words "my angel" written in a fancy loopy print.

"Thanks. Mom was a great photographer." His voice sounds sad. "What does your mom do?"

"She puts bad guys in jail." It comes out with a bitter edge that I don't expect. Skyler gives me a funny look, so I explain. "That's what my dad used to tell me, probably to make her look like some kind of superhero." I turn and run my hand along the clothesline. "My mom is a federal lawyer. She lives in the other Washington."

"Do you ever talk to her?"

I clip and unclip an empty clothespin so I don't have to meet his eye. "She called right after Rachel's funeral, but she just talked to Dad. I don't think she wanted to deal with an emotional teenager." I look up to see if I'm dumping too much on Skyler, but he looks like he gets it. I smile and try to sound more positive. "She's okay. I just don't think having a kid was part of her master plan. What about you, you ever talk to your mom?"

"No, she's dead." It comes out in a voice that's so cold I have to look to see if it's really Skyler talking.

"I thought—"

"She died a couple of years after she left us. But I didn't find out about it until the end of eighth grade. I was doing a research paper at school, and I decided to see if I could find her. I found an obituary." His voice is so emotionally removed that he could be reading a cereal box. "When I asked Dad about it, if he knew, he said she was dead to us the minute she walked out the door."

"Oh." I'm not sure what to say. I want to ask him what happened to her, but he looks so distant that I'm afraid to. "I'm sorry."

"Not your fault." He sits down at the computer and clicks the mouse. "The file's up."

He stands up from the computer and looks at me expectantly. I was so eager to see what Rachel left for me, but now I'm afraid. What if it is just a school assignment, or just pictures of us? Maybe she didn't get the chance to do what she wanted to. Maybe she died too soon.

I take a breath and cross the room. When I sit down, Skyler puts his hands on my shoulders, like he's helping me brace myself. I stare at the page in front of me, a jumble of pictures with the words "Journey Map" at the top. There are a lot of pictures of me and Rachel together, but most are just her. I can trace her transformation through the pictures, from my friend who always had something to laugh about to the sullen, hardened girl who never smiled.

"What's this?" I touch a picture stuck in the middle of the others, almost like it was added as an afterthought. I make the picture bigger and realize it's a football jersey. More specifically, it's Evan's football jersey and the number eighteen. Below it are written the words, "Making the cut," but it doesn't look like Rachel's handwriting.

"Looks like a football jersey," Skyler says casually, but I'm sure he knows who wore number eighteen.

I can't tell Skyler that I know whose number it is, and I can't tell him that I'm worried that his brother might have had something to do with Rachel's murder, so I pretend it's no big deal. "Rachel always had a thing for football players."

"Most girls do," Skyler says, and I catch the bitterness in his voice.

"Could you print this for me so I don't have to try to get into Dad's computer again?"

"Sure." Skyler takes my place at the computer and prints off the picture. I reach to get it, but he stands up, blocking my way. "Can I show you something?"

I'm distracted, wondering if there's any way I can make sense of the mass of pictures Rachel left for me, but I say, "Okay."

He moves the backdrop mounted on the wall, revealing a cupboard underneath. He pulls out a stack of pictures and shuffles through them before he sets the rest back inside the cupboard. "I want you to look at something, but I'm afraid . . . I mean, I know it'll be hard for you."

Now he has my attention. "What is it?" He hands me the picture, like he's not sure he should show it to me. I gasp when I see what it is—a picture taken from Rachel's front porch, through her shattered bedroom window. There's a dark spot on her carpet. I cover my mouth and look away, even in black and white I know what it is.

"I'm sorry." Skyler takes the picture from me.

Everything inside me is churning like it's going to go in reverse. I have to swallow a couple of times to make sure everything stays down. "When did you . . . how . . . why?" I lean against the counter to steady myself. I can't believe Skyler took that picture.

He puts his hand on my arm. "I don't want you to think I'm a creep or anything like that. Eric lets me go with him on calls sometimes, because he knows I want to be a forensic photographer." He looks at me like he's begging me to understand. "I want my pictures to help people, catch bad guys, like what your mom does. I only showed you this because I wanted to see if there was something the police missed, something you might catch because you knew her so well."

"What else did you see? Did you see her after—" I swallow back another wave of nausea.

Skyler shakes his head. "No. This was after they took her away. I don't usually go with Eric when there's a body involved anyway." He looks at me sideways, like he shouldn't have said it that way. "He thought it was a drive-by with no victim when he said I could come."

I take a breath and look at the picture again, avoiding the dark spot at the bottom. The mirror over Rachel's dresser is shattered, and the wall behind it is marked with bullet holes. Then something catches my attention on the far side of the room, at the edge of the photo, there's a picture hanging at an odd angle. "That picture is crooked."

Skyler looks too, but he shakes his head. "It could have been like that for a while."

"No. Things like that really bugged Rachel. She wouldn't have left it that way."

"Maybe it got knocked sideways when the bullets came through?" But Skyler doesn't sound sure of that.

I look at it closer. "Maybe, but there aren't any holes in the wall by it."

Skyler takes the picture from me and studies it too. "Might be important. I could mention it to Eric."

"No. It's probably nothing." I say it too quick. Skyler is giving me a strange look, but I keep thinking about what Rachel said about not trusting the police. "Do you have any more?"

"No. I only got one shot off before Eric told me I had to leave because it was a murder investigation." He gives me a guilty glance. "He doesn't know I took that one."

"Can I keep it?" Now I sound like the creepy one, but there might be more to the picture. "If I have more time to look I might see something else."

He hesitates. "I have the negative. I can make you another copy." He goes to the closet again and gets out a shoe box full of negatives, strips of developed film. He sorts through them, pulls one out, and puts the box back in the closet. Then he slides the strip into a black machine and turns it on.

Another picture is projected on the table below. It's a picture of me from Evan's party. "What's that?"

Skyler looks embarrassed as he moves the negative so the picture from Rachel's room is showing instead. "I was just messing around." He turns a knob on the projector and the picture gets bigger. "We can blow it up so you get a closer look at the wall."

"That would be great." I lean forward and study the image on the table.

"You're right, I don't see any—" Skyler freezes and I hear it too, someone yelling his name. He swears under his breath and goes to the door, opening it just a crack. His face goes pale.

"What's wrong?" I walk across the room to him.

He shuts the door. "My dad's home."

"Oh." I wonder if Skyler is going to be in trouble because I'm here. It doesn't seem likely, considering what Evan told me about their dad being "cool" with parties at their house. Whatever it is, Skyler looks scared.

"Skyler! Skyler!" His dad's voice is getting closer. "Where the hell are you?"

He reaches over and turns off the projector. "Stay here. I'll come get you when it's safe to come out." The way Skyler says it, combined with the tone in his dad's voice makes me afraid, so I nod. He slips out the door.

I sit on the desk chair, waiting, listening to muffled yelling outside the shed. It sounds like Skyler's in deep trouble. I'm worried about him, but I also wonder if I'm going to make it home before Dad gets there and what he'll do if I don't. I stand up and pace the room, wondering what I could say to my dad or to Skyler's dad if I get caught.

While I think about that, I go back to the projector and turn it on again. I mess with the knobs on the side of the projector, making the picture bigger until the image goes blurry. I don't see anything else so I turn it off.

It still creeps me out that Skyler took the picture, but I guess his reasons are good ones, and if it's something that will help me . . . I glance across the room. The cupboard behind the backdrop calls me to it. Skyler said he only had one picture of Rachel's room, but what if he has other pictures, like some from the other murder, the one in the old house? He said he didn't go on murder investigations *usually*. Maybe that one he did. But I can't ask him about it without explaining why I want to know.

I strain my ears to hear if he's coming, but the yelling sounds far away. I open the door to the cupboard and grab the stack of pictures. A bottle of pills comes out with them. I pick it up and read the label, aripiprazole, a medicine I've never heard of before. The prescription is for E. Cross, which I guess could be Evan or Eric. Then I see the date. They're like ten years old.

I put the bottle back and look through the pictures. Immediately I'm both disappointed and relieved. I shuffle through them, but they're just pictures of the football team at some party, in stupid poses, their shirts off, flexing or whatever. I set them back in the cupboard, embarrassed that I went through Skyler's things.

Something else catches my eye, the box of negatives. I pick up the first one and hold it up to the light, it's the same stuff, the football team trying to act cool. I put it back in the box and pick up the next one. The first couple of pictures are more football team, but down the strip they get weirder.

It's hard to tell, because the negatives are reversed—dark where they should be light and light where they should be dark—but they look like close-ups of bloody wounds. I pull the negative of Rachel's bedroom out of the projector and put the other one in. Then I turn on the light.

At first I think these might be pictures from another murder investigation, but the next one is a kid who was in our class but moved in the middle of last year. He's grinning as he holds up an arm dripping in blood. I'm totally confused now. Are these just the football team goofing off again, maybe from Halloween or something?

I pick up the next negative and put it on the projector. It's more close-ups. One picture looks like a guy's chest, but his face isn't in the picture. The wound on this one is bigger, big enough that I can tell it's a number crudely cut into his chest—20.

I step back, shocked, thinking about Evan's lumpy tattoo. I pick up the first negative again and put it in the projector. All the wounds are shaped like numbers.

One of them is 18.

I hear someone outside. I put the negatives back in the box and slam the cupboard shut, but it's too late. He's already seen me.

CHAPTER
16

"Jaycee, what are you doing here?" It isn't Skyler, it's Evan.

"Waiting for Skyler." I try to force my voice to stay casual, but my heart is racing.

"Well, he's in deep. He was supposed to be doing the hay today. *Not* hanging out with you." Evan's accusing tone makes me feel even guiltier.

"He didn't tell me that. He said he would meet me at the church and—"

Evan's blue eyes snap with anger, all the fake tenderness I saw in them before is gone. "He's not supposed to be out here anymore either. This is my space. The computer's mine."

I wonder if that means the pictures in the cupboard are Evan's too.

His voice softens, and he sighs. "You'd better let me take you home. If Dad catches you here things will be worse for Skyler."

"Okay," I say reluctantly. I glance over at the picture

Rachel made, still sitting on the printer. When Evan turns his back to go out the door I grab it, fold it in half and tuck it inside my shirt, underneath the scarf I'm wearing.

I follow Evan outside. Compared with the false light of the darkroom, the sun feels too bright. I blink and stumble forward. Evan puts his hand on my waist to steady me, then he leans into my ear. "My bike is behind the big barn, go around back and meet me there. I'll tell Dad I have to go somewhere."

I sneak around the back of the Cross property, feeling like a criminal, wondering where Skyler is and what it means to be "in deep" with his dad. Then I see him, kneeling on the side of the barn, one hand cradled against his body. He looks hurt.

"Skyler," I whisper. He looks up, afraid at the sound of my voice. "Are you okay?" I go closer and kneel down next to him, watching for his dad.

"I told you to stay in the darkroom," he says without any emotion.

I lean closer to him. "Are you hurt?"

"I cut my hand cleaning up the mess he made." He indicates a beer bottle that must have been broken against the shed. There are trails of brown liquid in the dust on the side of the barn.

"Let me see." I gently pull his hand away from his chest. There's a piece of glass embedded in his palm, and it's streaked with blood. His white shirt is stained with blood too.

He looks down, like it's the first time he's noticed the glass and pulls it out without flinching.

I suck in a breath. I've seen a lot of blood today, but this is real and not in black and white, and it's Skyler's blood, which makes it more awful. "That looks . . . pretty bad." It's still bleeding. I unwind the scarf around my neck. It's silk, a present from my mom, but I wrap it around Skyler's hand and tie it tight, knowing it will be ruined.

He looks up, like he's surprised that I'm being nice to him. "Thanks."

"Do you want to get out of here? We could go to my house, hang out until your dad cools off." I know I'll be in deep too if I bring Skyler home, but somehow I can't compare my dad's anger with what I've seen of Skyler's.

He shakes his head. "I'm okay." He forces a smile that fades as a shadow falls over both of us. Skyler jumps to his feet, but it's only Evan again.

"Jaycee, c'mon. You need to leave." Evan's voice has an urgency to it that I can't ignore, so I stand up too.

Skyler gives him a dark look and then turns back to me. "I don't want you to go anywhere with him."

"Don't be stupid, Skyler," Evan says. "Either I take her home or we sit around and wait for Dad to find out she was here."

"No. I'm taking her home." When Skyler stands in front of Evan it's painfully obvious how much smaller he is than his brother.

"Dad will—" Evan starts.

"Maybe I should—" I say.

"No!" Skyler faces Evan, gripping his fingers so tightly that blood seeps through the scarf. "You stay away from her."

"What's going on here?"

I turn around, expecting to see Skyler's dad, but this time it's Eric.

"Skyler, what did you do this time?" Eric reaches for Skyler, but he shrinks away. "Let me see." Eric's voice is commanding but still gentle. He takes Skyler's hand and pulls it toward him. Then he unwinds the scarf and uses it to wipe away the blood. "I don't think you need stitches." He rewraps Skyler's hand and steps back, looking at me, like this is the first time he's noticed me. "What are *you* doing here?"

"Allow me to introduce Skyler's girlfriend, Jaycee, the lawyer's daughter," Evan says. "Skyler left the field to be with her, and Dad's home."

Eric swears under his breath, looks at Skyler, and shakes his head. He turns back to me. "I'm sorry, Jaycee, but you need to leave. This isn't a good time."

Evan rolls his eyes. "I offered to take her home, but—"

"She's not going anywhere with you." Skyler stands between me and Evan.

"Calm down." Eric pulls his keys out of his pocket and hands them to Skyler. "Take my truck. Take Jaycee home, and then go finish the field. I'll handle Dad."

"But—" Evan starts to say.

"I said I'd take care of it," Eric says, giving Evan a dark look.

"Whatever," Evan says. "Your funeral. See you later, Jaycee."

I'm not sure what to do, but I follow Skyler to his brother's truck. He isn't even watching for his dad, but I am, and I don't see him.

Skyler lets out a long breath once we're in Eric's truck. He starts it up and peels out backward. "I'm sorry about that. Could you let me know if there's anything else I could possibly do to screw this up?"

I force myself to smile, not sure how to take everything I just saw. "It's okay. I'm sorry I got you in trouble. Sorry I made you come here."

He takes in a breath like he's trying to calm down. "It's not your fault. I didn't think Dad would be home this soon."

"What's going to happen when you get home?"

"Guess that depends on whether I go home. Eric's got a full tank of gas." He looks at me. "What do you think, Jaycee? You want to get away from here, run away with me?" I'm stunned into silence, but he laughs and the tension fades. "Relax, I'm kidding."

I'm glad to see the hardness leave his eyes so I joke back. "It's not a terrible idea. I mean, I'm probably going to be in trouble when I get home too. I just think maybe we should, I don't know, graduate from high school first."

He rolls his eyes. "Details."

I grab his hand. "Look, I was serious about you coming to my house, at least until your dad cools off."

"No. Thanks. I need to finish my work. By the time I get home Dad'll be cooled down and sobered up."

"What if he isn't?" I ask seriously.

"Then I'll be outside your window at midnight. Pack a suitcase." He winks at me, but his eyes still look sad. I wonder if there's something more serious going on between him and his dad than what he's telling me. When he kisses me good-bye, he acts like he doesn't want to let me leave.

By some miracle, Dad isn't home yet. I change my clothes, leaving Rachel's picture in my bottom drawer. I'll have to look at it later.

The Sunday paper is where Dad left it on the kitchen table. A picture of Rachel is splashed across the front again. This time, she's wearing a low-cut white tank top, a pair of cutoff shorts, and no shoes. It looks like a recent picture, and deliberately sexy. Next to her is a smaller picture of a grizzled Mexican man in an orange jumpsuit and shackles.

Arrest Made in Murder Case

LAKE RIDGE—Police arrested Jose Ortiz, 65, in connection with the shooting death of Rachel Sanchez after a gun alleged to have been used in the crime was found in his room at the Lake Ridge Motel. Sanchez was found in her bedroom, dead of a gunshot wound, Saturday, June 16. Ortiz has a long arrest record, including drug trafficking, running a prostitution ring, and assault charges. Police say he has ties to a Mexican gang prominent—

"Where have you been?" Dad comes in and shuts the door behind him. "Why weren't you at church?" His tone is even, but there's something behind it. I know I'm busted.

"Didn't Taylor—"

"Before you answer that question, I should probably tell you that Mrs. O'Dell said she saw you leave church in Skyler's truck." His eyebrows hood his eyes with disappointment. "What do you have to say for yourself?"

The article I just read, with the picture of Rachel, and everything else today boils up inside of me. Dad's accusations hit me hard. I shove the newspaper at him. "What about this, Dad? When were you going to tell me about this?"

He looks at the picture of Rachel on the front and then calmly sets the paper down on the table. "We were talking about you. Now isn't the right time to—"

"It's never the right time!" I yell back at him. He looks stunned, so I push forward. "She was my best friend, and you won't even tell me anything about what happened to her. I have to find out about it by listening to the gossip at church."

He folds his arms. "Okay then. Let's talk about Rachel. A year ago the two of you were very much alike, good girls who got good grades, did what your parents asked you to do, stayed out of trouble. And then little by little Rachel changed. She started sneaking around with boys her mother didn't approve of. She changed the way she dressed and how she acted; she went to parties where there were drugs and alcohol. Maybe she got addicted, maybe she needed money to get high, maybe she just sank so low that she didn't care enough to get out the trap she had laid for herself. One year ago she was just like you, and now she's dead."

He stops to let that sink in. I blink, too shocked to speak.

"Now let's talk about you. You get some creepy text message from God knows who, you leave church and sneak off to Skyler's house after you promised not to be alone with him."

He pounds his hand on the table and I jump. "Can you understand why I might be upset? Can you understand why I might be afraid?"

I take in everything he's saying and slump into a chair, all the anger drained out of me and sucked into the hole in my chest. I feel very small and very ashamed. "I'm sorry, Daddy."

He sinks into the chair next to me. "I saw a lot of bad things when I was a lawyer, Jaycee. A lot of kids, younger than you even, who got into bad situations in the name of a little fun, in the name of a little freedom, situations they couldn't get themselves out of. Situations like the one Rachel found herself in. I thought we were safe here, but . . ." He breathes in. "Don't you get that I'm worried? Don't you get that I only want to keep you safe?" He cups my chin in his hand. "I don't want to lose you the way Araceli lost Rachel."

He turns away, and for a second I see something like tears in his eyes. I wait while he composes himself. "So no more sneaking around with Skyler and no more secret text messages."

I can only nod.

He puts his firm face back on. "You're grounded. You'll spend tomorrow working at the office with me. You will have no contact with Skyler or any of your other friends at all this week, do you understand?"

I nod again, but I'm thinking about how shattered Skyler looked when I got out of the truck. I'm not sure I should stay away from him for a whole week.

—　—

Later that night, after I'm sure Dad is asleep, I pull the sheet of pictures Rachel left me into my bed and study it with a flashlight, under the covers the way I used to sneak read when I was a little kid.

The first picture was taken at the end of ninth grade. Rachel and I are standing together in the middle school gym after our graduation dance. She's in a strapless red dress that makes her look like a Latina model. I'm wearing a pink frilly dress that someone from the church loaned me. It makes me look like I'm ten. We have our arms linked and both of us are smiling. It hurts my heart to see us together like that, so happy.

The next picture is something from the Catholic church, a baptism or something. She's standing next to Eduardo, a young mother holding a baby, and a group of people I don't recognize.

There's one more of the two of us from last summer. We're sitting on the sweetheart log at the edge of the park, where kids have carved and crossed out initials for so many years that they blur into each other. I used to imagine that Evan would carve my name next to his on that log; now I wonder if Skyler will.

The next pictures look like Rachel took them herself, maybe with her cell phone. They document how she changed. Her nose gets pierced and her hair gets bleached, her eyebrows are plucked thin and her makeup gets darker, but that isn't what I notice the most. It's that she doesn't smile anymore. Her face is pained, and then hard, and finally, hopeless. Only the last one is different. Rachel is wearing a white dress and the sun is shining behind her hair like a halo. She has her eyes closed like she was laughing. She looks like an angel. I'm not sure why she put that picture last. Maybe she wanted me to know wherever she is now, she's okay.

There are other pictures, mixed in with the self-portraits. The first ones are graffiti from the old house. There's only one other picture with Eduardo in it. It's a close-up of the symbol on his back. If I didn't know he had the tattoo, I wouldn't even know it was him. I wonder what their relationship was like. During the last couple of months it seems like they were always together, not holding hands or kissing like most of the couples at the school, they were just together. I wonder if he was the one she was talking about that night. I wonder if he's the one who sent her the text.

There are numbers written in between the pictures, so small that I didn't notice them before: 20, 22, 34, 44, 66, and finally, Evan's jersey with the 18 and the words "making the cut."

I think about the bloody 18 I saw on the negative. Could it have been the beginning of Evan's tattoo?

I concentrate on each individual picture, trying to make sense of it. It meant something to Rachel, enough for her to go to the trouble of hiding that little chip in the cross. It frustrates me that there isn't more, that she was so cryptic.

I close my eyes, half thinking, half praying for some kind of guidance, except I'm not sure if God helps kids who defy their dads and leave church with boys.

Something that Skyler said about the other picture sticks in my mind.

I wanted you to see if there was something the police might have missed, something that you'd know because you knew her so well.

That stops me. I look at the pictures again. If Rachel created this for me, if she was worried about someone else finding it, then there have to be things only I'll recognize. I have to look at it that way, in the light of ten years of friendship.

Y ou got it?" Dad says. I don't, not really. I finally fell asleep last night after staring at Rachel's pictures for hours. I stared at them until my eyes hurt, but I couldn't figure anything out. My head is a jumble of everything that's been going on. I can't focus on the explanation Dad just gave me of his elaborate filing method.

"Jaycee, did you hear me?"

"Yeah, sure, Dad." I turn my attention back to the piles of paperwork; they look overwhelming. "You know, you could just scan all this stuff in and save it on a computer."

"Never trusted keeping things on a computer," Dad says. "Computers are machines; they crash and files get lost. I prefer to have everything where I can reach out and hold onto it if I need to."

I wonder if he feels that way about me too, because he settles down at his desk while I work at a little table to the side, within arm's reach. I'm not sure why he spent so much time explaining everything when I could ask him a question any time I needed to.

He makes phone calls while I file. Every few minutes I glance out the window, toward the school playground, thinking about the conversation I heard, the pictures from Skyler's house, and the pictures Rachel left for me.

Dad notices. "I know you'd rather be out enjoying the sunshine. I'm sorry I have to punish you."

I doubt that. I turn my attention to the filing. It's mindless, and I kind of like creating order, sorting the piles into neat folders in Dad's filing cabinet. Then I come across one that looks different than the other papers. The label at the top says CONFIDENTIAL. I stand up and set the pages in front of Dad. "Where does this go?"

He looks down at the paper and then looks up at me sharply. "Did you read it?"

"No." I automatically feel guilty, even though I didn't read it.

"Did you see any names on the file?"

"No."

His face relaxes. "I'll take care of this one. I thought I'd taken all of those out. Any that are marked confidential please give to me immediately and don't read what they say. They go in a different file."

"Okay."

He takes a ring of keys out of his desk, unlocks the bottom drawer of the file cabinet, and thumbs through the tabs. I know I shouldn't watch him, but I do. I keep ruffling through the pile on the desk so it doesn't look like I'm watching him, but I can see names on the files. I read the first few: Asher, Brown, Chandler, Cross.

Cross?

He shuts the drawer. "I appreciate you showing that to me without looking at it." He goes back to his desk and puts the keys back in the drawer. I nod, but I'm burning up with curiosity about whatever that file says about Skyler's family. How much does my dad know about his dad and what goes on there?

"Once you've finished that paperwork you can dust my shelves. I have a meeting with the sheriff in about twenty minutes."

I turn back to the files, trying to keep my mind off the one I saw in the drawer. I would never look at Dad's confidential files. Before. I've done a lot of things in the last couple of weeks that I didn't think I'd ever do, a lot of things that would shock my dad.

I keep thinking about the file and the key while I work.

Finally Dad stands up. "The meeting should only be about an hour, and then we can head home for lunch."

As soon as he's gone, I open the drawer and take out the key ring, rolling it between my fingers and contemplating what I should do. I'm not even sure I want to see what's in there. The rumors are that Skyler's mom had an affair and left his dad and the rest of the family when Skyler was really young. Maybe they're divorce papers.

I guess I wouldn't want Skyler poking around in my family's

business, not that there's much excitement there, but maybe there's something in the file that will help me help him.

I put the key into the file cabinet and it turns with a little click. The Cross file has CONFIDENTIAL across the top, just like the other files. I reach for it, but as I glance over my shoulder I pull another file out instead. This one says: CHANDLER and LEGAL COUNSEL.

I lean over to put it back in the file, picking up a couple of words: football hazing rituals, cutting, plausible deniability, lack of evidence. Coach Chandler is the football coach and was my geometry teacher last year. I remember hearing about this. It was a few years ago, some kid accused the football team of some kind of hazing and brought a lawsuit against the school and the coach, but nothing ever came of it. Dad helped Coach Chandler out because he couldn't afford a lawyer.

I look at the file again. This time the word "cutting" stands out. I think about the pictures I saw in Skyler's darkroom, or maybe it's Evan's darkroom and they're Evan's pictures. It looks like the hazing ritual is still going on. I contemplate taking the file, maybe even telling Dad about the pictures I found, but then I'd have to admit to Skyler and Dad that I was snooping. Also, crossing the football team would be social suicide for school next year. Besides, as sadistic as it is, the boys in the pictures looked like they were okay with what they were doing.

I shove the file back into the drawer and listen for footsteps as I pull the Cross family file out and set it on the floor in front of me. I take a breath and open it. The first page is a letter to my dad.

Mr. Draper,

I'm writing to ask for your help so I can get my son back. I made a lot of mistakes, I know that, but I can't leave Skyler with his dad. Wayne's older boys seem to be happy with the situation, but Skyler is a sensitive boy who needs someone who understands him.

Wayne is trying to have the state declare me an unfit parent so I can never see my son again. I know I shouldn't have left the way I did, and I know what the doctors or my ex-husband may have told you about my illness, but I'm doing much better. I'm taking my medications. I'm working as a housekeeper and making extra money on the side doing portraits. I have a little apartment and I know I can take care of him. Please, I'll do anything to get him back.

Sincerely,
Megan Dial (Ellen Cross)

Underneath there's a copy of the letter Dad sent back to Skyler's mom.

Dear Mrs. Cross,

I'm glad to hear that you're doing well. I hope your condition continues to improve and that you have success with your photography. However, I cannot in good faith get involved in this case. I'm not well acquainted with you or your circumstances. As far as your mental health is concerned, I'm not a physician and therefore I have to leave that to their evaluations.

Know that your son is doing well and seems happy. I will keep an eye on him, and if his circumstances change I'll do my best to make sure he's taken care of.

I wish you the best,
Travis Draper

My heart hurts for Skyler's mom, and for Skyler. I wonder if he even knows she was trying to get him back. I didn't realize until now that Eric and Evan had a different mom than Skyler, but it makes sense. Skyler is smaller and his hair is darker than his brothers'. Knowing what I saw of Mr. Cross, I wonder if Dad should have gotten involved.

The next page in the file is another letter to Dad, this time from an attorney.

Mr. Draper,
I am writing to you because we found correspondence between you and Megan Dial in her personal papers. We regret to inform you that Ms. Dial took her own life on the 6th of this month.

The late Ms. Dial's will leaves a large sum of money from a family trust to her son, Skyler Cross, with explicit instructions that the money not go to

her ex-husband. As the attorney settling her estate, I'm endeavoring to transfer the trust fund for her son through a Mr. Ortiz, a friend of Ms. Dial's who lives in the area, but I have met with some resistance from Ms. Dial's ex-husband. I was hoping you could assist me with this. Please contact my office at your earliest convenience.

I've also been entrusted with a brief note that the late Ms. Dial left for her son. I've enclosed a copy of the note. Perhaps you can decide the best time and method for getting it to him.

Sincerely,

Jason B. Kirk,
Attorney at Law

It's all pretty terrible. I glance through the letter again and the name Ortiz stands out, the same last name as the man who was arrested for Rachel's murder? It's probably just a coincidence. Ortiz is a common enough last name, but then again—

I reach for the last page in the file, the note from Skyler's mom to him, but the door to Dad's office opens. I shove the papers into the folder and stuff the file back into the drawer, but when I slam it shut the lock catches and it bounces back. I'm stuck on the floor with the drawer open and the file half hanging out. I turn to face Dad, trying to form some explanation. Instead, I see Skyler.

I stand up quickly to block the file from his view. "Skyler, what are you doing here?"

"I came to see you. You didn't answer the phone at your house, so I figured you might be with your dad." He moves across the room and wraps his arms around me, leaning over my shoulder toward the file cabinet. "What are you working on?"

I step back from him fast to cover the open drawer. "You can't be here. I can't see you."

He looks hurt. "Why not?"

"I'm grounded. Someone from church saw us leaving together."

"Ouch, sorry." He looks miserable. "How long you in for?"

"A week. At least." I'm trying to keep an eye on Dad's office door, listening for footsteps and trying to keep my body in front of the file cabinet so Skyler won't know I've been digging into his family's business. "So you'd better go."

Instead of leaving, Skyler steps forward and brushes a stray piece of hair out of my face. "A whole week? I'm not sure I can live that long without you."

I step back again, banging my ankle, the sore one, on the corner of the open file cabinet. I bite my lip. "Sorry. But it'll be longer if my dad catches you here."

"Where is he now?" Skyler closes the distance between us again; now I'm trapped between him and the open drawer. He looks over my shoulder again.

I move to block his view. "At a meeting with Eric, at his office."

"How long is the meeting?" Skyler looks around the office, but he doesn't move away from me.

I chew on my lip and glance at the clock. "Not long enough." Then I bite down hard, what a dumb thing to say. *Not long enough for what?*

He grins. "I guess I can't take you out to lunch then." He reaches for my braid, lying on my shoulder, and rolls it between his fingers.

My face is on fire; I can't look him in the eye. "Nope."

He puts his face so close to mine I can taste his breath. "And kissing you right now would probably be a bad idea."

I'm having a hard time breathing, either because I'm scared of getting caught or because I do want him to kiss me. "Definitely a bad idea." Even as I say it, I lean closer to him.

He pulls away, drops the end of my braid, and leaves me hanging. "I guess I'll just go then." He turns toward the door. I fight the urge to follow him and make him finish what he started, at least kiss me good-bye. He sets a white box on top of the files I was working on. "I'll leave this here for you. Kind of a 'sorry my family is weird' and 'thank you for saving my life' gift." He looks over his shoulder, giving me the same grin that I've seen on Evan. "I guess I'll see you later."

It takes me a second to compose myself after he leaves. When I hear his feet on the stairs, I bend over and straighten the files in the drawer. The note from Skyler's mom is still poking up. I listen for footsteps again and pull it out.

There are only four lines on the paper, written in the same

loopy scrawl I saw on the picture in the darkroom, but the handwriting looks more shaky:

Good-bye, angel.
Don't give in to the demons.
I'm sorry for everything.
I love you.

The second line is chilling. It makes me think of what the letter said about Skyler's mom being mentally ill. She must have been slipping out of reality when she wrote the note. I wonder if Skyler has ever seen it.

I push the files all the way in and lock the drawer, but I stay on the floor for a while, thinking about how hard things have been for Skyler. His dad is obviously a jerk and his mom killed herself. Maybe that's why he was alone so much at school.

I stand up, looking at the box he left. I cross the room and pick it up. Then I sit down in Dad's big chair and slide my finger along the taped side, my heart dancing with anticipation, listening for any sign that Dad is coming back from his meeting. A little afraid of what I'll find, I open the box. Inside is a phone. A nice phone. A really nice phone. One with Internet access, like Rachel's phone. I pick it up and hold it in my hand in disbelief. The hand-me-down, ancient cell the FBI guy took from me was nothing like this. My stomach twists with a sort of embarrassed guilt, the kind you get when someone gives you something that you know you can never pay them back for. Almost like Skyler can read my thoughts, the phone buzzes.

Ur welcome. Call me l8tr

Before I can figure out what to say back, the doorknob twists again. I slide the box into the recycling bin under the table and slip Skyler's present into my pocket.

Dad walks in; behind him are three men. "Did you finish the filing, Jaycee?" he says without introducing his guests to me.

"Yes." I study the men who are with him, trying not to stare. They hover in the doorway. I'm sure they're migrants, they're all in worn jeans and stained long-sleeved shirts, holding their hats, looking nervous and out of place next to Dad's white shirt and tie.

"Good, thank you. I need you to go home now, so I can help these gentlemen," he says.

"Do you want me to get you some food?" I ask, but he's already at his desk, looking distracted.

"No. I'll get something later. Go ahead and take the truck. I'll grab something in town and walk home when I'm done here." He motions for the men to come in.

"Okay," I say, trying not to look too eager.

"Straight home, Jaycee," he reminds me.

"Sure, Dad." I answer easily enough, but inside I'm shaking. This was exactly what I was hoping for, freedom from Dad and access to the truck. I cover the phone in my pocket with my hand as I squeeze by the men on my way out.

I'm almost out the door when he stops me again. "Jaycee, there's a town meeting tonight. That FBI agent and Sheriff Cross are going to talk about gangs and what the community can do to stop them. I think I should be there. If you want to come," he hesitates, and I see his inner struggle to shelter me from everything, "I think it might be a good idea if you came too."

"Okay, Dad. I'll go." I feel a little surge of triumph mixed with fear. I know it's a big leap for him to let me go to the meeting, like he's finally letting me see that there are bad things in the world. It almost makes me feel guilty for what I'm about to do.

I start out heading home, but once I'm out of sight of Dad's office I go around the corner toward the park. One of the pictures of me and Rachel was taken at the Sweetheart Log. I might as well start there.

It's too hot for anyone to be playing outside, so the park is pretty much deserted. I go to the tree, kneel beside it, and scan the letters that are carved there.

I look for Rachel's name, and then my name, then our initials. The carvings blur together, and I can't find anything. I sit down and take the paper out of my pocket. I position myself exactly where the two of us were sitting on the log, but I still can't see anything.

I look from the picture to the log, but nothing comes. Hot

and frustrated, I think about heading home, but then the bells at the Catholic church chime one o'clock. The picture of Rachel and the group at the baptism was taken there. Father Joseph might know who was in the picture.

The sanctuary is empty. The candles in the front aren't lit, but it still smells like burned incense. I've been here with Rachel a few times, so I know Father Joseph's office is through a door behind the pulpit. I go to it quick, before I lose my courage.

When I knock he calls, "Just a minute."

While I wait, I pull out the collage. Rachel was standing almost where I am now, on the other side of the podium, with a big group. The woman in the middle is holding a baby wearing a long white gown. As the door opens I fold the paper so only the picture from the baptism shows. I stand forever, watching the clock tick by precious minutes. I'm not sure what Dad will do if he finds out I didn't go straight home.

Finally Father Joseph comes out of the office. "Why, hello, Jaycee." He looks surprised to see me. He's older than my dad, with a large bald patch down the middle of his round head, pleasantly plump wrinkles across his tan face, and a surprisingly small body. "What can I do for you?"

I show him the picture. "I was hoping you could tell me who these people are."

He takes the paper from my hand. "What is this for?"

I prepared myself for this one, even rehearsed the lie while I was waiting. "I was thinking about putting a scrapbook together for Araceli."

He pats my shoulder. "That's a nice idea." He peers back

over the picture. "The baby's name is Esme. They named her after her grandmother, Esmeralda. The boys are the baby's cousins: Beto Ramos, Eduardo Perez, and Manuel Romero. The woman in the back . . ."

I don't hear anything else he says. I'm stuck on one name, Manuel Romero, the boy that died in the old house. Rachel met him, at least once. I can't think of a delicate way to say it so I just jump in. "Did Rachel know him?"

"Who?" Father Joseph looks startled.

"Manuel Romero, the boy in the picture, did Rachel know him. Were they friends or . . . something?"

He shakes his head. "I couldn't say if she knew him. He wasn't here very long before . . ." He sighs. "Manuel was in some trouble in California before he came here, gangs I guess. His uncle had hoped to straighten him out." He rubs the silver hairs left on top of his head. "Why do you ask?"

I look at the worn wooden floor. "I just think it would be ironic if . . . if they were somehow connected."

"That would be a sad irony indeed." His usually smiling wrinkles droop across his face. "It's always sad for me to see young people heading down the wrong—"

"Do you think his family would be okay if I went to visit them? To find out some things . . . for the scrapbook," I add quickly.

A strange look crosses his face. "They don't live here anymore. They moved soon after he died. I don't know where they went. Sorry, I'm not very much help."

"No. That's okay," I say. I wish I could talk to Manny's

family, but it sounds like that's impossible. "I need to get home. Thank you anyway."

He grips my hand. "I hope you're doing okay." His pale-brown eyes meet mine. "This is such a hard thing for you young people." I nod but can't answer him around the lump in my throat that his kindness brings out. "Give your father my best," he says and releases me.

I nod again.

Once I'm back in Dad's truck I make a quick decision. I know I'm pushing it, but now that I know what I'm looking for I need to go back to the Sweetheart Log.

I go over it again, looking for the initials RS and MR, but I can't find them. Finally I step back, hold the picture up, and compare the log to what I see in front of me. The image is small, but I can make it out. The letters—their initials—are there, carved just below Rachel's leg in the picture. I go back to the log and look at that spot again, but they aren't there now. A big chunk of the log is missing where they should be. There are a lot of initials on the log that have been crossed out or carved over, but this one looks like it has been gouged out.

The message is clear. Manuel and Rachel did have something going on, and someone wasn't very happy about it.

The tiny town hall is packed with people, all talking at once. Eric is at the front. He's talking to Agent Herrera, who's half paying attention and half scanning the crowd. Dad leads me to a seat near the front of the room, next to Claire and her mom. I wish it was in the back, because Agent Herrera picks me out immediately. I avoid his gaze and try to make myself smaller as Eric calls for quiet.

"Thank you for coming," he says when the room has quieted to a buzz. "I know this is a busy time of year for all of you, so we will try to keep this meeting as brief and as informative as possible. First, I would like to assure all of you that we are working closely with federal authorities to insure the safety of—"

"What about the man you arrested?" The question comes from the back of the room. Without turning I recognize Mrs. O'Dell's voice. "The man who had the gun."

Several cries of "yeah" and "what's going on with that?" filter through the crowd.

"Agent Herrera of the FBI has taken over the investigation. He will answer all questions." Eric steps back, looking relieved to let someone else handle the crowd.

Agent Herrera steps forward. "The gun in question was legally registered to Jose Ortiz and was determined not to be the murder weapon. The suspect was not the Jose Ortiz we originally thought he was, so he was released."

"Then what have you found out? Anything? My wife is afraid to leave the kids alone." This time the question comes from Brent Thompson, father of Mitch Thompson, one of the captains of the football team.

"We are looking into several leads." For a second Agent Herrera's eyes find mine again. I try not to turn away because I don't want to look guilty.

"What about the gang connection? I heard the girl who was killed was part of a gang." I don't catch who asks that question.

"We are investigating a possible gang connection, but at this point we can't say whether the victim was the target, or if this was a random act." Agent Herrera says "the victim" like Rachel wasn't a real person. "At this point we haven't seen any other evidence of gangs in Lake Ridge."

"So what can we do to keep ourselves safe? As a single mother," Claire's mom says the last part pointedly, reaching for my dad's arm, "I need to know how to keep this from happening to my daughter."

"I'll tell you how to keep all of us safe," Brent Thompson again. "It's time for the police department to start checking green cards again. We all know that ninety percent of the migrants who come here are illegals and are already breaking the law. How do we know where they came from or what they're capable of? It's time to get rid of the bad element that's invaded this town. What do you say, Sheriff, how about doing your job?"

Eric looks uncomfortable; he clears his throat. "Unfortunately it would be impossible to check all the documents of all the people who come here to work on a seasonal basis. We have to rely on the employers to—"

"Like they care," Brent says. "All the farmers care about is cheap labor. It doesn't matter if the people they bring in are gang members or murderers or—"

"Easy for you to say," William Harris, who owns one of the biggest farms around, breaks in. "I want to know how I'm supposed to harvest my crops if I have to keep track of everyone who comes to me looking for a job."

Brent turns around to face him. "That's part of your responsibility as—"

"This is not an immigration issue." Agent Herrera's voice cuts through the arguing. "We have reason to believe that the person who committed this murder was someone the victim knew, someone who lives here."

The room goes silent again for a few seconds, and then the buzzing reaches a fevered pitch. People are throwing out accusations about Rachel: "I heard she was a gang member," "a drug dealer," "a prostitute." "How do we know she wasn't working with the illegals?" And then the questions get stupider: "How do we know *she* was here legally?" "What about her mother? I heard she had ties with a gang in Mexico."

I try to shut it out. Rachel and Araceli have lived here longer than we have. Rachel was born in Pasco.

"Quiet down." Eric's voice booms through the noise. "This kind of speculation will get us nowhere. What's important is that we come together as a community and send the message to whoever did this, that gangs and violence will not be tolerated in Lake Ridge. We can do this by watching out for our neighbors like we always have, but maybe we should step things up a bit. Keep an eye out for anything strange, watch for and report graffiti or anything that looks like it could be gang related. We do not want this kind of element in our town."

"Your sheriff is right," Agent Herrera says. "Experience has taught me that the best defense against gangs is a strong community. It isn't the responsibility of the people in this town to find out what happened." He's looking at me again. "Leave that to the proper authorities. We just ask that you keep a watch out and report any suspicious behavior. Sheriff Cross and I have outlined some points we would like to go over . . ."

The meeting drones on. A lot of talk about neighborhood watches and graffiti patrols. Agent Herrera doesn't offer any solid answers. I feel like coming here was a waste of my time.

Just as the meeting is ending, Dad stands up. "In the spirit of community cooperation, I would like to invite everyone here to help with the cleanup at Araceli Sanchez's house on Saturday. I think it would go a long way toward creating a sense of community."

Some of the people are nodding in agreement. Others, like Brent Thompson, are shaking their heads. I see it in their eyes: "She brought this on herself."

When the meeting is over, I get up quickly. I'd like to leave before Claire's mom gets her hooks into Dad and makes him talk to her all night, but more important, I want to leave before Agent Herrera sees me. I lose on both points. Claire's mom already has her arm looped through Dad's, talking about how scary it is to be a single parent these days, and Agent Herrera is walking toward us.

"Miss Draper, I have something to return to you, and I have a few questions," Agent Herrera says.

Claire's mom's eyes get really big. Dad untangles his arm from hers. "What kind of questions?"

Agent Herrera's eyes bore into mine. "We found some things on your daughter's phone that we would like her to explain to us."

The four of us—me, Dad, Agent Herrera, and Eric—all squeeze into the sheriff's office in the back of the town hall building. Agent Herrera takes the chair behind the desk, Eric perches on the edge, and Dad and I take two chairs across from them.

"I thought you might want to have this back," Agent Herrera says, sliding my phone across the desk. I take it and turn it over in my hands, waiting for the blow to fall and the questions to come.

Dad starts first. "What did you find out about Rachel's phone?"

Agent Herrera leans forward. "We traced payment of the phone bill to a bank account in Spokane. Unfortunately, the person the account was registered to doesn't exist. The account was opened with false documentation about eighteen months ago. We haven't been able to determine who was actually paying the bill. We've continued the cell service, hoping that someone will attempt to use the phone and then we can get a trace on it. So far, that hasn't happened. It's possible that the phone was destroyed by the murderer."

"I don't see what any of this has to do with Jaycee," Dad says.

Agent Herrera looks from Dad to me. "The phone records we recovered show that a large data file was sent from the victim's phone number to Jaycee's phone number on the night of the murder. Perhaps a video file?" He catches my eye, holding my gaze. "Do you know what was on that file? Was that what you deleted?"

I'm confused, looking to Dad for help. "I deleted a text message. I don't think there was anything attached to it. I didn't see anything like a video file." I look around the room. "I promise."

"We aren't saying we don't believe you," Eric says gently. "We're just trying to find out what happened."

"Did anyone else have access to your phone that night?" Agent Herrera says.

"There was this guy at the party, Peyton Harris, he—" I stop myself, realizing that Dad doesn't know anything about the party yet.

"Go on," Agent Herrera says, all three of them are watching me closely now.

I look down at my hands. "I was at a party, at Skyler's house. Peyton Harris stole my phone." I turn to Dad, trying to get him to understand. "I didn't want to go to the party, but Claire and Taylor were going. I . . . I wanted to call you to come get me, but I couldn't find my phone because Peyton had it. Skyler got it for me. Then he took me back to Claire's house. He didn't want to be at the party either." Dad looks so disappointed that I want to disappear. "I'm sorry. I should have told you—"

"How long do you think this boy had your phone? Did you see him do anything to it?" Agent Herrera says.

"I don't know. He hid it in the laundry room. He was just messing around. I didn't know about the message, if I had . . ." But I can't answer that question. I deleted Rachel's text, would I have deleted something else, like a video file? I don't know. I only know that whatever she was trying to tell me was important. I wish I had seen it.

Agent Herrera leans back, like he's tired of all of this. "Unfortunately, without the victim's phone, we have no way of finding out what was on that file, or on the message she sent you. By the time we knew to look for them, the data had been recycled by the cell phone carrier." I hear the accusation in his voice, this is my fault. I should have come forward sooner. "If you find anything else, please bring it to my attention, or to the attention of Sheriff Cross, immediately."

I think about telling them about the card in the cross, the pictures, the gouged-out initials, and everything, but Rachel's words keep coming back to me, *don't trust the police.* She said it more than once. There had to be a reason.

Dad answers for me. "She will."

She was sneaking around with a guy. Going to parties she wasn't supposed to go to. She had a phone her mom didn't know about. All these things described Rachel before she died.

And now they describe me.

I expect a lecture on the way home, for Dad to get mad again, but instead he sounds sad. "I'm sorry you didn't feel like you could tell me about the party. I would have come and got you, no questions asked."

I want to erase the hurt from his face, so I say, "I would have called you, but Skyler offered to take me home. It was just easier, and after Rachel . . . I didn't think the party was important enough to make you worry about it."

"I guess I'm glad you have a friend like Skyler," Dad says. "And I'm glad he has someone like you. I know he's struggled a lot, especially since his mom died, but he seems to be doing well now. Just promise you'll be careful. Remember what I said about you two not being alone. I meant it."

I think about the phone and a hundred other things that maybe I should tell him about, but I can only manage, "Okay, Dad."

"I mean later. Right now you're still grounded." He sighs. "Another thing, I talked to your mom again last night. She wants you to come stay with her for a little while, until things get settled down here."

I'm annoyed that Mom called again, but that she didn't bother to talk to me. "Why did she talk to you about it, and not me?"

"Maybe she wanted to ask me about it before she brought it up to you."

"So what did you say to her?"

He won't look at me. "I said it might be a good idea."

I laugh, but then I realize he's serious. "You honestly think DC is safer than Lake Ridge?"

"No, but . . . it might not be a bad idea to give you a break from everything here. Besides, your mom misses you. You haven't been to see her for a long time."

I roll my eyes. "That's her fault, she's always too busy. She's always making promises she can't keep."

"She's doing her best," Dad says. "We both are." He's silent for a while and finally he sighs. "Look, maybe I've been too tough on you, about a lot of things. I know I'm just a dad who doesn't get what a teenage girl wants or needs, but you have to trust that I'm trying to do what's best for you. I don't want you to think you can't come to me with anything."

"Okay, Dad," I answer, but inside I'm squirming. There's

too much I can't tell him. "But I don't want to go stay with Mom right now."

He breathes something that sounds like a sigh of relief. "Okay."

— —

I think about my conversation with Dad for a long time after he goes to bed. I need to cut back on the lies, starting with the phone. I can't keep it, but I don't know how to make Skyler understand why.

I start with: Thanks for the phone, but I can't keep it.

His answer sounds hurt: Don't u like it?

I love it, but it's too expensive.

He answers: I have money, don't worry about it.

I don't ask him where the money came from. I already know he has a trust fund from his mom. I wonder if my dad helped set it up. I wonder if his dad knows about it.

My dad won't let me keep this.

Don't tell him.

I don't need it anymore. I got my other phone back from that cop.

But this one is better. U don't have to use ur dads computer.

I can't think of an answer for that. He's right. The phone does give me access to the Internet whenever I want it. Despite everything Dad said, I don't think I can ask him if I can use the computer without getting a lot of questions. Maybe I should hang onto the phone just for a little longer.

He texts back: This is just for us. Don't give anyone else this number.

I like that idea. Kind of like the note-exchange place Rachel and I had in the old fireplace. I text back: K.

He ends with: I have to be up early tomorrow, TTYL. Luv you. Night.

That stops me. On top of my guilt I have another nagging question: is "luv you" in a text the same as "I love you?"

I feel like things are happening fast between me and Skyler, maybe too fast. I was kissing him in the church parking lot, something I'd never dream of doing before. I've known of him my whole life, but in some ways I feel as if I barely know him. We went to grade school and middle school together, but until the end of this year, we'd never really talked.

Rachel talked to him sometimes, but she talked to everyone. I remember they sat together on the way home from the eighth-grade field trip. Some guys were teasing him on the bus, I'm not sure what about, but she left me alone and sat by him. I wonder if he remembers that. I wonder if he heard her tell me she thought he was weird the day he was behind us on the way home from school. I hope not.

I glance at the text again. Maybe he's as nervous about this as I am. Maybe that's just what having a boyfriend is like. I wish I could ask Rachel. I'm sure she wouldn't think he was weird now, not if she got to know him.

I answer simply: Night.

Then I try to put it out of my mind. I have other things I need to worry about. I put the page of pictures on my bed, pressing out the wrinkles with my hand, trying to make sense of it. I think about what I found out today. I'm sure now that Manny was the guy she was talking about. She was in love with him, and then she found him dead. I feel sick, thinking about how she cried all night, and how she wouldn't talk about it. It must have been so horrible for her. I know she was afraid to go to the police, but why didn't she tell me?

I wonder how long she knew Manny, but I'm not sure it matters. In just a few weeks Skyler has become a huge part of my life, like I can't remember what it felt like not to have him in it.

Maybe I do love him.

I touch the new phone sitting on my bed beside me. Who texted her that night? Manny? Or was he already dead?

I look at the pictures again, trying to find something easy, something I can go after tomorrow if Dad leaves me alone. The number 18 stands out again. It was Evan's jersey number, but I don't think that's what she meant.

I search the number 18 and gangs on my new phone. I come up with a gang called the 18th Street Gang. I skim the article. Words stand out to me like "multi-ethnic" and "transnational." It says there are members of the 18th Street Gang in 120 cities and in 37 states. Are they here? Could Evan be part of a gang?

I push that idea out as soon as it hits my brain. Agent Herrera said there was no evidence of other gang activity in Lake Ridge, and the symbols were all for one gang, the Cempoalli.

I look at the paper again. The words above the number

don't make any sense. "Making the cut." It seems like that should mean something to me, but I can't figure out what.

I need to sleep, but first I have to check on one more thing. Something that's been bugging me. I pull up a Spanish to English translator and type in "boba." It comes up with words like "silly," "stupid," and "naive." I close the browser, disgusted.

I should have guessed.

I hide the paper and my phone in my bottom drawer, next to Rachel's broken necklace. That drawer is getting stuffed with too many secrets. I lie on my bed and try to turn my brain off by concentrating on what it felt like to have Skyler standing close to me, twisting the end of my braid in his fingers, inches away from kissing me. Then by remembering what it felt like when he kissed me the first time . . . and when I kissed him . . .

I'm drifting off, my brain getting fuzzy, when I think I hear something outside. I sit up fast, listening. I hear it again. It sounds like someone is standing by my window. I left it open to let the cool air in.

I stay in bed, too afraid to move.

The wind billows my curtains away from the window. Then I see it. A piece of paper stuck to my screen, fluttering in the breeze like a trapped moth, and making a soft scraping noise. I listen again, but I don't hear anything but the paper and the wind. I climb out of bed and creep across the room. The picture of Rachel's room is burned into my mind, so I avoid walking in front of the window.

As I get closer I realize the note is on the inside, slipped through an opening cut in the corner of my screen. I reach for the paper, free it with trembling fingers, and read the message inside.

The police couldn't save her, and they won't be able to save you. Keep your mouth shut and mind your own business, bitch.

The bottom is signed with a symbol I've come to recognize, the sign for the Cempoalli.

I slam the window shut and run to Dad's room. I pause outside and listen to him breathing. I reach up to knock, the note clutched in my fingers, but there's another piece of paper stuck to his door, no words, just the same symbol.

Rachel's words come back to me, *No one is safe from them.*

Not even my dad.

CHAPTER 22

"Jaycee, get up."

I jerk awake and look around my room, panicked until I realize that it's just Dad. I blink at the clock: 7:30. The last things I remember were the sun finally coming up and falling into an exhausted sleep. I struggle to sit up as he pushes my curtains open. "I need you to tell me the truth." I freeze midyawn, afraid of what truth he's referring to. "Were you in my office last night?"

I blink again. "No."

He taps his fingers on my windowsill, but he doesn't notice the rip in the corner of the screen. "I think someone was."

I sit up, wide awake now, a cold chill moving across my body. "What makes you think . . . ?" But I can't finish that sentence.

"When I went in this morning, some things were moved around. Rearranged like someone was looking for something."

"Is anything missing?" But I'm pretty sure what they're looking for wasn't there.

"I don't think so. I can't decide whether I should call the police."

"No." I say it too fast, and he looks at me suspiciously. "I mean, if nothing is missing, why would you bother them?"

He sighs. "It's probably just me getting old, misplacing things or forgetting where I set them."

He stares out the window a little longer and then says, "At any rate, you'd better get up. I'm taking those men to Spokane this afternoon."

"Why?" I slide my legs off the edge of the bed.

"They had some problems with the people they were working for. Worked for nearly the whole season and then they were sent away and told they wouldn't be paid. I can't do anything about it, but there's an office there that might be able to help them."

"Why you?"

"Because of my legal background. Because it's the right thing to do."

"Can I come with you?" I'm suddenly afraid of being left alone.

He looks at me like that's a strange question. "I'm borrowing a car from Mr. Hobbs, but there still won't be room for you."

"When will you be back?"

He shakes his head. "It'll probably be late. Considering everything, I'd feel safer if you were in town. I'll talk to Claire's mom and see if you can stay there tonight." He turns around to face me. "This doesn't mean you aren't grounded anymore. I expect you to stay at Claire's house tonight and go nowhere else. Do you understand?"

I nod, but I'm thinking about the notes and that someone got inside our house while we slept. My stomach hurts. Is finding out what happened to Rachel worth putting both of us in danger?

——

"Boba, aren't you on the wrong side of the lake again?" Eduardo appears out of nowhere. I jump when I see him, but control it enough to keep from hurting myself again. I try to keep my voice even and say casually, "Just going for a run." I convinced my dad to let me go for a run before he left for Spokane. My ankle feels much better, and I needed time to think about everything.

"By yourself?" Eduardo says it like I'm doing something stupid again.

"Is that a problem?" I say, but I've been thinking about what the note said the whole time I've been running. I'm actually glad to see him.

"This isn't the safest place for a girl to go running by herself," he says.

I glance around, trying to decide how much he knows about me being safe or not safe. "Okay, come with me then." He looks shocked by my invitation. "Unless you don't think you can keep up."

"Is that a challenge?" he asks.

"Consider it an invitation. Apparently I need protection,

we need to talk, and"—I can't resist a little jab—"you could use the exercise."

"Exercise?" He snorts. "Try cutting asparagus for twelve hours in the hot sun, then you'll know what exercise is." He breaks into a jog so I have to extend my stride to keep up.

"I have. It was miserable." I look across the field full of workers in long sleeves and broad hats. "Why aren't you working now?"

He shrugs. "I got fired." He points to his tattoo. "Someone saw this."

"I'm sorry," I say because I don't know what else to say.

"Doesn't matter," he says, "I won't be here very much longer. After I figure things out I'm gone."

"After you figure out what happened to Rachel?" I slow my pace a little because my ankle is starting to throb.

"Yeah, after that." He slows his stride to match mine. "Did you find anything else?"

"A note." I watch his face, testing him, because I'm half-convinced he was the one who left it in my screen, even if it was just to scare me.

He stops and looks at me, his expression guarded. "What did it say?"

"It said for me to mind my own business, that the police wouldn't protect me. It was signed with the Cempoalli symbol."

"This isn't good." He looks genuinely concerned. "They know about you, and they know you're looking."

My arms prickle. "Who knows?"

He looks at me like I'm an idiot. "The Cempoalli—the ones who left the note. You shouldn't stay here. Is there somewhere you can go, someplace safe?" I'm surprised at how worried he sounds.

I think about what Dad said about going to stay with Mom, but I can't leave now. "I'm not running away. Besides, you said no place is safe." I put my hand on his shoulder. "Look, stop. If we can't go to the police and we can't run away, the only thing left is for us to work together, figure this out."

"And then?" He stares through me with those dark eyes, not quite as comforting now.

"Then we go to the FBI or whoever, someone who will listen."

"And if they won't listen?"

"They will." I work at sounding confident, even though I'm not. "It's just like dealing with a bully on the playground; they think they're in charge because everyone is afraid to tell, but once someone does—"

He laughs. "Did you hear that from some motivational speaker or in Sunday school? Bullies don't do drive-bys. Bullies don't open up your gut with a knife."

I grimace at that image. "So you kill one of them, they kill one of you, and pretty soon everyone is dead?"

"As long as I'm the last one standing, it works for me."

I turn and face him. "That's completely asinine, you know that?"

"Where I come from, it's the law. Kill or be killed. Being part of a gang means survival."

"Well, where I come from, which is here, the law is the law, and being part of a gang makes you a bad guy."

"So you really believe the police will protect you?"

"Yes." I try to sound sure, even if I'm not.

"What if you're poor or don't speak the language or have the wrong color of skin or have a gang sign tattooed on your back?" He kicks at a big rock, sending it flying. "Everyone is equal, right? Just some people are more equal than others."

That sounds like something I've heard before. George Orwell? *"Animal Farm?"* I look at him in disbelief.

He shakes his head and smiles. "Didn't count on that, huh? A gangbanger who can read. How about this one? 'She doesn't need a priest but an avenger, so you go get the priest and I'll be the avenger.'"

I look at him, confused. "What's that from?"

He looks smug. *"The Count of Monte Cristo."*

"So you're the avenger and I'm, what, the priest?"

"Sounds about right."

"You obviously didn't finish the book, or you would know that by the end Edmond figured out that vengeance wasn't everything he thought it would be."

"Right. He had endless wealth, got the girl, *and* he got to see his enemies twist in the wind. Yeah, I can see where that would suck."

"Look, whatever happened in the story, vengeance won't ever be justice, it'll just be . . . wrong."

He shakes his head, disgusted. "That's the problem, boba, your idea of justice and my idea of justice are never going to mesh, so we can't work together."

I start running again. "Then I guess I won't tell you what I found in her cross." I want to bite my tongue. I had no intention of telling him I found anything in the cross. It just kind of slipped out because I was irritated with him.

He grabs my shoulder, jerking me back hard. "What did you find? Rachel's journal?"

I stand in front of him and rub my shoulder, still irritated and now a little afraid of him. "No. It was just a bunch of pictures, or one piece of paper with a bunch of pictures arranged on it. It was something Rachel made in school, but I think it means something."

"Show it to me."

"I don't have it, not with me, I left it at home."

"We need to get it now." He starts running again, completing the loop that will take us into town.

I match his pace, catching up despite the pain in my ankle. "I can't show it to you now. My dad's home and he wouldn't—"

"Wouldn't want you to show up with a guy like me?"

"No, it's just . . ." I try to come up with an answer that he can't turn into something that sounds racist.

Eduardo laughs. "Don't worry, it wouldn't be the first time someone's dad didn't want me around. When will he be gone?"

"He's home for the morning, then he's leaving for Spokane—"

"Are you going to be alone?"

"No. I'll be at Claire's."

"Good," he says.

"Good?"

"It's not safe for you to be alone."

I think about that as we get closer to town. How much danger am I really in? "Why don't you think the police can protect me?"

"Experience. They didn't protect Manny, and they didn't protect Rachel."

I think about that for a minute while we run in silence. I don't know anything about Manny or what Rachel saw in him. Why she was willing to put herself in so much danger to find out what happened to him. "Tell me about him."

"Who?"

"Tell me about Manny. I want to know more about this guy Rachel was so in love with that she gave up everything for him."

Eduardo breaks stride a little bit, but he doesn't turn. "What do you want to know?"

"Just anything. He obviously meant a lot to Rachel, but she never told me anything about him. I don't even know why." I watch him out of the corner of my eye, trying to judge his reaction when I say that.

His jaw clenches in pain. "He told her not to tell anyone; he was afraid someone would come looking for him. He was right."

"Why was he so afraid? Do the Cempoalli really hunt down former gang members just for leaving?"

"Depends on who you are, or why you leave." Eduardo is being vague on purpose. I think there's more to it than what he's telling me.

"Why do *you* think they came after Manny?"

He waits for a few strides, looking around, I guess to see if we're really alone. "Because he crossed them, and you don't cross the Cempoalli."

"What does that mean, 'cross them'? What did he do?"

Eduardo stops running. I stop too. He looks around again and then leans closer to me. "Remember the person I told you about? The one who ended up in the Dumpster?"

"Yes." I'm afraid of what I'm going to hear.

"There was more to it. After he was killed, we had to make things even."

"Even? You mean like one of yours for one of theirs?"

He nods. "But it went too far."

"What happened?"

Eduardo is struggling with how much to tell me; I can see it in his face. "I wasn't there, but Manny was. He said too many people died. He wouldn't tell me anything else, but after we came here, he talked to that FBI guy about it, the one who took your phone."

"Agent Herrera?"

"Yes. Manny gave him everything he asked for, betrayed his homies in exchange for protection, and what did he get?" He starts pumping his fists, like he's working himself up again, like when we were at the cemetery. "I told Manny we couldn't trust him, but he didn't listen. He would have done anything for her. He wanted Rachel to see that he had changed, that he wasn't ever going back. He ended up getting both of them killed."

I think about what Father Joseph said about Manny's family moving. "Is that why your uncle left, because he was afraid too?"

"Yes."

"Then why did you stay?"

His jaw clenches in pain again. "Because Rachel wouldn't leave, and I told Manny I'd take care of her."

There's something about the way he says it that makes me understand why Rachel told me to trust him. Despite all his faults, Eduardo is loyal, so loyal it's almost scary.

"Why are you still here then, if she's . . . if Rachel's gone?"

He has his head down, and he's breathing hard. I don't think it's because of our run, more like he's trying to get control of his emotions. Finally he answers, "I made a promise."

"What did you promise?"

He starts running again without answering, but I can guess that it had something to do with getting revenge. He doesn't say anything else until we're almost to town, then he says, "I've come far enough. I'll leave so you don't have to be seen with me."

"It's okay. I don't . . . care." My protest sounds weak, even to me. I'm not sure what Dad or Skyler or anyone in town would say if they saw Eduardo and me together.

"No. It's better if you aren't seen with me. Just don't go running by yourself again."

I shrug, trying to sound brave. "I've been running the same route all summer. I'm not afraid."

He looks up at me, his eyes sad. "That's the problem, boba. You should be."

CHAPTER 23

M aking out in the church parking lot." Taylor finishes the black heart she's painting on my toenails. "I'm impressed, Jaycee. I didn't think you were that kind of girl."

"We weren't making out." I pull my toe away and smudge the heart so it turns into more of a glob.

"That's not what I heard," Claire says, flipping to the next page in the magazine she's looking at. "I heard it was all hands and tongue and steamy windows."

I shake my head, annoyed with their prying, wishing they would sneak out and go wherever they're going. I need to be alone so I can think.

"How long are you grounded?" Taylor's question cuts into my thoughts. She's started over on my big toe, like it was the most important thing she has to do with her life. It probably is.

"One week," I say, then, "Ow," as Taylor moves my leg by gripping the sides of my ankle, sore again because of my run.

"That sucks," Taylor says.

"You're lucky you have us," Claire says. "We'll make sure you get the chance to see your boyfriend tonight, grounded or not."

I look at the two of them. I'm still not sure if "boyfriend" fits my relationship with Skyler, but I kind of like the way it sounds.

"Not only that, we're going to do the whole makeover fairy-godmother bit. I have your outfit all picked out." Claire gets off the bed and goes to her closet. She comes back with a little white tank top and a pair of cutoff jeans—really short cutoff jeans.

"I can't wear that."

Taylor shakes her head at me. "You don't honestly expect to hold Skyler's attention with what you have on."

I look down at what I'm wearing. When I picked it out I thought it was cute: a flowered yellow shirt, capris, and sandals.

"You look like you're eight. That shirt does nothing for your"—Claire snickers—"boobs." She throws the tank top at me. "This will help. We're going to Evan's party and there will be girls there who know how to catch a guy's interest. Skyler's gotten kind of cute. You need to make sure his attention doesn't wander."

"I can't—" I try again.

"Look, hon." Taylor recaps the nail polish and blows on my toes. "The sad thing is we're kind of living through you this summer. You're the only one who has anything interesting going on. This town is too small and it's been too hot for anything exciting to happen."

212 / Jennifer Shaw Wolf

Except that my best friend was murdered, something they seem to have forgotten again.

"I really, really can't I—" But as I'm trying to come up with the right words to plead my case, I get a text. Without thinking, I get my phone out of my pocket.

What r u doing 2night?

Before I can reply to Skyler, Taylor grabs my phone. "Where did you get this?"

I turn red and stumble through, "Dad got it for me to replace—"

"This is so cool." She cradles the phone in her hands. "It has everything on it." She strokes it with her hand, as if it were a kitten, and then starts texting something back to Skyler. I reach for my phone, but she holds it out of my reach and hits send.

"How did you ever afford that?" Claire sounds jealous. "Your dad selling drugs to the migrants on the side?"

"Maybe that's why he took them to Spokane," Taylor says. "To pick up his next shipment."

I'm annoyed that I let them see the phone, annoyed that they're implying my family is poor, and annoyed that Taylor is still texting on my phone. "Give me back my phone!" I reach for it, but she climbs up on the bed, and she's a lot taller than I am. I climb up after her. She starts jumping on the bed, holding the phone out of my reach.

"Girls!" Claire's mom is at the door. "I'm trying to get some sleep. I have to work tomorrow."

I plunk down on the bed and so does Taylor. Claire's mom

takes in the outfit her daughter is wearing, a low-cut red shirt and a short jean skirt. "Going somewhere, ladies?"

"Just doing makeovers and trying on each other's clothes, Mom," Claire says innocently.

Her mom doesn't look like she buys it. "It's time to call it a night. I promised Jaycee's dad she'd get to bed early."

"Sure, Mom." Claire is all innocence. "But can we watch a movie while we fall asleep?"

Claire's mom glances at me. "Nothing inappropriate."

As soon as she closes the door Claire picks up the clothes she picked for me and sets them on the bed in front of me. "So what are you going to do?"

Taylor fluffs her hair. "I already told Skyler you were coming, but if you want me to take care of him tonight . . ."

I look at Taylor, with her perfect body and her perfect blond curls, and then picture her and Skyler together. It hurts just thinking about it. "Fine. I'll come." I take the clothes and go into Claire's closet to change.

An hour and a half later, the movie, a steamy romantic comedy my dad would have never let me watch, is over. Claire's mom is asleep, and I'm dozing on the bed, too many sleepless nights getting to me. Claire elbows me. "Time to go," she hisses.

Guilt and fear hit me. "I don't think I should—"

"Shut up." Claire puts her finger to her lips. "Your man is waiting."

Taylor yawns and stretches. "You've totally screwed up your hair," she says. "And we don't have time to fix it again."

Claire creeps across the room and opens her bedroom

door, listens, and then motions for us to follow her. I hesitate, but I really do want to see Skyler. We take the same path we took the night of the last party, down the hall, through the back door, and toward Claire's huge backyard, illuminated like daylight in the full moon. I look around, feeling exposed, because of the outfit or the moon, I can't decide which. Taylor nudges me from behind.

I grip my phone through the pocket of Claire's shorts and look behind me. As I do, something moves behind the slats in the fence. I can't see what it is, maybe just a cat. Maybe I'm getting paranoid because of the note and Eduardo's warning, but I'm positive something or someone is moving with us on the opposite side of the fence. I freeze.

"What are you stopping for?" Claire hisses.

"I think someone might be over there." I say it as quietly as I can, gesturing toward the fence.

Claire huddles closer to me, but Taylor says, "Where?"

"Through the fence," I say.

Claire moves behind me, but Taylor creeps over to check it out. She's almost to the fence when she lets out a scream and jumps back. Claire screams too, turns toward the house, and runs. I'm frozen in place.

Then Taylor laughs. "Peyton Harris, what the hell are you doing hiding behind that fence? What are you, like, some creepy peeping tom?" Claire stops running and turns around. Taylor walks closer to the fence and peers through. "And Mitch Thompson, what are you guys doing?"

Peyton peers over the fence sheepishly. "Hi."

"You didn't answer my question." Taylor stands with her hand on her hip, which is thrust out so it makes her skimpy shorts look even skimpier.

"We were just wondering if you girls needed a ride to Evan's house," Mitch says.

"Hells, yeah!" Taylor answers.

Claire walks up behind Taylor. "Quiet, all of you." She glances back at her house, but the windows are still dark. "Perfect. Now I don't have to borrow my mom's car."

"Jaycee's with me." The voice that comes back through the fence is Evan's. I didn't know he was here too.

Claire and Taylor both look at me, eyebrows raised.

"I told you that outfit would work," Taylor whispers.

"Whatever, just shut up, okay?" Claire hisses. She sounds annoyed, and I don't think it's just because we're all talking too loud. "Look, we have to get out of here now, before my mom wakes up." Claire and Taylor pile into Mitch's car, I follow Evan to his dad's truck.

"Where's your motorcycle?" I say as he holds the door open for me.

"It might rain," he says.

"It doesn't look like it's going to rain to me," I answer. "Why were you guys really hiding behind the fence?" Maybe Evan didn't bring the motorcycle because it was too loud for sneaking around.

He smiles. "Okay, you caught me. I came looking for you. I wanted to make sure you were coming to the party. You didn't answer the text I sent."

I touch the bulge in my pocket and then I realize he must mean my old phone. I haven't even turned it on since I got it back.

He pats the seat beside him. "Why are you sitting clear over there?"

"I like to look out the window." I'm trying to figure out his game. Evan is all charm again, obviously he wants something from me. I'm just not sure what.

"I don't bite," he says, putting the truck into reverse.

"That's not what I've heard."

"Ouch," he says, but he smiles like it's a compliment. As we drive toward the house he drums his fingers on the steering wheel in time to the music on the radio. "I like what you're wearing, Jaycee. You look really good."

"Thanks." I tug my shorts down so they cover more of my thighs.

"You should have worn that necklace, the one you left in the fireplace. That cross would have been really sexy with that outfit." More finger drumming, not so in time with the music. "So what was so important in that bag of beads? Why did you hide it in the fireplace all this time?" He's fishing again, trying to find out if there was anything else by the fireplace. It occurs to me that two can play at that game.

I turn around and face him, staring pointedly at his arm. "Why do you have a tattoo of the number 18?"

He shrugs, like it's casual. "It's my lucky number, my football number."

"But why eighteen?"

He doesn't hesitate. "It's a family number. Dad wore it, and then Eric, and then me."

"Skyler?"

"No, Skyler always has to do things bassackward." He laughs. "His number was 81."

"Oh." I lean back. He's so casual about it, I don't think it could mean what I was suspecting, that Evan was part of a gang. Still, there are a couple of answers I need, answers that I think only Evan can give me. The warning from the note goes through my head, but I push it away. I just have to make sure I don't sound like I'm trying to get information. I keep my voice casual, conversational. "You said you took digital arts last year, didn't you?"

He shrugs. "Yeah, why?"

"I'm taking it next year, and I was wondering what kind of things you did in that class."

He rolls his eyes. "You should get out of it. I took it because it was supposed to be an easy class, but it was actually a lot of work."

I nod like I understand. "I hate it when elective classes give too much homework."

"Yeah, me too." He shakes his head. "The final project was a huge pain in the butt. We had to put a bunch of pictures together, and they couldn't just be random pictures, they had to represent something significant from our lives. Ms. Reeves called it a journey map."

"What?" The word catches in my throat. That was the title Rachel put at the top of the page of pictures.

"Yeah. Stupid, right? And it took forever to do. To top it off, after I thought I was finished, she said we had to pull a picture from someone else's project and add it to ours to show how all our journeys are connected or some sh—" He looks at me. "Crap like that." He grins. "Your friend Rachel took one from me. She stuck a picture of my football jersey smack in the middle of her collage. That's what made me decide to ask her out for New Year's Eve."

I try to think what reason Rachel would have for putting Evan's jersey on her picture, but I can't think of anything. We're almost to his house. I can see lights and hear music blaring. I clench my toes in my borrowed sandals because it reminds me of the night Skyler kissed me, the night Rachel died.

I'm almost out of time, but he brought it up, so I ask, "What happened just before Rachel left the New Year's Eve party? Don't tell me you really don't know why she left." The conversational tone is gone. I want him to take this question seriously.

He puts the truck in park and kills the engine. For a minute I think he's going to get out without answering. Instead he starts drumming his fingers on the steering wheel again, even though there isn't music coming from the radio anymore. He shakes his head. "I think Peyton must have said something to her. I went in the kitchen to get a drink for us and when I came back he was standing in front of her in the living room. She flipped out, ran in the bathroom, and started puking. He had his shirt off, and I know that Peyton could stand to hit the gym once in a while, but no girl has ever reacted like that before."

I ignore his stupid attempt at humor. "Didn't you ask her what happened?"

Evan shrugs. "She wouldn't talk to me after that at all. I told you, she had someone else take her home. Peyton said he was coming in from the hot tub and she freaked out when she saw him."

"And you believed him? You don't think he tried something?"

Evan looks annoyed at me, like I'm questioning his authority or something. "It was my house, and she was my date. Peyton's not that big of a jerk or that stupid. She probably just had too much to drink and she was so embarrassed that she hurled that she wouldn't let me take her home. Anyway, she went out with him a couple of times after that. If he had tried something she didn't like, do you really think she would have gone out with him?" He opens the door, clearly done with the questions from me. "Are you coming in or what?"

"Yeah. Give me a second." I'm trying to think. What would Peyton have done that made Rachel so upset she threw up? Maybe Evan's right, maybe she drank too much and got sick, but I think it was something else. I never saw Rachel drink, not even once.

Evan stands with his hand on top of the door, waiting for me. "By the way, Skyler won't be here tonight. He's got to get the hay baled before it rains or Dad will kill him."

I drag myself out of the truck, miserable already. I'm stuck at a party I'm not supposed to be at, that I don't want to be at, and now with no hope of seeing Skyler.

Evan hangs back, walking in with me. "We don't have to go in. We could just hang out here." He puts his hand on my shoulder. "Talk or . . . something." I push his hand away and give him what I hope comes off as a death glare, but he just looks confused. "What's up with you, Jaycee? I'm just trying to be nice."

"I'm with your brother. Don't you get that?" I snap at him.

He pauses on the front porch. "Okay, not to sound like a jerk, but why?"

I'm suddenly flustered, not sure how to explain my relationship with Skyler to Evan. "I don't know. He's cute and he's sweet, and . . ." I gather up my confidence. "Not full of himself, and not fake. Not like some guys I know."

Evan looks a little shocked at my honesty, but he laughs. "Okay then. So since Skyler isn't here what are you going to do tonight?"

"I'll probably hang out in his room, text him or something."

"Seriously? The party's out here. You should give us a chance, we aren't as bad—"

"I'm positive."

He shakes his head. "You're a hard one to figure out, Jaycee, but I like a challenge."

I get out of the truck and slam the door behind me. Talking to Evan is starting to make me feel dirty. He follows me to the front porch. "You're seriously just going to hang out in Skyler's room alone?"

I don't answer him. Luckily Claire and Taylor are already here. They provide a perfect distraction. Claire has her shirt all the way unbuttoned so I can see the strings and scraps of fabric that pass for her bikini top.

"Is the hot tub open?" Peyton asks.

Evan keeps his eyes on the gap in Claire's bikini top. "Yeah, I'll go get the cover off."

As he heads for the back porch, I have another thought. "Hey, Evan, do you still have your digital arts project?"

He stops. "Why?"

I try to sound casual. "I just want to look at it, so I know what to expect."

He gives me a funny look, like he's not sure if he should be suspicious or not. "Maybe. I haven't gotten around to throwing away my high school stuff yet."

"Evan, weren't you going to open the hot tub?" Claire sidles up beside him and puts her hand on his arm.

He looks down at her and hesitates only a second before he says, "Right," and goes outside.

As soon as they're on the back porch I head for Evan's room. I want to see if I can find his project and compare it with Rachel's. I need to hurry. If this party is anything like the last one, Evan's bedroom won't be vacant for long.

I pick his room out pretty easily. It's a disaster, exactly the kind of room I'd expect a guy like Evan to have. His bed is torn apart and covered with dirty clothes. A pile of dirty dishes is stacked next to the bed, and the garbage can is overflowing with pop and beer cans. The walls are decorated with sports stuff and pictures of girls wearing even less than what Claire is wearing. Guys can be so gross.

222 / Jennifer Shaw Wolf

His desk is covered with papers. It looks like the assignments from his entire high school career. I shut the door behind me, lock it, and then get started on the pile on the desk, not caring too much where the papers end up after I look at them. I think the only thing that would look suspicious in this room would be if I cleaned it.

The pile is like a reverse history of Evan's high school career, starting with unaddressed graduation announcements and letters from colleges. I can't help but skim the letters as I set them aside. They all start with the words, "We regret to inform you . . ."

I finally reach some actual classwork: essays, math papers, and notes. I'm about a third of the way into the pile when I see it, poking out from below a pile of old school newsletters. I grab the journey map, scattering the rest of the pile onto the floor.

I turn on the desk lamp and lean forward to study it. The back of Evan's jersey is the first picture on this one: the beginning of a journey instead of the middle, like on Rachel's. It's the same picture, down to the three words above it, "making the cut." The rest are pictures of Evan playing football. They go from his freshman year to the end of his junior season, when they went to the state championship. Except for a couple of pictures taken at practice, Evan's senior year isn't here at all. The last picture is one that Rachel had on her picture, a black broken heart, maybe symbolizing the state championship game they lost junior year, the entire wreck of a senior season, or maybe the scholarships he didn't get. At the top is the grade, a big red A. I guess the whole thing is kind of poetic in a self-centered, poor-me kind of way.

I go back to the first picture and the three words above it, "making the cut." That part still doesn't make any sense to me. The football team doesn't do cuts, everyone makes the team. Maybe he meant that he got to play varsity his freshman year. Did Rachel mean to include the whole picture, words and all, or did she just plunk Evan's jersey picture in the middle of her collage to fulfill the assignment?

The door handle shakes, like someone is trying to come inside. I scramble to my feet. Someone knocks. "Occupied," I yell, stuffing the collage in the only place I can think of to hide it, in the front of my bra. Thanks to the push-up feature on my borrowed tank top I actually have a gap to put it in. I pile the papers back on the desk, wondering how hard it would be to get the screen off Evan's bedroom window and get out that way. Another knock.

"We're in here," I yell back, hoping it will discourage whoever is at the door if they think there's more than one person in the bedroom.

"Jaycee?"

I freeze halfway to the window. It's Skyler.

"Is that you?"

I stare at the door, weighing the consequences of Skyler catching me in his brother's room against sneaking out the window, but the window is next to the back porch and the hot tub. I'm sure someone will see me climbing out. I tuck the paper farther down my bra and go to the door.

"Jaycee." He looks dumbfounded when I open it. He looks over the top of me. "Who is in here with—"

"I'm by myself. Hiding out." I try to look casual, but I know

I'm not pulling it off. "I thought you'd be here, so I came with Claire and Taylor, but Evan said you had to finish the hay."

"I broke down. Something's messed up with the baler. I don't know how to fix it, and I can't get ahold of my dad, so I came home." He looks kind of dazed. "What are you doing in Evan's room?"

"Your room was occupied?" It comes out as more of a question than a statement.

He shakes his head. "They aren't allowed in my room. Ever."

I can't tell if he's hurt or angry or something else. Everything he says comes out cold and measured. He just keeps looking at me, like he can't believe I'm here.

"And why are you dressed like that?" he finally says.

"Claire and Taylor . . . these are Claire's clothes . . . they . . ." I suddenly feel really stupid for letting them dress me.

"I don't like it. It isn't you at all. Unless"—he looks beyond me, maybe still looking to see who I was sharing the bedroom with—"you aren't who I thought you were."

I lean against the door frame, so tired of trying to hold everything in and keeping secrets. Wanting to somehow erase the look on his face and prove to him that I am whoever he thought I was. Finally I settle on the truth. "I was looking for this." His eyes get big when I reach into my bra, but he looks away. When he looks back again, I smooth out the paper to show him.

"But why?" he asks.

The sounds of the party—loud music, squealing girls,

splashing from the hot tub—suddenly feel too close. "Can we talk about it somewhere else?"

Skyler waits so long to answer that I think he's going to say no. Finally he sighs, "I guess so."

I follow him out of the room and into the hall. Peyton and some girl I've never seen before are coming from the opposite direction. He has a towel around his waist and his skin is bright red, like he just got out of the hot tub. I start to turn away, not sure if he's wearing anything besides the towel. Then I see his chest.

"You two leaving?" He grunts to Skyler.

I don't hear how Skyler answers. I'm too busy staring at Peyton's chest and the number 34, standing out against the red, a scar carved into his flesh.

CHAPTER
24

W hat's up with Peyton's chest?" I whisper to Skyler when
we're outside on the way to the darkroom. It looks like
the number I saw in the pictures, only it isn't the same; that
one was 20.

Skyler's eyes get icy and cold, like it bothers him that I
noticed Peyton's chest. "Guys like him do stupid things."

When it comes to describing Peyton, "stupid" is usually a
corrective adjective, but I get the idea that there's more going
on than that.

"Why thirty-four? Wasn't that his jersey number? Why
would he, why would anyone—" I'm a breath away from admit-
ting what I saw in the darkroom. "Is that part of the whole
hazing thing that happened a few years ago?"

Now Skyler looks scared. "How do you know about that?"

I backtrack. I can't tell him I was snooping in the darkroom. "My dad helped Coach with the case, I remember him
talking about it. Is it still going on?"

Skyler lets out a disgusted but shaky breath. "We aren't supposed to say, but since I don't have any loyalty to any of them anymore, I guess I can tell you." He turns around to see if anyone is listening. "Yes, it's still going on. They call it 'making the cut.'"

I catch my breath, gripping the piece of paper tighter in my hand.

"They take the players that, according to them, are the least worthy to be on the team to some secret location. Then they make them do stupid things to get on the team, one of which is carving their jersey number into their skin. 'Supposedly'"—he makes air quotes—"the coach knows nothing about it."

"That's insane," I say. "Did you have to do it?"

"No." His voice goes cold again. "If you're good enough, and you have someone to vouch for you, then you don't have to do it. Lucky for me, I had Evan." He says "lucky" like it has a bitter taste to it.

"But Peyton was pretty good, right? And Evan has a tattoo with his number on it, and a scar. I'm sure he didn't—" I stop when I see the icy look Skyler gives me.

"No. The great Evan Cross didn't have to 'make the cut.' He did it voluntarily." He shakes his head. "Peyton too. Most everyone on the team does it at some point, out of some twisted sense of loyalty. I didn't want to. I was never much of a team player. Maybe that's why Evan jumped me so hard in practice." He rubs his wrist, like the memory actually causes him physical pain.

I stay back, afraid of the anger I see in him. "Wait. Evan was the one who broke your wrist?"

"Stupid, freak accident, at least that's what he told Dad." He keeps his eyes straight ahead. "But I knew the real reason. He didn't want me on the team. He didn't want me to screw up their perfect season."

"But they didn't have a perfect season. They lost every game."

"I know. Ironic, isn't it?" Skyler flips the lights on in the darkroom, shuts the door behind us, and crosses his arms. "Any more questions about my brother and the football team, or are you ready to tell me what's really going on? Why were you in Evan's bedroom anyway?"

I hold out Evan's assignment. "I found this. It's just like the paper Rachel left for me."

Skyler takes the paper from me, but he barely glances at it. "Yeah. They were in the same class. So?"

"She put that file on a micro-SD card, hid the card in her necklace, and left the necklace in a place only I could find it. It has to be important." I'm talking fast, trying to convince him that I'm not completely insane.

He looks at the paper again, licks his lips, and then talks slowly, like he's worried about hurting my feelings. "Why are you doing this?"

"Doing what?"

"Digging up stuff about Rachel, trying to figure out what happened. It could be dangerous, and I don't want—"

"I can handle it," I snap at him. He's starting to sound like Eduardo.

"I didn't say you couldn't. I just think . . ." He sighs. "Rachel is dead, Jaycee. Nothing you do is going to bring her back."

"I know that." But when he says it, I wonder if somewhere inside I thought figuring things out *would* bring her back.

"Why don't you just take all this to the police and let them figure it out?" He waves the paper in the air like he's annoyed.

"It has to be me. I'm the only one who . . ." I don't know how to explain it to him. His brother is the sheriff. I can't tell him Rachel didn't trust the police, or that I'm not sure if I do either.

"I know you and Rachel used to be close, but that doesn't mean—"

"She asked me to help her. She tried to call me the night she died, but I ignored her because I was—" I cover my mouth. I've said too much. Now he'll know how horrible I am.

"Was with me," he finishes.

I nod, afraid if I open my mouth I'll start crying.

He sets the paper down on the table and puts his hands on my shoulders, his blue eyes soft with concern. "That doesn't mean it's your fault that she died."

"What if it is?" I grit my teeth to keep the tears from falling.

He pulls me against him, even though I go stiff and don't return his embrace. He breathes into my hair. "No. It's not your fault. I promise, it's not your fault."

"But I have to do something. I can't just pretend it never happened. I can't let everyone condemn her and say it was her fault. I can't—" I close my eyes and lean against him to keep from crying.

He holds me for a long time without saying anything. Finally he kisses the top of my head. "Okay."

"Okay what?" I look up at him.

"Okay, I'll help you. I'll help you find out what happened to Rachel."

I pull away, shocked. "What? Wait. No. You don't have to—" I think about the note in my room and the symbol on Dad's door. I can't drag Skyler into this mess too.

He puts his finger on my lips. "Yes, I do. To keep you safe. Besides, I have access to things you don't. Things like crime scene photos and coroner's reports and—"

"Wait, you can get that kind of stuff?" The idea scares me and excites me at the same time.

"Remember how I said I wanted to be a crime scene photographer? Eric lets me look at that kind of stuff sometimes. I don't think he's supposed to but . . . he does, and anyway, I know where the files are in his office. I might be able to get you what you need."

"You'll help me?" I feel like a huge burden has been taken off my shoulders. If Skyler helps me with this, I don't have to be all alone.

He smiles, but it's kind of a sad, resigned smile. "On a couple of conditions. First, don't do anything stupid without me. I mean it."

I nod. His concern makes my stomach do flips. "And second?"

"Give me tonight."

"Tonight?"

"Forget about all of this, just for tonight, and be with me."

"I can't . . ." Now my stomach is doing an entire tumbling routine.

"Not like that." He ducks his head. "I just want to spend time with you, away from all of this." He sweeps the room with his hand, but I get the idea he means more than just the room or even Rachel's death.

I look around, thinking about how nice it would be if I could forget, even if it was only for one night. "Okay." I breathe.

"Great." His smile gets bigger. "But first, will you please change out of that outfit and wash off some of this?" He brushes his hand across my cheek. "You don't need it, any of it."

I'm not sure how to take that. "What am I supposed to wear?"

"Hold on." He goes to the back of the room, moves aside the backdrop, and opens a drawer under the cupboard. He pulls out a white dress. "This was my mom's."

"Oh." The idea of putting on his dead mother's dress kind of freaks me out.

He must realize how strange this is for me. "Not *hers* hers. She used it as a costume for some of the pictures she took, but I think it will fit you."

"Why do I have to—"

"Trust me. You'll see." He hands me the dress and then heads toward the door. "You have ten minutes and then I'm coming in, whether you're ready or not."

I still feel stupid, but it feels good to slip out of the too-tight shorts and suffocating tank top and pull the dress over my head. It's soft, flowy white cotton with a round neckline and a wide blue ribbon that I cinch tight at the waist because it's too big. I retrieve my phone from the pocket of Claire's shorts, frown at the time, 12:45, and slip it into the pocket of the dress.

Then I walk over to the sink and use a paper towel and some soap to scrub off the layers of makeup that Taylor so carefully applied. I look in the mirror above the sink to make sure I don't have streaks of mascara. My skin looks even paler against the white dress, and the sloppy bun Taylor made is falling out and looks frizzy. I wish again for Rachel's sleek dark hair and tan.

"I'm coming in," Skyler announces. I notice Evan's paper, still sitting on the cabinet. I pick it up and slip it into the dress pocket. The door swings open and I turn. Skyler stands at the door and whistles. "You look amazing."

"Thank you." I feel my face get hot, but for once it feels good.

He crosses the room, wraps me in his arms, and kisses me for real, finally finishing where he left me yesterday. "You ready?"

"Since I don't know what we're doing, I guess so."

"Cool." He reaches behind the door and gets his camera. Then he digs around in a cupboard under the sink and gets a couple of small cylindrical, yellow canisters.

"What's that?" I ask suspiciously.

"Film for the camera." He opens a hatch in his camera and puts the film inside.

"What are you planning to do with it?"

He gets an evil glint in his eye. "Trust me."

"I don't want to—"

He stops me with a kiss. "Remember, you promised, tonight is mine." He shoulders his camera bag, puts one arm around my waist, and we walk out of the darkroom.

We walk away from the noise of the party, behind the shed and up a little path. He stops. "How's your ankle?"

"It's good," I answer.

"Let me know if I go too fast." He pulls me behind him, clinging to my hand. It's still bandaged with my scarf.

The little dirt path leads to a hill on the far end of the Cross property. I huddle next to Skyler as we pass the duplexes that serve as temporary housing for the migrants that work on Skyler's dad's farm. Most of the lights are out, but outside one of them is a little knot of men talking, their cigarettes glowing red. Their eyes follow us as we walk away.

I stumble as the path gets rougher, and Skyler stops. "Is it your ankle?" I shake my head and show him my bare feet. He laughs. "Where are your shoes?"

I look down, embarrassed. "I left them in your darkroom."

He shakes his head. "I guess I have to carry you again."

"You can't. I'm too—" I start, but he picks me up before I can finish. I cling to his neck as he carries me the last few steps up the hill. At the top he sets me down in the middle of a bunch of white wildflowers. I fall back on my butt. Embarrassed, I scramble to get up.

"Wait. Stay there," he says.

"What?"

"No, seriously." He takes the camera out of the bag. "You look great."

I rise up on my knees. "Remember, I hate pictures. I always come out looking horrible."

"But I'm a great photographer, remember?" He kneels down next to me and twists a piece of my hair between his fingers. "Besides, your looking horrible is not possible. Just relax." He pulls out the bun Taylor spent half an hour on and runs his fingers through my hair. "The moonlight behind your hair makes it look like a halo. Lie back."

"What?"

"Trust me."

I lie down among the wildflowers. He brushes through my hair with his fingers until it circles my head. "Relax. You look like you're in pain."

"There's a rock under my head."

He laughs. "Pretend it's a pillow. Close your eyes."

I close my eyes and try to relax. He runs his finger over my lips, and I open my eyes. He shakes his head. "Eyes closed. Pretend you're having a really great dream." I close my eyes again. "Are you dreaming about me?"

"You!" I open my eyes and beat my fist on his chest.

He stops my fist and then holds my hand against his chest. "Sorry. I couldn't resist. Please close your eyes and stay still, for me." His lips curve into a sexy pout that makes his dimples stand out again.

I lie back down and close my eyes, but I can't relax.

He's taking forever. "Any day now," I say with my eyes scrunched shut.

"Hold on a second more, I'm waiting for the perfect expression. This is film, so I don't have unlimited pictures."

I try to think of something nice, something that will make me look like I'm having a good dream. All I can think of is how cold the ground is, how hard the rocks are under my head, and what will happen if my dad finds out I went to another party, or worse, that I'm here alone with Skyler. Then he kisses me. As soon as his lips touch mine, everything else rushes from my head. I smile and he takes the picture.

"Perfect," he says.

"Mmmm, yeah," I murmur. Then I sit up, embarrassed. "How will you know if it's perfect until you get it developed?"

"That's the fun part of taking real pictures, the anticipation." He puts the camera in the bag and lies down next to me. "And if it doesn't work, we'll come back again." He slides his arm under my head, cradling it against the rocks. "And again." I snuggle up next to his body and forget about being cold. "And again."

"That sounds nice," I say as he nuzzles up against my cheek.

He kisses my cheek. "It does, doesn't it?"

"But I want a picture too, and I'm not as patient as you are." I pull my phone out of my pocket and then lie down on his arm again. I hold it above us and snap a picture. I look at it. I don't look stiff or horrible in this one either, just happy.

He reaches for the phone. "Let me see."

I hold it out of his reach. "If I have to wait, so do you."

"Oh yeah?" He buries his face in my neck and blows on it. It tickles, so I start laughing. He reaches for my phone again, straddling my waist and pinning one of my arms against my body. I'm trying to get away, trying to hold the phone out of his reach, and laughing so hard that I'm crying. He leans over so his face is close to mine. I stop laughing and look into his eyes. He brushes the hair out of my face, curling it around my ear and sliding his hand down my cheek. "You're beautiful, you know that?" he says.

His expression is so intense that I don't even close my eyes when he leans in and his lips touch mine. I kiss him back, dropping my phone and wrapping my arms around his neck, pulling him closer to me. He relaxes his body on top of mine so our legs are tangled together, my bare toes sliding against the cool leather of his boots. He moves his hands down my back, and I close my eyes, letting go of everything—all the pain of losing Rachel, all the frustration at not knowing what happened, all the pressure of being the good girl who always does everything right.

I let it all go, just for a few seconds, just until I feel something desperate about the way he's kissing me, and I feel it in the way I'm kissing him back. I want to keep going. I want to close my eyes and melt into him and forget everything. But I can't. I'm too afraid that this will get out of my control like everything else.

"Stop." I push his mouth away from mine. His lips move down my neck, leaving feathery, butterfly-wing kisses that churn up everything inside me again. "Stop. Please."

He finishes one last kiss on my shoulder, so soft and tender that for a heartbeat I regret pushing him away. He rolls onto his back and stares up at the sky, breathing hard. "I'm sorry, Jaycee. I don't want you to think that's the reason I brought you up here. I just . . ." He breathes out. "Wow." He rolls over on his arm and his expression changes. "Are you okay?"

"Yeah . . . I just . . . we need to do something else." I stand up, brushing dirt and dried grass off my back.

He picks up my phone and hands it to me, his hand lingering on mine. "I have an idea."

"What?" I say. His eyes are full of mischief again.

He picks up his camera bag and twists it over his arm. "You want to go into the darkroom with me, see what develops?"

I laugh, glad to get rid of some of the tension. "Is that some kind of photographer's pick-up line?"

"Yeah, that's exactly what it is. I actually heard Evan use it once. So, do ya wanna?"

"Do I wanna what?"

"Go to the darkroom with me." He indicates his camera. "I could show you how to develop the film so you could see for yourself how beautiful you are."

"How long is that going to take?" I ask.

"About a half hour, depends on how fast of a learner you are."

"Sure," I say. "I'm always open to new developments."

"Ugh." He rolls his eyes. "That one was worse than mine."

— ▬

"You have to hook the leader on the little tabs, here." Skyler is trying to guide my fingers, but I can't seem to make them work right.

"Does it have to be so dark?" The darkroom is so black I can feel it pressing around me like a fog.

"Absolutely pitch black, or you'll end up with a black strip and no pictures." He moves my hand to the other side of the plastic film roller. "There, I think you've got it. Start turning the crank."

I roll the film out onto the little wheel while Skyler keeps his hand on my wrist. For a second I wonder what my dad would think about me fumbling around in the pitch black with Skyler, but I guess it's better than what we were doing in the meadow. The wheel starts clicking.

"Okay, you're done. Now we can put it in the developer tank. The lid has a seal that keeps light out, so we can turn the light back on. If you really want to." He touches my face and then kisses me, but he misses and ends up kissing my nose.

I giggle and lift my mouth up to meet his. "I think we'd better."

"Right." He turns on the light and sets the canister on the cabinet. "Now we put the developer in and let it work for fifteen minutes, but we have to agitate it."

"You mean like make it angry?" I giggle again. I'm not sure how late it is, but the lack of sleep is getting to me and making me act silly.

He starts pouring in the developer. "No. I mean you have

to shake it. But you have to get it just right; the more you shake, the higher the contrast."

"So it has to be 'shaken, not stirred'?" I say in a bad James Bond imitation.

He starts moving the bottle back and forth. "Something like that." He shakes his head. "How come you're so silly tonight? Are you sure you didn't have anything to drink at the party before I got there?"

I can't tell if he's kidding. "No. I just get loopy when I'm tired. Once when I slept over at Rachel's we got so silly that we made this video, *The Jay and Ray Show*. We told really stupid jokes and laughed until we almost peed our pants. I wonder if she still has it. I mean . . ." As soon as I say it, I realize my mistake, Rachel doesn't still have anything. "I wonder how long she kept it."

Skyler looks sad for me. "You miss her a lot, don't you?"

"All the time."

"I'm sorry."

I spin the desk chair around and make an effort to lighten the mood again. "It's not your fault. But it feels good to forget it all for a while and just be here with you."

He kneels down in front of me, stopping the chair from spinning. He crosses his arms over my legs and looks up at me. His eyelashes frame his blue eyes, and for a second I glimpse the innocent little boy I saw in the picture. "I wish I could help you forget it all forever. I wish I could take you away from here, someplace where you'll never have to be sad again."

I rest my elbows on the arms of the chair and lean on my hands. "Now you're the one who's drunk. There isn't any place like that."

He stands up, kisses me on the top of the head, and goes back to the bottle. He looks so sad that I wish I hadn't said anything. "If there were a place like that, would you go there with me?"

"Definitely." I spin the chair again. "Actually, that sounds kind of perfect. Can we go there tonight?"

He puts the bottle down and crosses the room to me again. He traces my lips with his finger. "Maybe not tonight, but someday, I promise."

CHAPTER 25

I'm frozen. Backed against a wall that's wet with paint. Someone is in the curtains, his back to me. Rachel screams from upstairs and he turns. His eyes, blue and hard, fall on my face for a second before he slips away.

My eyes flutter open, and I'm face to face with another pair of blue eyes. I scream.

Skyler startles backward. "I didn't mean to scare you. I was just watching you sleep."

"What time is it?" The darkroom is pitch black. I dig for my phone. It says 4:45.

I don't remember falling asleep. I remember Skyler getting a pillow and blanket out of the cupboard, saying that he sometimes slept in the darkroom when his dad was mad at him. I remember him lying on the floor beside me while he explained about little silver crystals clinging to the places where the film was exposed to light. I remember watching him move the bottle back and forth hypnotically and me getting sleepier and sleepier while I lay against his chest.

"I have to get back. Now!" I scramble to my feet.

Skyler scrambles with me. He stands up and heads to the door. "I'll get my truck. Meet me behind the barn in five minutes. Where you met me before." He goes outside and breaks into a run.

I stuff my phone in my pocket. We are so so busted. I can already picture Dad's face, pinched with pain and disappointment, as he escorts me onto a plane that will take me to live with Mom and away from Skyler forever.

I hear Skyler's truck roar to life. I turn around to pick up Claire's clothes, and stop when I see the picture. He's blown it up big. I'm sitting in the meadow, my hair fanned out around my face like a halo in the moonlight. My eyes are closed and I look like I'm having a good dream. Underneath the picture he's written, "My angel."

I walk outside and break into a run, meeting Skyler and the truck behind the barn. "I'm so dead, so dead, so dead. My dad is going to send me to a convent and we aren't even Catholic," I moan as Skyler drives toward Claire's house.

Skyler looks scared too. "I'm sorry. I should have woken you up sooner. I'm so stupid."

He pulls around to the alleyway where Evan and the other guys were hiding. I stop at the gate; the house looks quiet. I turn over my shoulder and mouth "bye" to Skyler.

He leans his head out the window of his truck. "Sorry again."

He looks so miserable that I turn back around, stand on my tiptoes, kiss him, and whisper, "It's okay. I'm good. Thanks for giving me a night to remember, I mean, a night to forget."

He smiles and tucks a piece of my hair behind my ear. "No. Thank you." When I turn back to the house I think I hear him whisper, "Love you."

I keep walking without turning around, too embarrassed to answer that, but I'm glowing, floating, one hundred percent in love. Nothing in my life before compares to what it feels like to be with Skyler. It's like he fills a place in my heart that I didn't know was empty.

I head across the lawn, hoping the back door isn't locked, but maybe not even caring if I get caught. Then I hear Claire hissing, "Jaycee, over here." She's on the trampoline in the corner of the yard, tucked into a sleeping bag. "Where have you been, young lady?" I keep my eye on the house as I make my way to the trampoline. "We're telling my mom my room was too hot so we came out here," Claire says. "All night, huh?"

"We fell asleep," I say, not wanting to explain anything, not wanting to mess up my great mood with Claire's prying. I climb on the trampoline.

"Don't make it move," Taylor groans. "Oh, I'm gonna hurl again."

"Don't worry. I've 'fallen asleep' a few times too," Claire smirks.

"Nothing happened," I insist, my face turning red. Why does she have to turn everything good into something that sounds dirty?

Claire looks me over, probably taking in my change in outfit. "Yeah, just like nothing happened the night of Evan's last party."

"Wait, what?" I stop, halfway on the trampoline.

"Don't make it move," Taylor moans again.

Claire gives her and then me a disgusted look. "We all know that Skyler took you home that night, and that he didn't come back."

"Nothing happened that night either." I guess it shouldn't surprise me that Skyler didn't go back to the party. He said it wasn't his thing.

She pats the other sleeping bag. "Well, whatever *didn't* happen, you'd better get in before my mom comes looking for us. You can share all the gory details later."

"Nothing—" I start again.

"Shut u-u-up," Taylor moans again. "I'm gonna hurl."

— —

At breakfast Claire's mom cusses us out. "You girls shouldn't have gone outside to sleep. It's not safe. There have been too many bad things going on around here lately."

I glance at Taylor, who's staring at the french toast Mrs. Rallstrom made for us like it's the enemy. She's so obviously hungover that I can't believe Mrs. Rallstrom hasn't picked up on it.

Mrs. Rallstrom turns to me. "Your dad called this morning, hon. He said that things got held over until today and so he stayed with a friend last night. He sent two messages: 'Don't forget about the cleanup at Araceli's today' and 'I trust you.'" Claire snorts into her juice. Her mom gives her a stern look. "I can give you a ride home whenever you'd like to go."

"Thank you," I say, but it doesn't come out very sincere. I'm remembering what Claire's mom said about Araceli at the church.

"What about you two?" Claire's mom turns to Claire and Taylor. "I think it would be nice if you went too."

"I have to work," Claire says.

"I don't feel too good, Mrs. Rallstrom." Taylor punctuates that remark by running for the bathroom.

"You girls didn't leave the dip I made out all night and then eat it, did you?" Mrs. Rallstrom cringes at the sounds coming from the bathroom. "It's supposed to be refrigerated."

— —

The cleanup at Araceli's starts after lunch, so Claire takes me home on her way to work.

I bring the white dress with me. When I get home, I spray the stains on the back, thinking about where the mud and grass came from, remembering how it felt to lie down in Skyler's arms, how it felt to have him kiss me. I think about the last thing he said to me. An odd mix of guilt and elation churns in my stomach. Is this what love feels like?

While the clothes wash I take a long shower, enjoying the quiet of the house, privacy, and freedom. Then I go to my dresser to find clothes, but I stop before I get to it. Something about the way the drawer is half-open looks off. I open it. My clothes look like they've been moved around, unfolded and pushed into the corners. I open my next drawer and find the same thing. My hands go cold. Someone was in my room.

Someone touched my things and pawed through my clothes. I try to convince myself that it was Dad, spying on me, but I don't think it was.

I pull the bottom drawer open and dig through it, getting more and more frantic, until I finally pull it all the way out and empty it onto the floor. The pieces of Rachel's necklace and the paper are both gone.

I sink to my knees in the mess. Why did I leave them here?

Did some stranger come into my house and go through my things? One of the gang members? I dig again, looking for a familiar symbol, dreading the thought of finding it, but it isn't here. Maybe it was someone else.

I sit back and think. Maybe it was Eduardo or Evan. Both of them were interested in what I found in the fireplace. Both of them knew I wasn't home last night.

I think about what Eduardo said about me not being alone, it's daylight and all the doors are locked, but now I'm afraid. I pick up my phone and text Skyler.

What r u up to?

He doesn't text back.

I breathe in, walk around my whole room, trying to see what else has been moved. My jewelry box has been rifled through. The pile of books Dad left for me to read has been restacked neatly. I know I left them scattered on the floor and under my bed.

I try Skyler again.

I need to see you.

He doesn't answer.

I stare at my phone, trying to shake the creepy feeling that permeates everything around me. I go to the front of the house and make sure the door is locked. I go to the back door and do the same. It's too early to leave for Araceli's house, even if I am walking. I don't want to get there and have to hang around Rachel's mom, trying to figure out what to say.

I need to figure this out before it gets worse. Now, while Dad is gone, safe in Spokane. I get out the paper I stole from Evan's room. The picture and three words, "making the cut," stand out.

Making the cut. Skyler said it meant cutting your jersey number into your flesh to prove your loyalty to the team. I go through the pictures Evan has of the football team, one by one, to see if I can tell if any of them have scars that are numbers, but none of the pictures are big enough. Then I see something else that makes me stop. He's standing behind Evan and Mitch. His face is turned to the side in profile, a little blurry, and I've only ever seen one other picture of him, but I know it's Manny.

Evan and Mitch are both wearing captain's jerseys, so the picture had to be taken at the beginning of last year, their senior year. The one Manny is wearing is a solid-black practice jersey, the kind of jersey the guys wear when they first start football, before they have their own uniform.

Manny was trying out for the football team? It seems like a stretch to me. A former gang member, someone who was hiding out, getting involved in high school sports. But maybe

248 / Jennifer Shaw Wolf

it isn't such a stretch, especially if he was trying to prove to Rachel that he was staying here.

I think about what Skyler said about the cuts. If Rachel had seen a number carved into Manny's chest, then seeing Peyton's number scar would definitely have freaked her out.

I dig my yearbook out of my closet and flip through the pages to the football team. I want to see if one of the pictures I saw in Skyler's darkroom was Manny, but I don't know how old the pictures were or what number Manny might have worn. I scan the team picture. Manny isn't in it, but neither is Skyler. The picture must have been taken after Manny died and after Skyler broke his wrist.

I take a deep breath. There's only one person who can help me. It's time to test how far Skyler is willing to go on his promise. I need to see the pictures of Manny's body to see if he had a number scar on his chest. I just hope I'm brave enough to see what Rachel saw. I write and erase the text three times before I hit send. I end up with:

If u can, I need to see the crime scene photos and autopsy report from when Manuel Romero was murdered.

Then I add:

Please. Luv u.

I brace myself for the questions that are sure to come back, because I just admitted that I'm not just looking into Rachel's murder, but Manny's too.

Skyler still doesn't answer, so I go back to the yearbook, trying to put a timeline together. The football team starts practice a month before school starts, at the end of July. Manny died three weeks later, the second week of August and the last week of summer vacation. Did Rachel know about Manny playing football, or did she find out about it when she saw his picture in Evan's collage?

You wouldn't approve of my methods.

Is that why she went out with Evan? What was she trying to find out?

Evan keeps coming up in all of this, the date with Rachel, the night by the fireplace, the pictures in the darkroom, even in my dreams about the night at the old house.

I glance up at the clock to see what time it is, but I see something else, a face in my mirror. Someone is watching me. I freeze, wondering if this is what happened to Rachel, not paying attention and then there he was with a gun. I turn around slowly and face Evan.

He taps on the window. "Open it."

I shake my head, pointing at my bathrobe.

He rolls his eyes and slips his hand through the slit in my screen, like he already knew it was there, then he slides his fingers around the edge of my window and pushes it open. I back toward the other side of the room, but he doesn't try to come in. "I knocked on the front door, but you didn't hear me. What were you looking at that was so interesting?"

I step back, wondering how long he was watching me. "Why are you here?"

He arranges his face into a pseudo-innocent expression. "I thought you might like a ride to Araceli's house, to help with the cleanup." He indicates the helmet under his arm. "I brought my bike." He grins again, sure that I'll go with him.

"Where's Skyler?" I ask suspiciously.

"Busted, thanks to you. He was supposed to finish that field last night. I woke up to him and Dad screaming at each other. I think he's grounded until retirement."

"He said he broke down, that he couldn't finish because—"

"Yeah, Dad's not buying that." Evan doesn't sound like he believes it either.

My heart hurts for Skyler, and I feel guilty for getting him in trouble. That must be why he hasn't answered my texts. "Is he okay?"

"He's survived worse. Besides, the smile on his face this morning makes me think it was worth it." Evan's expression makes me flush red. "But he's cool with me giving you a ride. I told him I'm not interested in stealing his girlfriend." He winks. "Get dressed. We're late as it is."

I check the time on my phone. He's right, we are late. I was so absorbed in my own thoughts that I lost track of the time. "I'll walk."

"The cleanup will be over by then." He has a point, and as much as I hate it, if I'm going to make it at all, it has to be with him.

"Give me ten minutes." I shut the window in his face, hard, lock it, and pull down the blinds.

— —

Even if we weren't thirty minutes late, Evan's bike would have made a scene when we got to Araceli's house. As it is, everyone stops what they're doing—painting or scrubbing graffiti or planting flowers—when Evan's bike announces us with a roar of his engine and a cloud of smoke and dust.

I keep my eyes down but glance around to see who is here. The crowd is an interesting mix of people. There's a big group from the town's Mexican community, including Father

Joseph. There are a few kids from school and a handful of people from church, including Mrs. Francis and Mrs. O'Dell. I guess they'll even do yard work to find something to gossip about. They already have their heads together, probably whispering about the way I arrived. Eduardo is here too, watching me as I dismount from Evan's bike.

"Thanks," I say, my eyes drawn to the number on Evan's shoulder, a tattoo that might have started out as something he carved himself. I touch it. The number in the middle is raised like a scar, not just something made by a tattoo artist. Evan looks at me like he's afraid of what I've seen, or what I've felt, but he doesn't pull away until I do. When I look up, Eduardo is still watching us. He catches my eye and shakes his head at me before he goes back to scrubbing at some graffiti on the porch.

I put on my gardening gloves, step back, and take everything in. It hurts to be here again, but in a way it feels good; healing, to see people working together to repair the damage, like the "community" that they were talking about at the meeting. The police tape is gone, the yard has new flowers, and the graffiti is being scrubbed off. The broken window has been replaced with a new one that's so shiny it stands in sharp contrast to the old windows all around it. The patchwork quilt is still there, attached somewhere inside to cover the window like a thick drape. I wonder how many people have driven out here to try to catch a glimpse of Rachel's bedroom. Besides that, the only thing that looks really different is the door. Once it was a brilliant red, and now it's black. It looks ominous, a permanent reminder that something bad happened here.

Evan joins the group of kids from school. I climb up the porch and pick up a piece of sandpaper to work beside Eduardo, smiling as I kneel down. He doesn't even look up. It annoys me that he doesn't even acknowledge my existence. "Hey," I finally say.

He doesn't answer. I don't have anything else to add, so after a long awkward silence I go back to scrubbing at the red marks, trying to forget that I'm underneath the window where Rachel was killed. "Hey," I say again. Eduardo doesn't look up, but I push forward anyway, but in a whisper. "We need to talk. Someone was in—"

"*No me hables*," he says loudly. He looks around then in a quieter voice he adds, "Not here."

"Where then?" I whisper back.

He shakes his head. "Later." He stands up and looks toward the old house. I nod.

I look down at the half-rubbed-out gang symbol below me. It makes me think about Eduardo's tattoo and what Skyler said about the football team, marking themselves with their jersey numbers like they were trying to prove they belonged to something, like their own kind of gang.

When I stand up, I feel dizzy, like the heat or being here is getting to me. I lean against the front porch and look inside the house. Araceli is sitting at her kitchen table, looking out the window, not watching any of us, looking like we aren't even here. She looks so alone. I swallow away my fear and step up to the front door. I have to talk to her. I have to apologize for deleting the text. I have to apologize for everything.

I tap on the door, but she doesn't move, so I push it open

and go inside. "Araceli?" I call. I walked through this door a thousand times after school with Rachel. I can't believe she'll never walk through it again.

Araceli doesn't answer, not even when I step into the kitchen and I know she can see me. I stand in the entryway, not sure what to do. Everything I mean to say dissolves on my tongue and I'm left with, "Are you okay?" It's a stupid question, one that I hate people to ask me, but at least it gets her to look up.

We stay still for a long time. Finally she says, "What did I do wrong, mija? Why did I lose her?" Pain closes off my throat, and I can only shake my head. "I tried to keep her safe, tried to teach her the right things, but they said—"

"Rachel wasn't killed because she did something wrong." I cross the room and stand in front of her.

"Then why did you stop being her friend?" Araceli's tone isn't accusing, instead it's imploring, like she really wants to know. "She loved you so much. You were such good friends."

I sink into the chair opposite her. "Because of a lot of stupid things. Things that I regret. Things that weren't her fault."

She looks out the window again, far away. "I didn't want her to have a life like mine. My mother was very strict. She wanted me to stay Mexican. She wouldn't let me speak English at home. She wouldn't let me make friends or talk to anyone at school. But I was pretty, so I found friends. The wrong friends. Friends who wanted something from me. Friends like Rachel's dad."

She reaches across the table, and I take her hand. "I never wanted Rachel to live the way I did. I wanted her to be a normal kid and have friends. Friends like you." She shakes her head. "What did I do wrong?"

I don't have an answer for her. I can only think of everything I did wrong, everything I might have done to push Rachel away. Everything I should have done to help her. Araceli stands up and goes to the fridge like she's done talking. She takes out a big glass pitcher full of lemonade. "I made lemonade and cookies for everyone who came to help. Please take them outside and tell them thank you. I don't feel well. I'm going to go lie down." She stands up and goes to the back of the house to her bedroom. She shuts the door behind her.

I stare at the pitcher of lemonade and the cookies, little pink frosted cookies like Araceli used to make for Rachel's birthday. I wonder when she made them. I stare at the closed door to Araceli's room, and then toward Rachel's room. I'm afraid of what I might find, but I have to make this right somehow. I leave the lemonade and cookies on the front porch and then go back into the house, drawn to Rachel's bedroom.

At the closed door I hesitate, and look toward Araceli's room again. The whole house is quiet, almost reverent, the sounds from outside muffled. I whisper a prayer for courage or forgiveness as I push open Rachel's door.

The top mattress from the bed is missing, and there's a big patch of carpet cut to the bare floor where the dark spot was in Skyler's picture. The things that were taken from the room and the things that were left seem odd to me: the dresser is empty, the big mirror that was on Rachel's wall is missing, but most of her pictures are still up. The wall has little red markings all over it, to indicate blood, bullet holes, or something else, I don't know.

I cross the room to the closet. Inside is the red dress Rachel wore to eighth-grade graduation, the one that was in the picture. The folding doors squeak as I open them, and for a second I'm afraid someone will come to see what I'm doing. I hold my breath, but no one comes.

The dress is in the back, long and full and brilliant red. I touch it, remembering how beautiful Rachel looked. I pull it out and lay it on the bed, running my hands over the skirt and up underneath. I don't know what I'm looking for, but the dress was on the collage. It had to mean something. I go through every inch of it, every bead, every scrap of lace, but I don't find anything. I look up, defeated, and come face-to-face with the same picture on the wall, still crooked like in the photo that Skyler took.

I almost laugh at myself for overlooking the obvious and hang the dress back up in the closet. I reach up and take the picture down to look at it closer. As I do, the cardboard on the back slips out of place.

I gasp as I realize there's something inside the frame, a folded piece of paper. I unfold it slowly and realize it's a note, written in Spanish. The handwriting is messy, like a guy's handwriting. I can only make out a couple of words: *te adoro, no le digas a nadie,* and in big letters, *olvidame.* I unfold the last corner and something falls out, another micro-SD chip.

My hands are shaking as I sit on the very edge of Rachel's box spring. I slide the chip into my phone. There are three video files on it. I start the first one.

The camera is pointed toward a guy sitting on the couch in Rachel's living room. It's Manny. "Smile, baby," Rachel says. She's holding the phone.

"Rachel, put the camera away." I recognize Eduardo's growl. The camera turns to the other side of the couch where he's reading some thick book. He barely looks up.

"Ed's right, Ray. You don't want to get caught with pictures of us on your phone."

Rachel sets the phone down on the coffee table, but she leaves the camera on. I can't tell if she did it by accident or on purpose, but the phone is on its side, so I can still see most of the couch. She curls up on Manny's lap. "I think you're lying to me. There isn't really a gang, you just don't want me to tell anyone we're together, just in case you find someone better when school starts."

"Wait, you mean there's someone around here who's hotter than you are?" Manny pretends to be shocked. "Why haven't you introduced her to me yet?"

Rachel gets off his lap and slides closer to Eduardo. "Because I'm saving her for *el guapo* here. Ed, how do you feel about redheads?" She puts her hand on his arm, and I see his expression change. There's no mistaking the way he looks at her. Despite everything Eduardo said about Rachel and Manny, it's obvious that he felt something for her too.

"Your friend is too good for Eduardo," Manny says, pulling

her away from him. Then his voice gets serious. "You haven't told her about us, have you?"

She leans against his chest. Eduardo goes back to his book, but I see him watching her out of the corner of his eye. "No. But I'm tired of keeping secrets. No one is coming for you here. Lake Ridge is the last place on earth, literally."

He kisses her head. "A little longer, okay? Agent Herrera promised us protection if I tell him everything, but I need to be sure. Soon we can just be hick farm boys like everyone else here. I might even play football again. I was pretty good when I was a little kid."

Eduardo laughs, and Manny gives him a dirty look. "What?" Rachel says.

"He doesn't think they'll let me on their team," Manny says.

"Gringo sport anyway," Eduardo grumbles.

"I think football players are sexy." Rachel slips her arms around Manny's neck. "The tight pants and the big shoulders, mmmmm." They start kissing. The look Eduardo gives them is pure jealousy.

The video ends.

I sit, thinking about what I just saw, and why Rachel left it for me. Did she want me to understand why she didn't trust the police, because they didn't protect her or Manny? Was it so I'd know Manny was going to play football, or why she had to keep him a secret from me, or was it something else? Was it the way Eduardo looked at her?

The next file is Rachel sitting on her bed, alone. She looks like she's been crying. "I've watched the video I took on my phone a thousand times. I can't believe it's all I have left of him, that he'll never kiss me or hold me or—" Her voice breaks, she struggles for control, and then she gets mad. "I have to find out who did this. I have to make them sorry. I have to make them understand what they took from me. He told me to forget him, but I can't. I won't ever forget."

I've never seen Rachel so upset. Not even the night Manny died. I'm starting to understand how much he meant to her.

There's one more video file on the chip. I open it up. This time the screen stays black. It takes me a second to realize that there are muffled voices coming through the speaker.

"We can work on it out here." I strain to recognize the guy's voice, but it's too muffled. I put the phone to my ear so I can hear better.

"What is this?" The second voice is Rachel. She must have turned the phone on in her pocket or something.

"My darkroom. What do ya say, shall we step inside and see what develops?" Evan. The guy with her is definitely Evan.

Rachel laughs, light and flirty. "I just need a piece of your project, the picture from the beginning, you in your football jersey with the words underneath. What does that mean anyway, 'making the cut'?"

"It's top secret," Evan flirts back. I recognize the fake charm in his voice.

"You can tell me." The phone jostles around, and I imagine her leaning into him. "I won't tell anyone."

"I could maybe be persuaded to tell you if . . ."

The phone bounces around, and I can't hear anything for a couple of seconds. I can only imagine what they're doing.

Then I hear a sound like a door opening and someone yells, "Evan, what are you doing?" It's Skyler. He sounds really mad.

"Get out of here, kid. Dad said you can't be out here anymore," Evan yells back.

"This is my place. My mom said—"

"Your mom is dead." I hear shuffling and yelling and things banging around, like they were fighting. The door slams, but I can still hear Skyler yelling from outside.

"Maybe I should go—" Rachel says.

"Ignore him. I locked the door. He'll go away in a little while," Evan says.

"But is he okay? I mean, he sounds—" Rachel tries again.

"He'll be fine." More jostling, I imagine Evan putting his arms around her. "Let's talk about something else, like you. What are you doing for New Year's?"

The video stops. I don't know if Rachel turned it off, or if it got turned off by accident. I think about everything I just saw. Evan took Rachel to the darkroom at least once, and she felt like she needed to record their conversation, but why? Did she think Evan had anything to do with what happened to Manny? I hear the door to Araceli's bedroom open. I freeze, afraid that she'll find me in here. I'm not sure how to explain what I'm doing or what I found. I hear her go into the bathroom. Quickly, I put the phone with the note in my pocket. Then I put the picture back together and rehang it, straight, and brush my fingers over Rachel's face and mine. I stand up and look around the room again, remembering two girls giggling on a checkered bedspread, a secret phone, and a text message that would take us somewhere we shouldn't have gone.

I make my way out of the dark house and blink in the too-bright sun. The crowd is packing up the tools and drifting away. I catch a glimpse of Eduardo. He looks toward the old house again and then back to me. I nod to show him I understand.

"You ready to go?" Evan appears in front of me, blocking my view of Eduardo.

"I can walk home," I say. Eduardo turns and goes the opposite direction, away from the old house.

Evan follows my gaze. "Are you sure? We could go to the lake or something."

"No. Thanks." I turn to go.

Evan grips my wrist. "I really think you should come with me."

I turn around to make a snarky comment, but the look in his eyes stops me.

"Or, more important, I don't think you should go with him." He nods toward Eduardo.

"With who?" I try to look confused.

He doesn't buy it, and he doesn't release his death grip on my arm. "You know who I'm talking about. That Mexican kid, the gangbanger, the one you were talking to before, the one you went running with yesterday."

I stare at him, and everything inside me gets cold. "How do you know that? Were you following me?"

"I saw you with him, it doesn't matter how. It's not like you were trying to hide it."

"If I was going to talk to him, or I went running with him, why would it be your business?" I try to make it come out brave, but I'm scared of the change I see in him.

"Because you're supposed to be with my brother." He says it quietly and through clenched teeth because the people around us are starting to stare.

I look at him, incredulous. "So it's okay for you to come into my bedroom, and for you to hit on me at a party, but if I talk to another guy I'm cheating on Skyler?"

"It's not just that. It's *who* you choose to talk to." Evan pulls me closer to him and glances at the people watching us. "Those people are dangerous, especially him."

I lock my eyes on his. I'm done playing games with him; it's time to get some things out in the open and see what his reaction is. "Are you sure *they're* the ones who are dangerous? What do you know about the things that are missing from my bedroom? Or about the pictures in the darkroom?" I lean closer, breathing into his ear, "What do you know about 'making the cut'?"

His eyes get hard, but I see fear behind them. He smiles as

he turns toward his motorcycle, still holding onto my arm. "I'd be happy to take you home, Jaycee." I don't understand what he's doing until I see the crowd around us. He leans closer and whispers, "Stay out of it. You don't want to end up like her." He tugs on my arm and says out loud, "We need to go now." Evan starts walking, dragging me with him, but before we get to his motorcycle, he runs into a wall of people, Father Joseph at the center.

Father Joseph puts his hand on Evan's arm. "I promised her dad I'd make sure she got home safely, so I think she should go with me."

Evan looks from Father Joseph to the group of people gathered around us. He slowly lets go of my arm. "Sure. I need to get back to work anyway." He looks at me with a smile that's loaded with malice. "I'll see you later, Jaycee."

After he leaves the crowd dissipates, and I'm left standing with Father Joseph. He says, "Let me take you home."

I glance through the trees, toward the old house, where Eduardo is waiting. I'm afraid, but now more than ever I need to get to the end of this. "No. I'll be okay. I'd rather walk."

He hesitates, opens his mouth like he wants to argue, but then nods. "Be careful."

"I will," I answer.

CHAPTER
28

Approaching the old house, even in the daylight, is creepy. I creak up the front porch and peer into the windows. It looks exactly the same as it did the last time I was here. I don't see any sign of Eduardo anywhere; maybe I misread what he was trying to tell me.

I leave the porch and walk around the side of the house. The front of the house is bare, but this side is tagged with graffiti. I get my phone out to take a picture of the symbol so I can compare it to the one on the note that was in my window.

Before I can push the button, someone grabs it out of my hand. "Bad idea." I wheel around to face Eduardo, completely freaked out. He turns the phone off. "You don't want to be caught with that on your phone." It's the same thing Manny said to Rachel on the video.

In a heartbeat the adrenaline rush turns from fear to anger, anger toward him. I reach for my phone. "Why not? You wear it on your skin."

He holds the phone out of my reach. "That's different, boba."

I glare at him. "I found out what that means, 'boba.' I'm not stupid."

"Oh really? Then what are you? Not smart."

"I got a 4.0 all last year—"

"Not books, boba, street smarts. You trust people too much."

"You mean like following a gangbanger to a deserted house and letting him take my phone and turn it off?"

"Something like that." He turns my phone over in his hand. "Where did this come from?"

I avoid his eyes. "My dad gave it to me, to replace the one I handed over to that detective."

"He win the lottery?" He smirks. My face burns red. He knows I'm lying. "If you were a Mexican, you'd get thrown in jail for having this, based on suspicion alone. If you have brown skin and can afford this phone, you must be a drug dealer." The chip on his shoulder comes out again. What did Rachel say? He hates white people and this town, and probably even fuzzy yellow kittens.

"Did you have anything important to tell me, or are you just going to give me your attitude again?" It irritates me that Eduardo acts like the whole world is out to get him.

He hands me back my phone. "Where did you really get this?"

I avoid his eyes, hating how transparent I am. "I told you—"

He shakes his head at me. "We won't get anywhere if we lie to each other."

"Fine," I say, staring directly into his eyes. "A friend gave it to me."

"A friend?" He looks at me skeptically. "Someone who wants to keep track of you?"

"What's that supposed to mean?"

"The Cempoalli all had the same kind of phone. Phones with trackers on them. When I left the gang, I threw mine away."

I look down at the phone again, but Skyler wouldn't do something like that.

"So is that from your *novio*?"

"Yes. Skyler gave me the phone, okay." I stare him down. "Why do you care?"

He shakes his head again. "You shouldn't trust him, boba. I worked on their farm. I saw things—"

"You mean between hits on your joint? Skyler told me you got fired for smoking pot."

"And did he tell you that his dad fired most of the workers that day? All the illegals, not just the ones who were smoking. That it was after most of the crops were already harvested? That he didn't pay anyone?"

I swallow and think about the migrants that Dad took to Spokane, people who worked all season and didn't get paid. "Skyler isn't like the rest of them."

"You can believe that if you want to, boba."

I study the circle in front of me, thinking about Evan's threats, the negatives from the darkroom, and Rachel trying to get information from the football team. "What if this wasn't made by one of the Cempoalli?"

"What?" He stares at me, his eyes burning through me.

"What if it was someone else?"

"Why would you say that? What did you find? Rachel's journal, do you have it?"

I'm sorry I said anything. "Look, I don't know anything yet. I'm still trying to figure some things out."

He looks suspicious. "Like what?"

I think about everything I've learned about Manny and Rachel and the football team. "I don't know yet. But . . ." I'm thinking of what Rachel told me to do, *work with Eduardo, trust him.* But she also said she couldn't give him everything because someone might get killed.

"But what?"

"It's kind of hard when I'm doing this all by myself." It comes out in a rush of frustration.

His expression doesn't change. "You shouldn't be doing this at all."

"But I am. We're in this together, so get used to it."

"Okay then. I have something to show you." He points to the house. "Inside." I see the challenge in his eyes. He doesn't think I'll come with him. He's right, the last place I want to go with him is in the old house.

I hesitate. "You know how to get inside?"

He nods. "I've been living here ever since I got fired because of my tattoo. Before that I was living with the migrants."

"You live here?" I think he's making a joke or being sarcastic until I see the tired, dejected look on his face. "You sleep here?" He nods. "Why? Why don't you just go live with your uncle, wherever he is?"

"I made a promise."

"But you can't *live* here. It's old and there's no running water or bathroom or—"

"You know of a better place?"

"Maybe you could stay with us. I know Dad would . . ." But I can't finish that sentence. I don't think even Dad would be willing to let Eduardo stay with us.

"Forget it." The hardness comes back into his face.

"But why would you want to live where Manny died? Doesn't that . . ."—I search for the right word—"freak you out?"

"It gives me a chance to look around, see if there is anything that might help me find out what happened."

"And you've found something?"

"One thing." He looks around. "Come with me and I'll show you."

I follow him to the back of the house, to another door with a padlock, but when he pulls on the metal plate it's attached to, the whole thing comes out of the cracked wood. He pushes his way inside. "Here it is. *Mi casa es su casa.*"

The windows are so dusty that the house is almost as dark as it was that night. It takes a minute for my eyes to adjust to the dimness. The room is just like I remember it, a big mirror on one side, the window with curtains on the other, but I'm on the opposite end of where I was then. Glass still covers the floor. The only indication that Eduardo has been staying here is a small pile of clothes in one corner, a rolled-up sleeping bag stuffed behind the couch, and . . . I move closer, a pile of . . . library books?

They're set on a little black table by the entryway, underneath the red circle. My stomach turns with nausea, even though I'm sure the paint smell is only in my memory. I squeeze my eyes shut and swallow a few times.

"Are you okay?" Eduardo is standing beside me. I'm surprised at the concern I hear in his voice. "Maybe you should go—"

"No, it's fine." I try to sound brave, but my face in the mirror across the room shows only terror as I reach to touch the symbol. I put my hand over a smudge on the side, left by my hand when I touched it before. It all feels surreal, this room has existed in my nightmares for so long, but right in front of me is solid evidence that I was really here that night.

Maybe someone else left evidence too.

I set my backpack down on the floor and go to the curtains, to the place where I saw the person with the 18 on his back. I move them aside and even get down on the dusty floor, looking for . . . I don't know what.

"This one isn't right." I look up, startled at the sound of his voice in the quiet room.

"What?"

He traces the circle with his finger. "The symbol is messed up."

"I know. I touched it when it was wet. When I was here before, the night I came with Rachel, the night Manny died. I got scared and backed into it."

"No, not that. The symbol in the center is reversed." He traces an eye-shaped marking with lines through it. "The dot is supposed to be above this, not below it."

I stand up and go to him. "Are you sure?"

He looks at me like I'm asking the stupidest question ever. "I'm sure. Whoever made this didn't know what they were doing. No Cempoalli would ever make that mistake. It's the Olmec symbol for twenty. We use it because there were twenty original members of the gang."

Twenty? That was the number I saw carved into someone's chest on the negatives at Skyler's house. If 20 is a Cempoalli number like 18 is one for the 18th Street Gang, "Would Manny wear a number that represented the Cempoalli?" I say the last question out loud.

"What do you mean?" Eduardo says.

"For the football team, is there any way Manny would have picked a jersey number that represented the Cempoalli, something like twenty?" Eduardo looks like he's thinking about it. "I mean, I know he was kind of betraying them, going to the police and everything, but—"

"Yes. He would have chosen the Cempoalli number for his football jersey."

"But why?"

Eduardo shakes his head. "You wouldn't understand. Even though we left them, even though we can't ever go back, they're part of us." He touches the symbol on his back. He looks so sad, so lost. For the first time it occurs to me how hard it must have been for him to leave his home, his family, even his gang, to come here. His best friend was murdered, and now he's living in an abandoned house, all alone.

I touch his arm. "You can't stay here, it isn't safe. I'll talk to my dad—"

He pulls away, shaking his head. "Don't worry about me. I can take care of myself." He slides something halfway out of his shirt, something black and shiny.

My heart stops as I realize what it is. "You have a gun?"

Eduardo looks nervous, like he shouldn't have shown me.

"Where did you get that?" I hiss.

He laughs, full of bravado. "Hick town like this? Everyone has a gun and nobody locks their doors. It's a gangsta's paradise. If you want I could get you one too." His face gets serious. "That might not be a bad—"

"Are you crazy?" I back away from him. "No. No guns."

He pulls the gun out in a smooth motion, like it was something he's done before. He turns it over, admiring it, and, I think, enjoying my reaction to it. "You'd change your mind if you knew all your enemies had them."

"I don't have any enemies," I say.

"Are you sure about that?" The way he says it, combined with the look on his face, makes my blood go cold.

I think about the note, and what was taken from my room, and the look Evan had on his face when he left Araceli's house, but I answer, "I'm sure."

He walks back to me, still holding the gun. "You should take this. I could show you how to use it."

"I didn't say I didn't know how to use it, I just—"

My phone buzzes. I pull it out of my pocket and the note comes too. Eduardo picks it up. "What is this?"

"A note. I think Manny wrote it to Rachel."

He reads it over, and I can see him struggling to keep his emotions in check.

"What does it say?"

"He says, 'If something happens to me, don't cry, forget you ever knew me.'"

"Why would he tell her that?"

"Because he knew if they caught up with him, if the Cempoalli found out that he was talking to the feds, they would kill him and anyone who was important to him."

I think about the video. "But he thought he was safe; he thought he was going to have a normal life. He was going to play football."

Eduardo nods. "Because he trusted Agent Herrera, but he was wrong. No one can keep us safe."

I glance down at my phone because I don't know what to say to him. I have a message from Skyler.

file attached. best I can do. in deep.

"What's the file?" Eduardo says, and I realize he's over my shoulder.

"It's the coroner's report on Manny. I asked Skyler to—"

"You told your boyfriend?" Eduardo bursts out.

"He can help us. He has access to things like this report. He will—"

"He has access to it because his brother is the sheriff, which means he will tell him everything you've found out. How could you be so stupid?"

"Skyler won't say anything to Eric, he—"

"Let me see it."

I hand over my phone, and he opens the file. His face goes pale as he looks at whatever is on the phone. He slams it down on the table, making the books jump.

"What did you see?" I ask, breathless.

"Nothing I didn't already know. They gutted him."

I put my hand on his shoulder, trying to comfort him. "I'm sorry—"

"Forget it, it's too late." He gestures at me with his gun. "If you find anything like that again, bring it to me, not the police, and not your novio." He spits out the word "novio" like it tastes bad on his tongue. He turns away, shoving the gun back into his shirt.

"Where are you going?" I step in front of him.

"There's something I have to do."

"Eduardo, wait." I put my hand on his shoulder, afraid of where he's going.

He pulls away. "If I find what I'm looking for, you'll be the first to know."

After he leaves I'm not sure what I should do. Follow him? Call the police and tell them about the gun? I don't know what the right thing is anymore. I keep getting deeper into this, and I'm not any closer to finding out the truth.

I turn over my phone, bracing myself to see what Rachel saw. The picture is just a drawing of a generic person, with red markings indicating wounds, a lot of wounds. I scan that first, examining the marks drawn on his chest, but I don't see anything that looks like it could be a number. I read the report, picking out words like multiple lacerations, punctured aorta, and extensive bleeding. It all sounds so clinical and sterile, not like it was talking about a real person, not someone who died right here in this house.

I read through it again. I don't understand a lot of the words and terminology, but I don't read anything that indicates that Manny might have had a number carved on him anywhere. The report mentions other scars, "scar tissue on right shoulder and left thigh, consistent with previous lacerations," but nothing about a scar on his chest at all. The picture I saw in the darkroom must not have been him.

I close the file, defeated. I feel like I've hit another dead end, and I'm running out of time. If I don't find out who killed Manny and Rachel before Eduardo does, he'll do something stupid and someone else is going to get hurt. I'm not sure what to do about him. Every time I think I've figured him out, something sets him off, he gets mad, and he runs.

I turn toward the stairs that stopped me before. The thought of going up there now is almost as terrifying as it was that night, but it's the only place left for me to look.

The stairs creak under my weight, and my feet leave prints in the dust. It doesn't look like Eduardo has ventured up here at all. At the top of the stairs is a long hall. There are two closed doors on my right. Light is streaming in through an open doorway at the end of the hall. I head there.

The room is empty except for a shattered mirror on one side of the room and bits of broken glass all over the floor. The floor is covered with a layer of dust, but in the far corner there are brown streaks on the wall and on the floor. This is where Manny died. I stand in the doorway and imagine Rachel coming up the stairs, thinking she was going to meet him here, instead finding him cut and bleeding. She must have gone to him, tried to help, and gotten covered in his blood. When she realized he was dead, she ran away, cutting her foot on pieces of glass.

I look around me at the walls covered in graffiti and imagine the scene she walked into. I would have been terrified too, terrified enough not to tell anyone, not the police, and not even my best friend.

I walk over to the Cempoalli symbols painted on the wall and study them, thinking about what Eduardo found downstairs. There aren't any that are reversed, but there are a couple of places that look like someone started to paint something and then covered over it, like he made a mistake.

I walk to the window. Half the glass is missing and another tattered black curtain hangs beside it. I look out across the yard. From here, I can see Rachel's front porch and her covered bedroom window. Someone standing where I am now could have seen everything that happened at Rachel's house. If the curtains were open, he could see into her bedroom.

I lean forward and something catches my attention. Wedged into a crack in the windowsill is something yellow. I slip my fingers around it and work it out. I hold it up to the light and realize that it's a film canister, like the one Skyler used the other night.

There's one word written on the side in red pen.

"Cuts."

Hey, Jaycee, what are you doing here?" Eric smiles as he leans out of the window to his sheriff's truck.

"Heading home from Araceli's house," I say casually.

He opens the door. "I'm not technically supposed to be giving anyone a ride in this car, but it's raining and it occurred to me that I never got the chance to talk to you about where you were the night your friend was murdered. We could call it 'official police business' and then I could give you a ride home."

"That's okay . . . ," I start.

Eric's grin fades. "I insist." Something about the way he says it reminds me of Evan at Araceli's today, like maybe I don't have a choice. He gets out of the car, walks around to the backseat, and opens the door for me. "I'd let you ride up front, but I get in trouble for having young girls in the front seat with me." His grin is back, but there's something behind it. I try to shake off the urge to run, because I'm pretty sure he can arrest me for running away. I climb inside. Just before he shuts the door behind me I see something on his hand, a faded scar that looks like the number 18.

"So," he says, "where were you the night Rachel was killed?"

I try to stay casual. "You heard what I said at your office. I was at Evan's party, and then I was with Skyler."

He looks in the rearview mirror. "About how long were you with Mr. Cross?"

"A couple of hours; then he took me back to Claire's house and I snuck back in."

His expression in the rearview mirror looks confused, like something I said didn't make sense. "What time did Skyler drop you off?"

"One forty-five."

"Are you sure?" He says it like that's important.

"Positive." I know almost the exact time Skyler kissed me because I turned my phone back on as soon as I got back into Claire's room. I was hoping he'd text me. Instead, I got the text from Rachel.

Sheriff Cross is quiet. I wait for more questions, but they don't come. Finally he looks back at me in the mirror, his face serious. "The other reason I wanted to give you a ride was to warn you. That kid you went running with yesterday is dangerous."

"How did you know—"

"It's my job to keep the people in this town safe. If that means keeping an eye on a known criminal, then that's what I do."

"A known criminal? Eduardo?"

Sheriff Cross is nodding. "I don't know if you are aware of the circumstances that brought him and Manuel Romero here, but they weren't good. I shouldn't tell you this, because it's part of an ongoing investigation, but I think you need to know, for your own protection. They were both part of a very dangerous gang in Los Angeles." He keeps emphasizing the word "dangerous." "Our office has been working closely with a gang task force in California, keeping tabs on them. I actually spoke to Manuel several times. He was cooperative, willing to ID members of his gang who were involved in a horrific murder. In exchange, we were giving him protection and immunity.

"But your friend Eduardo didn't want anything to do with it. He wouldn't talk to us, and he was pretty upset with Manuel for talking to the police. Said he was betraying his people or something like that."

It's all stuff I knew before, except the part about Eduardo not cooperating, but it sounds like him.

"But you didn't do a very good job of protecting Manny," I dare to challenge him. "Considering he's dead."

Sheriff Cross's eyebrows knit together in irritation. "We did what we could. We believe that Manuel was killed by someone close to him, someone who he trusted." He catches my eye in the rearview mirror. "Someone like Eduardo."

I see a huge gaping flaw in his story. "If Eduardo killed Manny, why would he stay? Why not just go back to his gang in L.A.?"

Sheriff Cross's nostrils flair, but something like a grin appears again. He delivers his death blow. "Because he hadn't finished the job." He looks up to see the effect that has on me. "I assume you know about the relationship between Manny and Rachel?" I nod. "We think that Manuel told Rachel everything that was going on, everything he knew, everything he saw. That she wrote it down in some kind of journal. Eduardo spent enough time with Rachel to find out what she knew, and then he killed her too." He's not even looking at the road now, just at me, emphasizing everything he says with the seriousness in his face. "He made it look like a drive-by shooting, but it wasn't. The bullet that killed Rachel was fired at close range. She knew whoever killed her, knew him enough to let him in her bedroom, and Eduardo doesn't have an alibi for the night Rachel died."

All of that sinks in. What if the sheriff is right? What if Eduardo killed Manny and Rachel, but then again, "Why is he still here?"

Sheriff Cross looks up. "Maybe he thinks there are still loose ends to tie up."

Everything inside of me drains out. I told Eduardo that I was there the night Manny died. He asked me to help him find Rachel's journal.

Were the guys I heard talking by the fireplace members of Manny and Eduardo's gang? Are they trying to find out what I know, what Rachel might have written down? And after they do . . .

"If you're so sure it was him, why haven't you arrested him yet?" My voice comes out small and weak.

"He's smart. He won't let himself get caught doing

something illegal." Sheriff Cross's eyes glitter at me in the rearview mirror. "But if you know something that we could get him on, then maybe we could hold on to him until we had more."

I keep it small. "He's living in the old house. Trespassing."

Eric smiles. "That might help, but I'm not sure it's enough. I know you think he's your friend, but that's just how he works. He's dangerous, Jaycee. He betrayed Rachel and Manuel. We have to get him off the streets before someone else gets hurt. We need your help."

I take a breath, thinking about the gun, and how Eduardo looked when he left. The words rush out. "He has a gun, one that he stole from someone's house, I don't know whose." I close my eyes, praying that I've done the right thing.

"Good girl, Jaycee," Sheriff Cross says. He opens his door, and I realize that he's stopped in front of Claire's house.

"What are we doing here?" I ask.

"I heard your dad's case was held over again in Spokane. He won't be coming home tonight. With everything you told me, I don't think you should be alone." He comes around and opens the door for me. As I get out, something wedged under the backseat catches my eye, a baseball cap with the words LAKE RIDGE HIGH STATE CHAMPS.

The same hat I saw in the light of the fire on the playground.

Where have you been, young lady?" Claire smirks at me when she opens the door. "And why did the sheriff drop you off? You trying to add to your Cross collection?"

I push past her without answering. I need to think about what I just did, and what I just heard. I need to— I stop when I see Skyler sitting on the couch.

"Oh, did I forget to mention you have a visitor?" Claire says.

Skyler stands up and crosses the room to me. He looks scared and confused. "Why were you riding in Eric's cruiser?"

I want to lean into his arms and sob out the whole story, but I can't in front of Claire. "What are you doing here?"

"You didn't answer your phone, so I came looking for you," Skyler says. "I'm worried about you, Jaycee. I think you should—"

"Don't say it, don't—" I've been through too much today to listen to one more person tell me I'm doing something stupid. Then I look at his face and realize he has his own issues. His lip is split and puffy and there's a bruise on his chin. I breathe in, shocked. "What happened to you?"

"Just a dumb fight." He looks toward Claire, watching us as if she were watching a movie play out in her living room. I realize Skyler probably doesn't want to talk about it in front of her.

"Here, let me help you get cleaned up." I walk him into the bathroom, shut the door behind us, and lock it. Then I turn on the sink. "It was your dad, wasn't it?"

He still won't look at me. I dampen a washcloth and sponge at the blood on his bottom lip. "And it isn't the first time."

He closes his eyes and shakes his head.

I put my arms around him and lean my forehead against his. "Oh, Skyler." He closes his eyes, and we breathe together. My heart breaks for him. Why didn't I see it before?

The bathroom door rattles. "Claire," I yell. "Give us a minute."

"Jaycee, what's going on in there?" It's Claire's mom.

"Nothing. I just . . . need some privacy."

The door rattles again. "Is someone in there with you? Claire, who went into the bathroom with Jaycee?"

I hear voices murmuring outside. I wonder if Claire will cover for me, try to get her mom away from the door or something. It surprises me how little I care. The only thing that matters right now is Skyler. It's not even that his face looks that bad. It's his expression. He just looks destroyed.

"I'm sorry. I didn't mean to get you into trouble," he says.

I gesture to the door. "I don't care about any of that. I only care about you."

He turns away from me, and his lips twist in the kind of grimace that means he's fighting back tears. "You wouldn't. Not if you knew who I really am. I'm nothing but a major screwup. I can't do anything right—not football, not farming; I can't even keep you safe." He slams his fist into the bathroom counter, so hard that it makes me jump back.

"Jaycee, come out of there!" Claire's mother yells through the door.

I don't answer her. Instead I wrap my arms around Skyler's waist and lean my head on his shoulder. "This is not your fault. None of this is your fault. You just have a jerk for a dad. You're smart and sweet and—"

He twists around and stops me with a kiss. His lips are pressed so hard against mine that I'm sure I'm hurting his mouth. He wraps me in his arms. "I love you, Jaycee. You're the best thing that's ever happened to me."

"I love you too, Skyler," I whisper back. It feels right to say it, but the desperation in his voice scares me.

He pulls away. "No one has ever told me that before. At least, not since Mom . . ." He swallows. I'm shocked and hurt for him. Wondering if he really means it. He wraps his arms around my waist. "I wish I could be the person you think I am."

"But you are, Skyler, you just don't—"

The door bursts open, and Claire's mom stands there looking more triumphant than shocked. "What are you two doing?"

I untangle myself from Skyler's embrace. "Mrs. Rallstrom, please."

She comes into the bathroom, pushes me aside, and takes Skyler by the arm. "You can't be here." Skyler grimaces and pushes her away. I notice fresh cuts along the scars on his wrist. I wonder if his dad did that too.

Mrs. Rallstrom backs away, shocked, like she just noticed Skyler's face. "What happened to you?"

"He got in a fight with one of his brothers, probably over Jaycee," Claire sings out, filling in the holes that Skyler left with her own version of the story.

"That's terrible." Mrs. Rallstrom steps closer to Skyler. "I'm going to call your dad, let him know what—"

"No!" Skyler looks terrified.

"Mrs. Rallstrom, you can't call his dad." I take a breath and try to calm down. "If you would just listen—"

"Don't." Skyler grabs my arm and takes me out to the porch. "You can't tell anyone. Please, Jaycee."

"But you need help."

"No!" he yells. "I don't need help. I'm leaving. I can't take this anymore. I have to get out of this town . . . I have to—"

"No, don't." The tears that have been threatening all day are back again. "We'll work it out. My dad can—"

"Come with me." He grips my arm harder. "You need to get out of here too. We'll just start over. I have mo—"

"She is not going anywhere with you!" Claire's mom yells, coming toward the door. "Stay right there until I have a chance to call your father."

Skyler ignores her. "Jaycee, please. You don't know everything that's going on. It's not safe here for either of—"

"Jaycee Draper, if you don't get in this house right now I'll—"

"Shut up, okay?" I turn around and yell at Claire's mom.

She looks like I slapped her. "Don't you talk to me that way. When I tell your father what a little—"

"Why don't you take care of your own daughter for once instead of getting into everyone else's business." I step in front of her and slam the door closed in her dumbfounded face.

Skyler smiles. "So you're coming?"

I shake my head. "I can't. Not now. I have to—"

"You don't have to do anything."

I lean over and gently kiss his puffy lip, just as Claire's mom gets the door open again. "I do. I'm sorry—"

"I'm sorry too." He holds me against him and kisses me hard again, ignoring Mrs. Rallstrom's threats. "I'll give you time to think about it. When you change your mind, call me." He slips something out of his pocket and presses it into my hand. "I love you."

"I love you too," I whisper back, the thrill of the words passed between us makes my whole body tingle.

"See you tonight." He smiles and backs away. I glance down at the picture in my hand, a smaller version of the one he had in his darkroom. Me, lying in the meadow, wearing a white dress, my eyes closed, smiling like I'm having a good dream.

— —

"You look—" Taylor starts.

"Dead," Claire finishes.

I had to show someone the picture, so I got it out when the three of us were alone. I'm sitting on Claire's bed, stuck here for a little longer. I finally convinced Mrs. Rallstrom *not* to call Skyler's dad, but she had a long phone call with mine after Skyler left. She wouldn't let me talk to him. She told me that he's starting back immediately, but it will be a few hours until he gets here. I'm not eager for that conversation, except I have a few things I need to tell him, like the truth.

"I was going to say angelic, but 'dead' kind of works too. With your hair fanned out like that and your skin all pale, you look like a dead heroine from a tragic poem, *Annabel Lee* or something like that," Taylor says. We both look at her. "What? Poe, right? We read it in Lit last year." We must still look shocked because she adds, "I read it." She touches my face in the picture. "You have such nice skin. I'm jealous." I think it's the first time she's said anything nice about the way I look.

"He probably Photoshopped it." Claire brushes her hair back from her face, showing an orange line of cover-up. It makes me feel better about my pale but clear skin. "You kind of look like a corpse."

"I still say angel," Taylor says.

"Whatever. Were we going to go to a party at the lake or are we going to hang around and talk about Jaycee's love life again?" She turns on me, a wicked sneer playing at the corner of her mouth. "Oh wait, I forgot, you're like grounded for eternity or something." I think her mom is letting her go out tonight, just to spite me. "Are you in, Taylor?"

Taylor looks at me for a second and then says, "I don't have a suit."

"You can borrow one of mine. It'll be only a little tight." She throws Taylor a wad of strings and then slips her feet into my white sandals. The ones she said looked like they belonged to a little girl. "Since you lost my shoes, I'm taking yours. See you later, Jaycee."

As soon as they leave I get a text from Skyler:

Meet me at your house?

I don't know how to answer. I agree that he needs to get away from his dad. I'm just not sure about how he plans to do it. I can't let him run away by himself, and I can't go with him. I open up my backpack and touch the roll of film I found in the old house. I had planned to ask Skyler if we could see what was on it, but it will have to wait. Getting Skyler out of here has to be my focus now, at least until he's safe. Rachel is dead. I can't do anything to bring her back. And Eduardo . . . I don't know if Sheriff Cross was telling the truth or not, but maybe it's time I let someone who knows more than I do try to sort him out. I'm not sure there was ever anything I could have done for him.

My phone buzzes again.

Come. I don't think I can live without you.

Somehow, I have to get out of this house tonight and convince Skyler to stay long enough so I can help him. Dad is going to be off-the-wall mad when he gets back, but he'll still help Skyler once I explain things to him. I know he will.

I text: I'll be there as soon as Claire's mom falls asleep. I'll call u when I get there.

I listen to the house around me. Somewhere downstairs the television is going. I wonder how long it will be until Claire's mom falls asleep. I open the blinds and stare down the road toward my house. There's a lot of darkness between me and it.

Skyler answers: You're my angel. I love u.

I pick up the picture he took of me again. He wrote the

same thing at the bottom of this picture, "My angel." I'm tired of waiting and worrying; I just need to get out of here. I pull my running shoes out of my bag and sling my backpack over my shoulder. Whether Claire's mom is asleep or not, I have to go meet him right now.

I slip my phone into my pocket, creep down the stairs, and head for the back door, the one I've snuck out of twice now, but never by myself. The TV drones on. No one comes out to see where I'm going. I pass silently through the back fence and to the dark alley where Evan and the other guys were hiding last time. I stop and listen—no footsteps but mine.

I cross behind Claire's house, down the empty road toward home, trying to ignore the darkness pressing in behind me. The urge to move faster, either home or back to Claire's house, is almost overwhelming. I break into a jog and then I run. I don't stop until I get to my house.

I grip my keys and walk up the stairs, but when I reach for the door I realize it's already open, just a crack. Did I forget to shut it tight when I left? Is Dad home?

Then I smell it. Spray paint fumes. Nausea hits me so hard that I have to lean on the windowsill for support.

"You shouldn't be here," someone hisses in my ear at the

same time he clamps his hand over my mouth, cutting off my scream. I struggle, but he picks me up and drags me off the steps, around the side of the house, below my bedroom window.

"Shhh, boba, it's me. Shhh." Eduardo says it like that should comfort me, like I should trust him, but my instinct is to bite him hard, scream, and run.

Before I can, voices float through my window. "Snooping little bitch. What do you think she knows?" I freeze and press into Eduardo, this time for protection. He doesn't loosen his grip, but he takes his hand off my mouth.

"Shut up and finish what we came to do." I strain to recognize either of the voices, but I can't, they're too muffled. "I'm almost done." A hissing sound comes through the door and the smell of paint cuts the air, the same smell as the night Manny died.

"If this doesn't stop her—"

"After this there's no way she'll keep looking." Panic seizes my chest. What are they doing in my bedroom? What if Dad gets home, what will they do to him?

"She turned in that Mexican kid today, said he had a gun." Eduardo's grip tightens around my waist. "And after tonight, when everyone sees this, she'll be sure it was him. Eric said—"

"No names!" the first voice says. "What if someone hears you?"

"But if she doesn't buy it, if she keeps looking?"

"He said he'd take care of her." Everything inside me turns cold.

The window squeaks as they push it open. In a heartbeat Eduardo is moving again, carrying me, dragging me, but this time I don't resist. He pulls me behind the bushes, and I curl up in a ball next to him and try to make myself invisible in the shadows.

One dark figure and then two jump out of my bedroom window. Their faces are covered with black paint, but I know who it is. Mitch and Peyton. More hissing, more paint fumes. I swallow at the bile that keeps trying to come up. They're painting the same symbols that were all over Rachel's door on the outside wall of my house. Eduardo grips something hard against his side. Without looking down, I know he has the gun. I stay breathless and still, more scared than I've ever been in my life, huddled against Eduardo and his weapon, not sure I trust either of them to keep me safe.

My phone buzzes. I grab for it in terror. Eduardo does too, both our hands scrambling in the dark. Somehow, one of us finds the button to silence it. The guys freeze. "What was that?" Peyton whispers. "Did you hear that?"

"Hear what?"

They stay still. Eduardo leaves one hand on top of mine, gripping it hard, like my phone might go off again. His other hand holds the gun.

After forever, one of them speaks again. "Let's get out of here." They throw the empty spray cans. I hear them clatter. One rolls across the lawn and lands in front of me. Without saying anything else they run, going in opposite directions. Eduardo rolls on his stomach and belly crawls out from under the bushes. I can tell he's moving to follow them, trying to decide which one to go after.

I crawl beside him and grip his shoulder. "No."

"Let me go, boba. They killed Rachel." His voice is stony and he won't look at me.

"You don't know that."

"Weren't you listening? They want to kill you too."

That realization sends ice through my blood, to replace the adrenaline that's been pumping since I left Claire's house. I swallow, but I answer, "We don't know that either."

"Let me take care of this, I promised Rachel—"

"We have to go to the police, we have to tell them—"

"Don't you have ears, boba? The police are part of this; no one will help us. We have to do this ourselves."

I move closer to him, wrapping my fingers around his arm, knowing that if he really wants to leave there isn't anything I can do to stop him. I dig my fingers into his arm and force him to look at me. "If you go after them, if you kill one of them, you will go to jail. I'll turn you in myself."

"Like you did today?" His face is so cold that I let go of his arm and shrink away. "They came for me. When I went back to the house all my things were gone and stuff was thrown around like they were looking for something." He gestures with his gun. "For this? Because you told them I have this?"

I scoot away from him. "Sheriff Cross said that Manny was cooperating with the police and that you were . . . I thought . . . I mean . . ." I look away, thinking of the cap in the back of the sheriff's car, knowing I've been played again.

"And you believed him." He stands up and I see something dangling from his neck. Rachel's cross.

I stare at it. "You stole that from my room," I say quietly. "You're part of this. One of them."

"No!"

"You were in my bedroom!" My voice gets louder, I don't care who hears. "You took—"

"Because you wouldn't give it to me. I had to know what she left behind."

"Then why are you here now?"

"I came looking for you, so I could show you this." He pulls a scrap of paper out of his pocket. It's a copy of a newspaper article. The headline says, FUTURE STATE CHAMPS? Below it is a picture of the entire football team, including Skyler and Manny. He puts his finger on Manny's picture. "I was right. He did choose number twenty."

"Where did you get this?"

"At the library. I told you there was something I had to do and that I would tell you what it was if I found it."

"I thought—"

"You thought I was going out to kill someone."

"You had a gun."

"You still don't trust me."

I shove the paper back into his hand. "How am I supposed to trust you? Rachel trusted you and now she's dead."

His face crumbles.

"Where were you the night Rachel died?" I stand up, suddenly furious with him, realizing that this is what's been bothering me all along. "Why weren't you there to save her?"

He won't look at me anymore.

"Answer me! For once give me a straight answer! If you're so tough with your gun and your street cred, why didn't you save her?"

His jaw is clenched. He grips the gun against his chest. For a second I think he's going to turn it on me, or himself. He takes a breath and his voice comes out shaky. "She wanted to go to that FBI agent, the one who let Manny die. I told her we couldn't trust him. We had a fight and I left. I was done with it, with her, with everything." He closes his eyes. "I was on my way back to L.A., hours away, when she called for help. By the time I made it back, it was too late. She was dead." He bows his head. "That's why I have to finish this tonight."

My anger drains away. Now I understand why he feels responsible for Rachel's death. I put my hand on his shoulder. "Then let's finish this together, the right way. The way she was going to."

He doesn't move.

"We'll go to Agent Herrera. I have his phone number, or we could go to his office. We could leave tonight." I can't stand the thought of Peyton or Mitch or anyone else being shot, even after everything they've done. "Too many people have died already."

He touches Rachel's cross. "No, the wrong people have died."

I do the only thing I can think of to stop him. I grab the gun.

He stares at me in shock as I turn it around and point it at his chest. "Listen to me. We're doing this my way. My dad is a lawyer. He can help."

Eduardo stands there, dumbfounded. He shakes his head. "You shouldn't point a gun at someone unless you're willing to pull the trigger."

"Who says I'm not." I point the gun to the sky, and I squeeze off as many rounds as I can before he wrestles it away from me.

"What are you doing?" he screams.

"Trying to keep you from becoming a murderer!" I yell back.

He checks the chamber and starts cursing me in Spanish. He raises the gun above my head. For a minute I think he's going to hit me with it. I cower away. "From now on, you're on your own, boba. Don't call me when they come for you." He stuffs the gun in his pants, turns, and runs away.

I watch him go, lacking the strength to follow. There must be at least one bullet left, or he has more somewhere. I turn and face the ugly red marks on the wall of my house, dripping as if they were fresh blood, just like the ones in the old house.

I breathe in the fumes and my stomach churns. I walk into the house, feeling cold, exposed. Alone. My shirt is streaked with dirt, my legs are scraped from getting dragged under the bushes. I'm more tired than I've ever been before, and I want to throw up, but I can't quit now. I need to make it to my room and see what they did to it before anyone else comes. Thanks to the gunshots, it won't be very long before the police get here.

I open my bedroom door.

Everything I own is destroyed. My drawers are torn out and thrown across the floor. The walls are painted with gang symbols and words in Spanish that I don't understand, but they seem threatening. My pillows have been torn apart and spray-painted red. My bedspread is in tatters. My mirror is smashed, and glass covers the floor. They did everything they possibly could to make me afraid.

It worked.

I stand at the door, for a second not able to move forward or backward. I force myself inside, avoiding what's left of my bedroom mirror and stirring through my destroyed possessions, my hands getting red with paint. Skyler was right. It isn't safe here, for either of us. I need to find him. We'll go to Spokane, to Agent Herrera's office, and I'll tell him everything I know. I open my backpack to put some clothes and my phone charger in it.

My phone buzzes again. I pull it out, my ears straining for the police sirens that still haven't come. Everything is eerily silent.

It's a text message, one line:

Meet me at the darkroom in 20—Skyler

CHAPTER 33

I zip the backpack closed and sling it on my back.

The sirens are finally coming, so I go the opposite direction, toward the fields, running faster than I've ever run before. I can't wait for the police to come. They won't help us.

When I reach the far end of the Cross family's property, where I first saw Skyler in the swather, I slow down and look at the shorn hayfield. The moonlight illuminates the bales of hay and the baler at the end. The field is still half-finished, and it's starting to rain. It will have to sit and dry again. By the time it's ready to harvest, Skyler will be gone.

I sprint across the field, avoiding the light from the house but listening for any sounds coming from it, yelling or something worse. I move from shadow to shadow, trying to keep my breathing quiet. Finally I make it to the darkroom. I pause to catch my breath and step inside.

The room is pitch black. Skyler isn't here yet. I reach up and turn on the light. Hanging from the little clothesline are the negatives Skyler developed when I was here before. I reach into my pocket, fingering the roll of film.

If we go to Agent Herrera he's going to want some kind of evidence. What do I have besides my word? I don't have Rachel's pictures, or her necklace, or even the video message she sent me. I still don't have anything concrete. What if he doesn't believe me?

I touch the roll of film again. This might be my last chance to find out what's on it.

I don't know how old the film canister is, how long it was wedged in the windowsill, or even what's on it, but it's all I have left. Skyler's darkroom equipment is lined up on the counter in front of me. I pick up the developer tank and turn out the lights. My hands are shaking as I work to roll the film on the little spool the way he taught me. It keeps slipping off and I have to start over. Finally I get most of it on. I'm not sure it's right, but it will have to do. I can't wait for Skyler.

I screw on the lid to the tank, turn on the orange safelight, and reach for the developer chemical. Skyler said something about the temperature being just right, but I don't have time for that either. I read the instructions on the side of the bottle, "Process for fifteen minutes, agitating for about twenty seconds every minute, don't overprocess." I set a timer on my phone and shake the bottle slowly, back and forth. I do it over and over again, pacing back and forth in between, wondering where he is.

The alarm on my phone goes off, and Skyler still isn't here.

I'm not sure what to do next, but the developer said not to

overprocess, so I dump the chemicals from the tank down the sink. Then I unscrew the lid and unspool a long length of black film. I think I ruined it, or that there was nothing on it to begin with. I get almost to the end before I see anything.

I hold the film up to the orange light. There are only three frames of pictures. The first one is similar to the one I saw before; the number 18, carved into someone's forearm. I hold the negative closer to the light, trying to figure out what the next picture is. I almost drop the film when I realize it's a picture of someone lying on the floor. Manny. His chest is bare and there's a dark spot all around him—blood. I force myself to look closer, but I can't make sense of the wounds on his chest. Then I realize the negative is upside down. I flip it over and pick out a shaky 20, carved into his chest.

The coroner's report Skyler gave me was faked.

I move to the third picture. I recognize the front window of Rachel's house. Through it I can see two people, Rachel and me. All three pictures were taken the night Manny was murdered, and the person who took them was watching us. Was it the person who sent Rachel the text? Why did he want her to come to the old house, what was he planning to do to her?

My phone buzzes, scaring me so much that I drop it on the floor. I scramble to pick it up. It's another text from Skyler:

Don't go home. I'll come get u.

I'm confused. Why would he tell me not to go to my house after he told me to meet him at the darkroom?

The door to the darkroom opens. I turn around, still gripping the negative. Before I can react, Evan takes my phone and turns it off. "I'm going to guess I'm not who you were expecting."

"No. You're not." I glance at the open door, wondering how far I would make it before he caught me.

He shuts the door and then turns on the regular light. The negative I'm holding goes completely black. I stare at it, not sure what just happened.

Evan takes the strip of film from me. "And I'm going to guess that you didn't use stop bath or fixer when you developed that."

"I didn't . . ."

"I've done that before." He drops the ruined film on the floor and steps on it. I edge toward the door, but he blocks my way. "You aren't going anywhere. We need to talk."

I back away, just out of his reach. "How did you get the number to my phone?"

"I figured out that Skyler had his own way of talking to you, so I stole his phone when he went to take a shower this morning."

"So you lured me here for what? To kill me like you killed Rachel?"

"No. I pretended to be Skyler because I knew you wouldn't come if you thought it was me."

It occurs to me that he didn't say that he didn't kill Rachel, but since I'm trapped, my only choice is to listen to him. "Okay, you want to talk, talk."

"You need to stop what you're doing."

"What are you talking about?" I'm trying to stay calm even though everything inside me is coming apart.

"All this digging around, sticking your nose in other people's business. You need to stop it." His voice is missing the charm and false flirting it usually has, sounding more like urgency bordering on panic.

"Why?" It's the only word I can make come out without my voice shaking.

"You're getting into dangerous territory. I don't want to see you hurt. I've seen this stuff before, gangs and . . ."

Somehow I don't think he's as concerned about me as he is about himself. I interrupt him, thinking about the pictures I just saw. "Tell me about 'making the cut.'" It feels like someone else is talking, someone braver than me, someone like Rachel.

"Jaycee, trust me when I—"

"No! Don't say that!" Something inside me snaps, and I forget that I'm supposed to be afraid. "I'm so sick of people telling me who I can and can't trust, I could throw up. From now on, I'll decide who I trust. And I'm not sure that includes you."

"Wait, Jaycee." He reaches for my shoulder.

I step away. "Don't even try to touch me."

He bites his lip and speaks slowly, every word precise, as if he wants to be sure I hear him. "Trust me when I say you don't want to go there."

I keep my eyes locked on his, anger and adrenaline replacing the fear. "Actually, that's exactly where I want to go. I want you to tell me about 'making the cut' and everything you know about that, especially what you know about the night Manny died." His eyes register more panic, but I press forward like I'm the one with all the power, not him. "Or should I take what I found to that FBI agent, or whoever will listen to me? Now, before you do what you did to her, before you make it so no one will ever listen to me again."

He leans against the wall, defeated. "You won't like what I have to tell you, Jaycee, and I'm not sure you'll believe me, even if I tell the truth."

"Try me."

He looks at his hands without saying anything.

"What if I start and then you fill in the blanks." I move closer to him. "'The cut' is a sadistic football ritual where you carve your jersey number somewhere on your body to show your loyalty to the football team." I touch the number on his arm, enjoying for a minute the sick thrill of being in control of him for once. "It's been going on for years. The coach supposedly knows nothing about it."

He doesn't look up. "Don't drag Coach into this, please. He didn't know. He wasn't there when it happened."

"Wasn't he there the night Manny died?" I feel like my trap has been sprung and Evan is stuck.

He grimaces and turns away. "It was an accident. We were just a bunch of stupid kids."

"Stupid kids who covered up a murder," I point out.

He runs his fingers through his hair and paces in front of the door. "It wasn't my fault. I was all for having Manny on the team. He was big and he looked strong. I thought we could use him. He carved the number into his own chest, deep, like he felt nothing, even when the blood was dripping down to his knees. But someone had to go."

"Go?" That word sounds much more ominous now.

"Not like that. Someone had to be cut from the team; it

was a respect thing. If we let everyone in . . ." He shakes his head like he's trying to clear his thoughts. "There were two of them who showed up, two who did every stupid thing we asked them to do. We put them up in the room together, in a kind of holding cell, while we decided what they had to do next. Then we heard something that sounded like fighting, like they were throwing each other around. Glass was breaking, and they were yelling. I ran up the stairs, we all ran up, but by the time we got there, Manny had a knife in his chest, and he—the other kid—had blood on his hands."

My stomach clenches. When I finally talk, my voice sounds way more steady than I feel. "If Manny was stabbed, how was that an accident?"

Evan closes his eyes. He looks sick or maybe just tired of holding the secret in. "He said Manny snapped, got mad about something and came after him with the knife they'd used to make the cut. He tried to defend himself and they both fell, Manny ended up falling on the knife. He was dead before we could do anything." Evan leans forward and puts his head in his hands. "There was so much blood."

I work on wrapping my brain about everything he just told me. There are still a couple of holes in his story that need to be filled, holes I'm not sure I want him to fill. "You didn't see the fight. How do you know it was an accident?"

He gets defensive, ready to put his wall back up. "I just did, okay. We all did."

"If it was really an accident, why didn't you just tell the truth?"

"Our football team, our senior year, my scholarship would

306 / Jennifer Shaw Wolf

have been over if we got caught. If anyone knew we were there that night. We decided to cover it up. Manny was a gang-banger. Eric said he was involved in some kind of murder in California. Maybe he . . ." Evan trails off without finishing that sentence.

I finish it for him, furious. "Maybe what? He deserved it? For trying to get away from that life. For where he came from?"

"No, not that exactly." Evan looks small and pitiful and horrible. I'm disgusted to think I spent so much time fawning over him.

"Because he was a Mexican you thought you could get away with it? Right?" With each question my voice gets louder, with each question I think about Eduardo and how right he was. "You knew the investigation would only scratch the surface, and then you could go off and play your stupid football game. And it didn't even matter because you lost. You lost every single game last year, and you lost your scholarship. Murder must be bad for team spirit."

He shrinks farther into the corner of the room, like a spider looking for cover.

"Don't you care about anything besides your stupid jock status? You threatened me, destroyed my room, you covered up a *murder*, all so you could play football?"

"That wasn't it . . . it wasn't all about protecting the team, it was—" He stops himself. He won't look at me anymore. Everything he has is working to hide one last secret.

"What then? What were you trying to protect? What would

make you—" Something horrible and dark fills my chest. I lean forward, trying to read his expression, afraid of what might be written there. "*Who* are you trying to protect?" It comes out as a whisper. I'm not sure I want to know the answer.

Evan just shakes his head. "You need to stop what you're doing, Jaycee. Trust me, you just need to stop."

I have to ask the question. "Who was with Manny in the room? Who killed him?"

"Jaycee, don't." His head is down.

"Who?" I put my hand on his arm, gripping the scar on his shoulder, 18 carved into his flesh, like in the picture from the negative I just saw.

He starts shaking his head. "He shouldn't have been there."

But the negative was upside down.

"I should have vouched for him." I stare at his scar, 18, like the number I saw in the curtains. It was Evan. It had to be Evan.

"I should have made sure he had a spot on the team."

There's a mirror in the old house.

I stop listening to him, pick up a marker that's lying on the counter, and draw the number 18 on my arm, trying to imagine it reversed. I look across the room at the picture of Skyler in a football uniform, 81.

"No!" I push him away. "You're lying to me. It was you, it was Peyton, it was Mitch, it was Eric—" I swallow hard. "It wasn't—" But Evan's face tells me what I don't want to know. "Skyler," I finish. Everything inside me goes numb.

I want him to tell me I'm wrong, but he closes his eyes. "You can't tell anyone what you know."

"I can't . . . I have to . . ." I'm not sure I'm still the girl who always does the right thing, but how can I keep this secret? Even if I love him.

"It destroyed him, Jaycee. He pretended to be okay, was calm that night, even told us what to do to make the scene look legit—" He swallows. "He stayed on the football team, went to school, held it all in. Then one night he lost it. I found him on the floor in his room, bleeding. He had cut the number out of his arm and slashed his wrists. I think he was trying to kill himself. We wrapped up his arm and drove him to the hospital. Dad told them it was an accident, a stupid freak accident. He didn't want anyone to think Skyler was crazy. He didn't want anyone to think he was like his mom. And I couldn't tell Dad why Skyler had done what he had done.

"But they didn't buy it. They kept him in the hospital and gave him some medicine that worked really well. He came back, normal again."

"Rachel?" The hole in my chest gets so big it chokes me. "Did he—"

"No!" He almost yells it, but his voice wavers. "You know he didn't kill her. You were with him that night. You were at the party together. I saw you leave in his truck. You were together all night."

I'm nodding, covering my doubt. Skyler took me back to Claire's house at least an hour before Rachel was killed. No one knows that but me. But he wouldn't have killed Rachel. He couldn't have. Manny was just an accident. "Who then?"

"I don't know," Evan says, but he won't look at me.

"One of the other guys? Someone who was still trying to keep what happened that night a secret, and Rachel got too close?"

He shakes his head. "No."

"What about everything else? The playground, the notes, my bedroom?"

"Peyton and Mitch and," he hesitates, "and me. We've been following you, trying to find out what you knew, trying to scare you into giving up. We were protecting Skyler, and all of us."

"Did you do the same thing to Rachel? Were you following her too?"

He hesitates, licks his lips. "Yes."

"The drugs in her locker—you planted those to get her in trouble, so no one would listen to her."

He nods.

"And when she kept looking, you killed her."

"It wasn't supposed to go that far, she wasn't supposed to get hurt—" He stops, realizing he said too much.

"Except that she did," I finish for him.

"It was an accident," he whispers.

"Another accident?" I explode at him. "She was shot through her bedroom window. How is that an accident?"

"She wasn't supposed to be home. She was supposed to be here." He takes a breath. "I invited her to the party. We had a tracker on her phone. It said she was here. Me and Mitch tagged her house, shot up her bedroom window to make it look like a drive-by. Something for her to come home to, so she'd be scared. Scared enough to quit looking."

The truth settles on me like a lead weight. "But she *was* home."

He grips my arms hard. "I'll tell them to leave you alone. They'll listen to me, but you can't tell anyone what I just told you. Promise me you won't tell anyone what you know."

The pieces slide together in my brain: the state championship hat, the faked coroner's report, the ride in the sheriff's car. "Does Eric know too? Has he been covering for all of you at the police station?"

"He knows enough." His hands get tighter around my wrists.

"Why are you telling me all this? How do you know I won't . . ." But I'm afraid of the answer to that question.

"You're everything to Skyler. He's okay again because of you. It was an accident. Nothing you do now will bring Manny or Rachel back. I know you don't care about Mitch or Peyton or me, but Skyler will get dragged into this too. Is it worth destroying all of us?"

I pull away, and Evan lets go of my wrists. "I need to think. I can't—" I hang my head. The fact that I'm even considering what Evan said makes it impossible to look him in the eye. "I don't know what to do."

Evan puts his hand under my chin and makes me look at him. "He's in love with you. That has to count for something." I look into Evan's eyes, so much like Skyler's that it hurts to look at him. He nods and backs away. "We'll give you time to think. I'm going to find him now. Dad got after him pretty bad today, and Skyler gets really down on himself. I'm afraid of what he might do." He stops in the doorway, picks up my phone, and hands it back to me. "I know you'll do the right thing."

"And if I don't?"

He looks at me, but he doesn't answer.

I think I already know.

CHAPTER 34

Evan leaves the darkroom, and I hear his motorcycle start up and fade into the night. I slide down onto the floor to think. Think about what I know. Think about who I need to protect. Think about Skyler, and Manny, and Rachel.

Then I remember Agent Herrera. His phone number is somewhere in Dad's office, but I don't think I have time to find it. I turn my phone back on, not sure how to even search for his number or what I would say to him.

Or if I want to say anything to him.

I have a string of missed calls, all from Skyler. He must be worried about me, wondering what happened to me, but I can't bring myself to call him back. How can I ever talk to him again?

I wish I could ask Rachel what to do. I wish she had left me more than a stupid picture and cryptic videos. I think about the file that Agent Herrera said she sent to my phone. She tried to give me more, but someone deleted it.

I look around me, completely overwhelmed. I have to do something, but I'm not sure what. I brace my hands behind me to stand up and something sharp digs into my palm. I pick it up. It's a piece of broken black plastic.

My phone buzzes. Skyler again, but I can't make myself answer it. I sit there, staring at his number on the screen, twisting the piece of plastic between my fingers, until the phone stops buzzing.

I stand up, almost on autopilot and go to the garbage to throw the piece of plastic away. I stop when I see letters on it, LOG and then the rest is broken off. I look at it closer. The letters look familiar. I look at my phone; it says LOGIC in the same type. I think the piece of plastic was broken off a phone like mine.

Rachel's phone?

Agent Herrera said that whoever killed Rachel might have destroyed her phone. Evan said she was here the night she died. Did she smash it herself? On the concrete floor in this room? I stand up and look around me. If Rachel was here, if she broke her phone, would she have kept it, thrown it away, or what? Did she have a chip inside it then? Could it still be here?

Frantic now, I push the drape aside and open the cupboard, ready to tear it apart, but it's completely empty. Somebody cleared everything out, all the pictures, all the negatives, all the evidence. I turn around and stare at the pictures covering the wall, thinking about where she hid the other chips. I start pulling them down, tearing the frames apart, looking for another chip, Rachel's phone, anything. In a few seconds the floor is covered with broken glass and frames and Skyler's mom's pictures. I stop. There are too many pictures, and I don't know how much time I have. I force myself to think. I look at the pictures again. They're hung at artistic angles instead of straight up and down. There's one, and only one, that's hung completely straight, conspicuously straight, if you knew what to look for. If Rachel touched any of them, that's the one. Ironically, or maybe purposefully, it's the picture of Skyler in his football uniform from eighth grade.

I take the picture down slowly and start to take off the frame, but I don't have to. Behind where it was hung, someone has gouged a hole in the drywall. Something black is inside. Rachel's phone.

I pull it out and look at it. It's identical to mine except the front glass has been shattered and parts of it are missing. I turn it over, looking for another SD chip, but there isn't one in the slot. I push the power button, thinking the file she sent me might still be on the phone, but it doesn't turn on.

Another dead end. I want to cry. Then I remember I packed my phone charger in my backpack. Maybe after being in the wall for two months the battery is dead. If Rachel's phone is the same as mine, maybe I can make it work.

I plug it in and then wait. The seconds tick by with nothing, then it finally glows to life. Even with most of the screen missing, it still works. I go to Rachel's messages. There are three outgoing texts.

The first message was sent to a number I recognize, Eduardo's. It's another video file. I pull it up and watch the video.

Rachel is in her bedroom. Her face looks shattered, fragmented by the glass that was broken out. "Eduardo, I'm so sorry for everything. I was so obsessed with finding out what happened to Manny that I forgot about everything else. I hurt you and Jaycee and Mom and everyone else who ever loved me. Please forgive me, but I have to finish this. Someone has to pay for what happened to him.

"I'm destroying this phone as soon as I finish tonight. I'm so stupid. They've been using it to track me. Everything is done now. I've hidden the important stuff so even if they get to me, they won't be able to find it. If something happens to me, give Jaycee the note. She'll know where to look for the rest. She's smart and good. Work with her. Don't be a pain in the ass." She rolls her eyes and almost smiles before she gets serious again. "I know I don't have the right to ask for anything else from you, but I have to ask one more favor, *cuidala mucho*." She touches her lips. "Please keep her safe."

Eduardo said he had made a promise that kept him here, and now I know what it was.

The second message is the one that was sent to my phone: another video message, the one I never saw. It never got through or someone deleted it. I close my eyes, remembering how my phone was missing at the party, how Skyler found it for me, how he took me home; how he rescued me. At least that's what I thought he was doing.

"I finally know who killed Manny, and I finally know why." She's standing in the darkroom. She turns the camera on a pile of pictures on the counter. They're all of her, more than a hundred of them. She shuffles through the pile and I see pictures of her from soccer, pictures from school, there are even pictures that look like they were taken through her bedroom window. She picks up the one from the collage, her in a white dress after the baptism. "This is the only one I've seen before. The one he gave me. He's been following me, taking my picture . . ." She swallows hard. "Since, like, eighth grade."

She picks up one of her and Manny kissing. "He knew about Manny. He knew about us." The video shakes and then goes black, like she had to put the phone down. Her voice is barely audible, and I can hear the pain in it. "I shouldn't have told Manny about the pictures or about him following me. He was just trying to protect me."

Then the video gets garbled, Rachel's voice cuts in and out. I catch a word here and there. "Agent Herrera . . . Spokane . . . he can help." I swallow the bitter irony. The night she died Rachel finally decided she could trust Agent Herrera, but I never got that message.

The phone dies again, so I shake it. Rachel's voice comes back. "He planned it that way. He wanted it to look like an accident." The video goes out completely and all that's left is her voice. I hear pure terror in it when she says, "And now he's watching Jaycee."

I step back, almost dropping the phone. Prickles of fear go up my spine, and I turn around to make sure I'm alone. I shake the phone, hoping to get the video back. What did Rachel see? Who was watching me?

Then her phone starts to vibrate. With shaking hands I check the incoming number.

It's Skyler.

JC?

He still has the tracker on Rachel's phone, and he probably has one on mine. He knew I had it as soon as I turned it on.

He knows I know everything.

Evan is lying to you.

Give me a chance to explain.

I stare at the phone, gripping it in my hand. I'm not sure how to answer him. I'm not sure if I should answer him.

Please, I love you.

My heart crumbles. This is Skyler, the guy I love. Even with everything I know, I still love him. My brain can't reconcile the two Skylers; the one who didn't want me to do anything dangerous without him and the one who killed Manny. Maybe there's something I missed. Maybe there's something Rachel missed. Maybe Evan is lying. The phone and the pictures could have been hidden in the darkroom by anyone at Skyler's house, his brothers or his dad, or someone else. Rachel never said his name. If I go to him now, he could explain everything and it will be okay. Everything will go back to normal.

But Rachel and Manny will still be dead.

Another text from Skyler comes through:

If you don't believe me I can't stay here anymore.

I stare at the phone, not sure how to answer him, not sure what he means. Is he still leaving? Part of me is relieved, maybe it's better if he just goes. But he sends more:

goodbye angel

don't give in to the demons

I'm sorry

I love you

I stare at the phone.

Don't give in to the demons.

Why would he say that? I feel as if I've read those words somewhere before but . . . It hits me like a punch in the stomach. I have read those words before. They're the exact words his mom wrote to him. He's not just leaving. He's going to kill himself.

Whatever he did, I can't let him do it.

I text back with shaking fingers: Wait! I'll come with you. Where are you?

He waits a few excruciating minutes before he sends back a picture, the old house, the upstairs bedroom, but I already knew that's where I'd end up tonight.

I text: I'll be there.

He adds one last message.

Don't call the police. Come alone.

I scroll down Rachel's contact list, praying he's not too far away, praying the message will get through, praying Eduardo will understand. I send the text.

I hope it isn't my last.

I run again, cutting through the fields that separate Rachel's and Skyler's houses. All I can think of is what Evan said about Skyler trying to kill himself before. I'm afraid of what I'll find when I finally get to the house.

Skyler was in love with Rachel—obsessed. He saw her with Manny, took their picture, and what? Did he decide to kill Manny then, or did Manny go after him? Self-defense, like Evan said? An accident? Rachel didn't think so.

He planned it that way. He wanted it to look like an accident.

But she didn't know him like I do.

When I get to the house, I stop to catch my breath and decide what to do. The moon reflects off the broken top window. Everything inside me is screaming that I shouldn't be here, the way it was a year ago. I can't change what happened that night, I can't bring Rachel back, or Manny, but maybe tonight I can finally do the right thing. Maybe there's one person left I can save.

I slip through the back door, the way Eduardo showed me. "Skyler?" I say it quietly. No one answers. I look around the room, my eyes searching the shadows, but I don't see him. I take another step inside. "Skyler?"

We shouldn't be here.

I pause as my eyes adjust to the dim moonlight coming in from the dust-covered windows. The window is reflected in a big mirror on the wall across the room. That's what I saw that night, the reflection of the window in the mirror, the reflection of the curtains, the reflection of a number—81 instead of 18. Skyler was in the curtains, not Evan. It was so dark and the mirror is so big that I couldn't tell the difference.

The wind catches the door, and it slams behind me. I jump and scream, my own voice scaring me as much as the slamming of the door. I look at the closed door, every instinct telling me to open it and run away.

Don't be such a baby, Jaycee, it's just an old house.

I take a breath—dust, mice, but no spray paint. I turn toward the stairs. Something moves above my head.

Did you hear that? I don't think we're alone.

I stop, listening for any other sounds, but all I can hear is my own breathing and my heartbeat in my ears.

Are you coming?

I start up the stairs. Each step creaks with my weight. The dark presses in behind me, but I force myself to keep going, I force myself not to look back.

I push against the closed door, my hand leaving a print in the dust over the faded red symbol for the Cempoalli. It swings open without a sound. "Skyler?"

I step inside. Little bits of moonlight reflect off the broken mirror on the floor. In the middle of the room is a pile of pictures and negatives. I step closer. Most of the pictures are of Rachel, but there are a lot of me too. I bend down and look at them. There are pictures of me running in the fields, playing with the little kids from church, even standing alone in the cemetery after Rachel's funeral. I wonder how long he's been taking pictures of me.

"Skyler!" I yell it this time, desperate. Maybe I'm too late, maybe he— Something glints at the edge of the pile. I pick it up. It's another SD chip.

I slide it into my phone. The file comes up, Rachel's face. I hit play and she says, "After you watch this, you'll know everything I know."

"Turn it off," Skyler says from behind the curtains. He's hiding there, just like he was that night. "I don't want to hear her voice again."

I stop the video and look up at him. I almost wish I could be mad at him, hate him or something, but he looks so sad, so all alone. Now I know he's been sick this whole time. "You kept that from me. Why?"

He keeps his head down. "I couldn't let you see it. I didn't want you to know what a monster I was." He tugs at his shirt sleeve, like he's trying to hide something, but blood is seeping through. The legs of his jeans are shredded, and he's holding a long piece of glass in his hand.

I move closer. "You're hurt."

"It's nothing." He folds his arms against his chest.

I tiptoe through the shards, my throat choked with pain.

I stop before I get too close, afraid of what he's become. "It's okay. I came to help you."

He shakes his head. "It's too late."

"It's never too late." My voice comes out gentler and calmer than I feel.

He stares at the blood coming from his wound. "I'm not a freak, Jaycee. I'm not crazy like Mom was. I don't even know how any of this happened."

"You were in love with her." I swallow away the bitter taste the truth leaves in my mouth. "You were in love with Rachel."

He doesn't answer.

I need him to talk to me, confirm or deny it, something. "You were in love with her, and Manny got jealous, so you . . ." But I'm not sure how to finish that. I start again, "Evan told me what happened to Manny."

Skyler closes his eyes. "He was so mad. He wanted me to leave her alone, to stop taking pictures of her, to stop following her, but I was only trying to keep her safe." The red stain on his sleeve looks like it's getting bigger. I need to do something to stop the bleeding.

I take another step closer. "Keep her safe from him?"

He nods. "Eric told us about him, that he was a gangbanger from L.A., that he was dangerous. I got that she didn't want to be with me. I got it when she freaked out after I gave her the picture I took, but I couldn't let her be with him."

I swallow away nausea. "So you killed him."

He finally looks at me. The wind blows through the broken window and the curtains billow on either side of him. His

whole face gets animated, pleading his case. "It was an accident, self-defense. They could all see that it was self-defense.
I wanted to turn myself in, but Evan said we couldn't tell anyone or the football team was over. That everyone would know
about the cuts. He said that Coach had been warned about it
once already.

"They wanted to make it look like a gang hit. They went a
little crazy trying to make it look real. The whole scene was
a mess, but no one doubted it, not the police, not even that FBI
agent. So I let it go. I made myself forget." He finishes the
story, his face drained of energy as quickly as it came.

"But you didn't forget." The cuts on his legs look bad, but I
don't think they're deep. But the one on his arm . . . I open
my backpack slowly and pull out one of the T-shirts I'd packed,
all the time moving closer to him. "You dug the number out of
your arm. You cut yourself, like tonight." I take his arm. He
barely flinches when I tie my T-shirt around his arm and press
it between my hands to stop the bleeding.

He watches me. "Thanks, Jaycee. You're the nicest person
I've ever met." He brushes my hair away from my face. His
hands are covered in blood. I close my eyes, but I manage to
stay steady.

I'm afraid to ask, but I have to. "What about Rachel? What
happened to her?"

He shakes his head. "She was getting too close to finding
out what really happened. They said they were going to shoot
up her house and make it look like a drive-by, just to scare
her. She wasn't supposed to be home. The tracking thing on

her phone said she was at my house. I checked before they left to make sure she wasn't home."

"But she was."

He keeps his head down. Part of me wants to comfort him, tell him that everything is okay, that it wasn't his fault. But I know it was. I finger the phone in my pocket, Rachel's phone. "That's why you got her that phone."

He jerks up his head.

I keep my voice even. "You were the one who sent her the phone, so you could keep track of her."

He shakes his head. "No. I did it because I heard Claire making fun of her, telling her she was poor, off-white trash, that she couldn't even afford a phone. I wanted to help her. I wanted to give her something to make her smile. I made it look like her dad sent it because I know what it's like to wait for a present from someone who doesn't care."

"Then why did you get me the phone?"

He doesn't answer.

"To keep track of me so you'd know when I was getting too close? So you'd know when it was time to kill me too?"

"No!" His face comes back to life, and he jerks his arm away. "I'd never hurt you. I love you. You aren't like her at all." He reaches out and rolls a piece of my hair between his fingers. I cringe but I don't move, afraid that running away right now would make things worse. "You have to believe me. I wanted to tell the truth, but they wouldn't let me. I never meant to hurt Manny. I never meant to hurt Rachel. I never meant to hurt anyone. You believe me, don't you, Jaycee?"

I want to believe him, that it was all an accident, but there are still a couple of things that don't make sense, like the third picture from the negative I developed. The picture of Rachel and me at her house. Someone was watching us from the window of the old house the night Manny died. "Who texted Rachel and told her to come here that night?"

His expression twists, and I back away as his eyes go dark. "I don't know. Manny, probably." Until now his voice has been carefully measured, but he says "Manny" like it was the foulest word he could utter and he stares at me with a hardness I've never seen in his eyes before.

He planned it that way. He wanted it to look like an accident.

I cover my mouth as I realize what Rachel meant by that. Skyler didn't kill Manny in self-defense. He killed Manny to keep him away from her. He planned it.

"But Manny was already dead by the time she got the text. You texted her. You wanted her to see that he was dead, that the gang had caught up with him. You wanted her to see that she'd made the wrong choice. You wanted her to be afraid."

A shudder runs through his body, and I know I'm right. "She couldn't forget him, even though he was dead. She couldn't let it go. She had to keep digging and digging, doing things she shouldn't have done. She destroyed herself trying to find out what happened to him." His voice is different, low and creepy with an edge of hysteria. I've never seen him like this. I remember what Eric said in the car, *Rachel was shot at close range.* If she was killed by accident, in a fake drive-by shooting, why would he say the bullet that killed her was fired at close range? Maybe he was trying to scare me. I look at Skyler. Everything about him feels dark, like he's a completely different person.

I think Eric was telling the truth.

I speak slowly, "After Manny was gone you watched her go through all those other guys, all the guys you couldn't stand, to find out the truth. But she didn't ever come to you. You were forgotten again, just like after Manny came. You couldn't have her, so you killed her." My voice comes out as a whisper.

"No, it wasn't like that." He grabs my shoulders. I shrink away from him, but he holds me tight. "Jaycee, listen to me. I was done with her. I'd already found someone else, someone better." His voice goes tender and he touches the side of my face. "I'd already found you."

I hold still, afraid to stay but more afraid to leave. "Is that why you took my phone at the party?"

"It wasn't me. Not at first. Peyton stole it when you came in, as a joke. You were so nervous that you didn't notice, but I did, because I was watching you. I took it from him. I was going to give it back. Then Rachel's message came through. She'd finally found out the truth.

"I couldn't let her tell you about Manny. I couldn't let her tell you what I really was. If you knew what had happened . . ." He closes his eyes. "How could you see me as anything but a monster?"

Everything inside me turns to liquid pain. "You killed her because of me?"

He doesn't answer.

"You drove me home, knowing that she was trying to call me, knowing that she wouldn't give up. After you dropped me off, you went to her house and you—"

He steps back, gesturing wildly with his hands. "I just wanted to talk to her, to tell her that I was sorry. That she needed to forget Manny, that he wasn't worth it, that she needed to let it go, but she wouldn't listen. She kept screaming at me to stay away from you. I tried to tell her that I was in love with you, that I would never hurt you. She said she would make sure I never came near you again. I couldn't let her keep us apart."

"So you killed her." I wait for him to deny it, but he nods his head yes.

He grabs my wrists, hard, so I can't get away. "You understand, don't you? Please tell me you understand. You're the best person I've ever known. When I saw you that night at the party, I knew you were better than any of them, better than Rachel would ever be. You're the only person since my mom who's ever loved me. You have to come with me. We'll leave here and never come back. Please, just say you'll come." He pulls me against his chest and buries his head in my neck. "Don't make me hurt you too."

My blood runs cold. Up to this moment, up until he said that he didn't want to hurt me, I didn't believe he *would* hurt me. Even when I knew he had killed Manny and Rachel, I thought I was safe because he loves me. Now I know I'm wrong.

"I believe you. I'll go with you," I say into his neck. I swallow hard, knowing if I don't play along with him now, I'll never make it out of this house alive. "I love you, Skyler. Just let me go home and get some things, write a note to—"

"No!" He grips my wrist, hard. I grimace and try to pull away, but he holds it tight. "It has to be right now." He runs his finger over my lips. "We can't tell anyone that we're leaving or where we're going. We have to destroy this place and everything in it. We can't leave behind any evidence."

He lets go of me and walks over to the window. His movements are quick and shaky now, like he's some kind of electronic toy, or like he's high on something, or maybe he's just lost too much blood. I glance at the door, waiting for the right moment to run. Skyler pushes the curtains aside. Underneath them is a can of gas.

I edge toward the door. He opens the can and starts pouring it over the box of pictures. "We'll drive to San Diego. I moved my money to an account there. Then we'll go to Mexico. That would be ironic, wouldn't it? Running away to Mexico?" He laughs loudly, like that's the funniest thing in the world.

"I guess so." I freeze as he looks at me again.

He keeps his eyes on me and pulls a lighter out of his pocket, flicks it open, and stares at the flame. "I should have done this a long time ago. But if I had, maybe I wouldn't have realized how much better you are for me than she was."

He drops the lighter, but before it lands, the fumes explode. The glass that's left in the upper pane of the window bursts apart and Skyler flies backward onto the floor.

I dash across the room and pull open the door, ready to run. Skyler screams.

I turn around. There are flames everywhere. "Jaycee!" His shirt is covered in flames. I hesitate only half a second before I run back to him, rip down the curtains, and throw my body over his to smother the fire. I'm pounding out the flames and burning my hands, but I don't feel it. I put out the fire on his body and crawl away. He lies there, stunned, as the flames spread around him. They roar up the curtain that's left, follow the trail of gas across the floor, and start consuming the pictures.

"We have to go!" I yell. The roaring of the fire gets louder.

I reach for his hand and try to stand, but he grabs me, wraps his arms around me, and then he rolls over so I'm trapped under his body. "No, Jaycee. It's over. I can't live like this anymore. We have to get rid of *all* the evidence."

CHAPTER 36

I scream. But it doesn't feel like the sound is coming from inside me. This is a dream, a nightmare. He's going to kill both of us. I struggle against his grip, but he's smashing me into the floor. I can barely breathe, and when I do I choke on the smoke and heat that's filling the room. The flames are everywhere. "Please, Skyler," I beg. "Don't do this. Let's just get out of here."

He kisses my forehead, slow and gentle, like he did in the field of flowers. "I'm sorry, Jaycee, but like I said before, it's too late. At least this way we can be together."

I struggle harder, pushing against him, beating my hands on his chest, but it's hopeless. He's too strong for me.

He kisses me. "Close your eyes. Pretend you're having a good dream. That you're dreaming of me."

I try to scream, to beg him to let me go again, but the smoke clogs up my throat. I dig my heels into the floor and push myself backward. Something stabs into my shoulder—a piece of the broken mirror. I drag my hand across the floor until I feel sharp edges. I close my fingers around it and grip the piece of glass so hard that it digs into my palm.

I raise it up and drive it into his shoulder with all the strength I have left. He yells, so shocked that I can push him off me. I crawl away, trying to find the door or the window, but in the dark and the smoke I'm disoriented.

Glass digs into my knees as I crawl across the floor, searching for a way out. The fire is so loud now that I can't hear anything else. My fingers brush the edge of something—the door. I reach up for the doorknob; it's hot and burns my hand, but I twist it, pull back, and crawl for the gap of fresh air.

Skyler grabs my foot. He's dragging me back into the flames. I choke on a mouthful of smoke, and my head swims, black and gray. I reach forward one more time, and my fingers close around something soft and hard at the same time. It's a hand.

"Jaycee!" The hand grips mine. "Don't let go."

I don't know if anything is real or not. Maybe I'm dying, but I cling to the hand because it's the only thing through the smoke that feels solid. Eduardo's face swims in front of me. He grabs my shoulder and pulls back hard; I feel like I'm being torn in two between Eduardo and Skyler.

"Let her go!" This time the voice is Evan's. He's running down the hall toward us. I'm not sure if he's talking to Eduardo or Skyler.

"No!" Skyler screams and tightens his grip on my leg. "Stay away from my girlfriend!"

With all the strength I have left I kick hard, shaking his grip on my foot.

Eduardo is carrying me down the stairs. "You came?" My

voice sounds like I'm underwater, like we're back at the lake. "I thought you said you wouldn't . . ." but I'm choking too much to finish that sentence.

"I'm sorry, so sorry I left you." His mouth and nose are covered with his shirt. I can only see his eyes. I focus on them, forcing myself to stay awake. We make it outside. The fresh air burns my lungs, but I gasp it in as he sets me on the ground.

He kneels beside me, brushing my hair out of my face. "You're okay, you're okay, you're okay."

But I'm not okay. I focus on his eyes and choke out one word, "Skyler!" But no one is listening. Flames and sirens and yelling people swirl through the blackness in my brain. I roll over on my stomach and gag out smoke. When my vision clears, Eduardo is standing above me; something in his hand glints in the light of the flames.

He still has the gun.

The curls of smoke are taking over my consciousness, but I can't black out. Eduardo is yelling something in a mix of Spanish and English at Evan. Evan is standing over Skyler, curled up in a ball at his feet. My heart lurches with fear and relief at the same time. We all made it out, we're alive, but now Eduardo is going to kill Skyler. I can't let that happen. I reach for his leg. "No." But my voice comes only as a hoarse whisper. I pull on his jeans. "No."

Eduardo's eyes are huge and wild. "He tried to kill you! He deserves to die!"

"No!" I yell it with everything I have left.

The flashing lights get closer, sirens are wailing. Eduardo points the gun at Skyler. "This is justice."

"Vengeance isn't the same as justice." It's her voice, Rachel. She's standing beside Eduardo, her hand on his arm. "Put the gun down. There's been too much killing already."

Eduardo looks horrified. I know he sees her too. The gun falls and he drops to his knees.

Rachel morphs into Araceli as she kneels beside me and gathers me in her arms. "Mija, mija, mija."

Eduardo is sobbing. Skyler isn't moving. Evan looks at me. "Are you okay, Jaycee?"

There's no way to answer that question. I bury my face in Araceli's chest as the sirens and flashing lights engulf us all.

My bedroom is full of flowers when I come home from the hospital. "People from the church," Dad explains. I nod and sit down on the bed. "Everyone has been praying for you."

"What about Skyler?" They're the only words I can get out. The only thing that's been on my mind since that night.

Dad and Mom exchange a glance. She was at the hospital when I woke up. I guess her daughter almost getting murdered trumped whatever she had going on at work. She sits on the edge of my bed. "You won't ever have to see him again. The judge has decided he's too mentally unstable to stand trial. As soon as he recovers from his injuries he'll go to some kind of state mental facility for children."

"I'm sorry." Dad is choking on the words. "This is my fault. I knew Skyler had problems. I knew, but I didn't think they were that . . . I'm sorry . . . I should have done more to keep you safe."

Suddenly I understand. "That's why you didn't want me to be alone with him." He nods. "And I didn't listen." I bury my face in his chest. "I'm sorry, Dad. I should have told you about Skyler and the phone and . . ."

Dad wraps his arms around me, dissolving into tears. "I should have listened more. I should have—"

Mom wraps her arms around both of us. "You can't blame yourself. No one knew how sick he really was."

I look up at her through my tears. "Is anyone praying for him?"

Mom looks at Dad again, her face full of doubt. "One of the hardest things I've learned working as a lawyer is that some people just can't be saved. Sometimes they're just too far gone."

Dad leans over and kisses my forehead. "Yes, baby, we're praying for Skyler."

I nod. "I'm glad."

Mom takes a breath and sits back. "I think"—she glances at Dad—"*we* think maybe it would be best if, after you're feeling better, you came home with me to get away from everything here. You could stay as long as you want to."

"I can't," I start.

"Please, it would make me feel better if you were close." Her voice is desperate and she looks so scared, vulnerable even. I've never seen her like this before; my mom is usually the tough city lawyer that no one can touch.

I look from her to Dad, thinking of all the times I wanted her attention, all the times I wanted her to acknowledge me, to show me that she did love me. Maybe it was always there but I didn't see it. Maybe I didn't give her the chance. I look back at Dad and imagine him all alone. I don't want to hurt either of them, but there's really only one choice. "I'm sorry, Mom, I can't. I belong here."

She looks down, fingering my satiny bedspread. "I knew that's what you would say, but the offer stands. You can come live with me anytime."

I reach for her hand. "I know."

— —

Life moves on without me. Mom has to go back to DC and Dad has to go back to work, so Araceli comes to stay with me during the day. She and Dad talk a lot in the kitchen, when they think I'm asleep. Sometimes I catch them holding hands.

Somewhere outside the fields turn gold and get shredded by monstrous machines, the air gets thick with dust, and the moon turns fat and yellow. For me, time stands still. The person I was is buried in the ashes of the old house. I don't think I have the strength to create someone new. Sometimes I think about going to live with Mom and just starting over, someplace where no one knows me, but that didn't work for Manny.

I'm not sure if it's been days or weeks or just hours when Araceli comes to my door. "You have a visitor."

There have been lots of visitors, shuffling in and out, people from the church or from town, bringing food or just checking in. But she hasn't ever brought them to me.

Sometimes I imagine that I died in the fire and that the

people who come are here to comfort my dad, to tell him how sorry they are for his loss and to find out what really happened. That I'm not here anymore, that I'm a ghost.

But it hurts too much for me to be dead.

My hands are still wrapped in white bandages to cover the burns and the cuts from the glass; my legs are burned and scarred.

My heart hurts the worst.

Every night I dream about fire, about burning, and about Skyler. When I wake up, I wonder if we'll end up together after all. If the purple walls around me will close in and dissolve into flames, and if what's left of my mind will collapse in on itself. If I'll end up next to him in the "facility for mentally ill children." Not quite the escape he planned, but maybe we'll be together after all.

Araceli is still standing at the door, waiting for me to say something. I'm searching for the voice to tell her that I don't want to see anyone, but Eduardo's head appears above hers. She steps aside.

He's holding a soccer ball.

He nods toward the ball. "I thought we could go outside, kick it around for a while."

I stand up. It's such a strange concept, so normal—going outside to play soccer—that I don't say no. But I don't want to kick the ball around. Soccer was Rachel's thing, and it hurts too much to think about doing it without her. "Can we go for a run instead?"

Eduardo nods.

Araceli smiles, bends over to help me put my shoes on, and says to Eduardo, "Be careful of her hands. They aren't healed yet."

——

He comes back every day. We run without talking, just our feet pounding together and our breath moving in and out. At first I don't even make a mile, my burned lungs and my sliced legs refusing to carry me as far as they used to. We build up our distance, little by little, as the last bit of summer fades away.

Finally it's the last day of summer vacation. Our run is over, and Eduardo and I are passing a bottle of water back and forth. He clears his throat and then finally asks the question that's written in everyone's eyes, the question that even Dad won't ask. "How are you?"

I shrug and turn away, but he touches my leg, just below the burn on my thigh and above the cuts on my knees. "Tell me what you're feeling, boba."

I take a deep breath as the thoughts swirl through my brain and refuse to come to order. In the beginning it's only single words. "Betrayed." Breathe. "Used." Breathe. "Hurt." Swallow. He nods. Then he waits. Something roils through my stomach and into my throat. I try to swallow it away, but it sticks and leaves a bitter taste in my mouth. "Jealous," I finally say and kick at a little rock under my foot.

He watches my foot, giving me the chance to get control. "In a crazy way, I'm still jealous of her, jealous of Rachel." I look up, waiting for his reaction, for him to condemn me, but his face is down and masked by my shadow. "I'm jealous that everyone wanted her; jealous that Skyler wanted her, jealous that he loved her first."

Eduardo shakes his head. "He didn't love her, boba. Obsession isn't love"—he puts his hand over a bandage on his back that's in the same place where the tattoo was—"any more than vengeance is justice."

I look up at him. "Where did you read that?"

He ducks his head like he's embarrassed. "Just made it up."

"That's really profound."

He smiles. "Thanks."

Across the lawn I watch the people going into church. A twist of guilt mixed with longing knots my stomach. I haven't been to church since the day with Skyler in the parking lot. Dad hasn't pushed me to go with him, but I know he wishes I would. I miss it, but I don't know how to face all those people who know everything about me and everything that happened.

Skyler's gone away, but Evan, Eric, and the rest of them are in big trouble. After the fire, the truth came out about everything. I think the biggest shock for the whole town was that the "bad element" they were looking for turned out to be homegrown.

"I'm sorry," Eduardo says.

"For what?" I turn and face the pain in his eyes.

"I shouldn't have left you that night. I shouldn't have—"

"But you came back when I needed you. You saved my life.

Besides, it was my fault you left. I shouldn't have told Sheriff Cross. I should have—"

He holds up his hand for me to stop. "I didn't give you any reason to believe I was innocent. I didn't give you any reason to trust me."

"Yes, you did." I put my hand on his leg. "You gave me every reason, but I couldn't see it." I turn back toward the church. "I didn't let myself see a lot of things."

"I didn't, either." He drops his hand to the water bottle beside him and grips it hard. "I know what you're feeling because I feel it too."

I reach over and put my hand over his, thinking about what I saw on the video. "Because you loved her—you loved Rachel—and she loved him?" He looks surprised that I figured it out, but he nods. "But you didn't ever cross that line, even after he was dead."

He looks at the ground. "No. But I thought about it. I thought about it a lot."

"You know you're the most loyal person I've ever met?" I say. He shrugs off the compliment, and I laugh. "We're kind of a mess, aren't we?"

He turns his hand over and takes mine, gently. "We're alive. After everything we've been through, that's something."

"I'm not sure I want to be alive." I lie back in the grass and close my eyes. "I'm not sure I can put the pieces back together and be something okay again."

He slides his fingers along the bandages on my hand. "I was wrong. You aren't boba. You aren't stupid or naive. You just see the good in everyone because you're good. Whatever you learned from all of this, don't lose that."

He reaches into the drawstring backpack he's brought with us every day but never opened until now. He pulls out a necklace, half of Rachel's cross, on a leather string with beads surrounding it. He holds it up and lets it cascade slowly into my hand. Then he touches the other half, strung on a leather strap around his neck. "I decided that this was the best way for us to remember her."

I sit up and look at the church. The doors are closed; everyone inside is probably singing the first hymn; then there will be a prayer, and the sermon. Suddenly, more than anything I want to be part of them again. To forgive, even if I can't ever forget.

I stand up quickly. "I need to go."

Eduardo stands up too; he looks almost scared. "Where?"

"Church." I point at the building. I'm sweaty and gross, wearing no makeup, and my hair is in an unflattering ponytail again, but I don't care what I look like. I just want to go back.

"Church?" Eduardo says it like it's a foreign word.

"Yes. Church. I have to go back. I need to—" I look at his perplexed expression. "Come with me."

He backs away, shaking his head. "I can't go in there."

"What? Are you afraid?" I tease him, hoping to get a reaction.

He doesn't answer, but he looks almost more scared than he did outside the old house.

"Please, I need to go back, but I can't do it alone." I reach for his hand. "Come with me, just for today, and I won't ever ask you for anything again."

"I doubt that," he says, but he takes my outstretched hand anyway. I grip it tight so he can't run away this time.

— —

We make quite a scene when we walk into the church. Two sweaty, grubby teenagers in shorts and T-shirts, the former gangbanger and the school goody-goody, walking hand in hand right in the middle of the opening hymn. More than once I think Eduardo is going to bolt, but I hold his hand tight, not caring who sees. Whispers follow us as we walk to the front. This time I don't listen to what they're saying.

We sit down in the front row, and Dad takes my other hand without saying anything, almost like he's been expecting me. I hold his hand and Eduardo's and close my eyes. I listen to the music and think about me and about Rachel.

She was my best friend for nearly fourteen years, but after she died I thought I didn't know her at all. I think about everything Rachel trusted me with—the soccer goal, her secrets, and finally, finding out the truth.

Maybe it was me I didn't know yet.

I know I'll miss her every single day, but the memories she left won't haunt me anymore. I'll remember the girl who never wore shoes, and our blood promise to always be friends. I'll remember girls who loved and trusted each other, protected each other, and sometimes even hurt each other.

I'll remember a friendship that will never go away.

ACKNOWLEDGMENTS

If I thought one book under my belt would mean I needed fewer people to get to this point, I was wrong. Not only do I have all the people who held my hand the first time around, I've gained another dozen or so whom I couldn't have made it through my second book without.

First, always, is my amazing husband, David, who still believes in me even when I don't. Close behind him are our kids, David (the younger), Sabrina, Zach, and Daniel, who provide me with endless inspiration. Then there's my extended family: my parents; my sister, Kristin Amrine, and sister-in-law, Angela Morrison (both of whom know this process all too well); my brothers and their wives; and the wonderful family I married into.

Special thanks go out to Guille Brooks for sharing with me her early life as a migrant farm worker, and to the lovely Silem Hernandez for being my Spanish tutor, Facebook buddy, beta reader, and one of the happiest, sweetest girls I've ever met;

also to my brother Stacey Shaw for beta reading/fact-checking and to my cousin JoLynn Hansen for all her Washington farm-girl expertise. Thank you to Monica Renda and Christie Carlson, my teen and teen-at-heart beta readers.

Something beyond thanks (I'm not sure what it is, but I assume it involves chocolate) goes out to my amazing editor, Mary Kate Castellani, for presiding as midwife over this process, and to Sara Megibow for believing in me and refusing to let me jump off the ledge. You're both amazing at your jobs, and I'm in constant awe of your insights and support. Thank you to everyone at Nelson Literary and at Walker Books for Young Readers for helping me through this process and for being the often unsung heroes who get great stories into the hands of the people who love them.

I could not have made this happen without the tireless (if not tearless) support of my critique group—Val Serdy, Blessy Matthew, Anastasia Carl, Joan Wittler, and Sarah Showell. I love you guys 99.9 percent of the time. I also owe a huge debt of gratitude to the fabulous Class of 2K12 for saving me a fortune in therapy bills and for helping me realize that it's okay (and even normal) to be a little crazy.

Thank you to all the other writers whom I've met and been inspired by, including the members of the Apocalypsies, the Harbingers, ANWA, SCBWI, and LDS Storymakers. It's so nice to know that I'm not the only one who hears voices in my head.

Finally, thanks to the Divine Creator and Author of the universe. I know I am nothing without you. I have been truly blessed.